Stealing God

JAMES GREEN

Luath Press Limited

EDINBURGH

www.luath.co.uk

MYS Pbk

First published 2009

ISBN: 978-1-906817-01-5

The paper used in this book is recyclable. It is made from low-
chlorine pulps produced in a low-energy, low-emissions manner
from renewable forests.

The publisher acknowledges subsidy from

Scottish
Arts Council

towards the publication of this volume

Printed in the UK by CPI Antony Rowe, Chippenham

Typeset in 11 point Sabon

FSC
Mixed Sources
Product group from well-managed
forests and other controlled sources
Cert no. SGS-COC-2953
www.fsc.org
© 1996 Forest Stewardship Council

Dominic, James and Joe

Acknowledgements

Dr Jackie Jacques MBChB, who knows about such things,
Fr Leon Pereira OP, who introduced Jimmy to Rome, and
Tanners Wines Ltd, helpful as always.

Chapter 1

IT WASN'T A place for Roman style or somewhere tourists 'discovered'. It was domestic Rome, unattractive, functional and none too clean, a side-street bar where locals met for a drink and a smoke.

At the end of the street the sidewalks of the busy Corso Emanuele were full of bright dresses, casual slacks and sunglasses. The Roman traffic churned noisily along the Corso but in the warm, spring sunshine no one wanted to notice the Eternal City's eternal chaos. Least of all the three men sitting in the bar. They were of similar age, mid-fifties, and looked at home at their table, as if this was just another lunchtime drink in their local. One of them looked at his watch. With his lived-in face, grizzled hair and rumpled shirt he might have been born and raised in such a street. But when he spoke his accent was pure north London.

'I'll have to go soon, the rector wants to see me.'

'What's up, Jimmy, smack on the wrist or a pat on the back?'

The question came from a small, balding man in a sweater. The accent was Australian. Jimmy smiled but didn't respond so the third man, a big man, filled the space.

'You don't expect him to tell you, do you? Jimmy never tells anyone anything if it's about Jimmy. I've been served up clams in chowder that I knew more about than I do about him.' He turned to Jimmy as if inspecting him. 'Eight months since we first met and I'll tell you what we know about you. You're a Duns College student, we got told that. You come from London, your accent tells us that. You've got plenty of money because Duns students have to be self-financing here and afterwards. That's common knowledge.' He nodded to the bottle and glass in front of Jimmy. 'You like beer not wine or spirits. And that's all.'

The Australian chipped in.

'Except that you don't talk about yourself.'

They were all smiling, it was banter between friends.

'That's right, Ron, he don't talk about himself.'

'What's to talk about? Anyway, neither of you came to Rome to get my life story so what's the difference?'

The big man laughed easily, you got the feeling he laughed a lot. He was wearing an overcoat and had a scarf hanging round his neck. The Jamaican accent explained why it wasn't time for him to get into short sleeves.

'Never mind why we came to Rome. We all know why we came to Rome, and you're right, it wasn't to talk about ourselves. But I tell you it isn't natural, Jimmy, for people working together not to know something about each other. A careful mouth is a good thing, a secretive one is something else all together. Secrets have a way of popping out at you when they can do the most harm.' Then he winked at the Australian before putting his elbow on the table and shielding his face with his hand. 'Confess, my son, tell me all and receive my absolution before it is too late and the fires of Hell engulf your immortal soul.' And he laughed a deep, West Indian laugh. The Australian joined in.

'Take him up on it, mate, he'll go easy on you. He used to be a copper back in Jamaica so he's seen it all. You can't shock Danny.'

Danny's big hand reached over and patted Jimmy's shoulder.

'That's right, you can't shock me.'

'Sorry lads, there's nothing to shock you with. I might bore you to death though, if I ever got going.'

'Don't tell me a life lived in London hasn't had its moments, mate. I can't believe that.'

'I don't suppose London's much different to Perth, Ron, if all you do is live and work there and raise kids.'

Danny laughed loudly and slapped the table with his hands, hard enough for the barman to stop reading the paper and look up and the few others in the bar to glance across at them.

'Information, Ron, information about Jimmy's dark and secret past.'

Ron joined in grinning.

'So, married with kids, who'd have thought you would let something like that slip...'

But the laughter died quickly and Ron and Danny looked at each other, then both looked down, away from Jimmy. It was Ron who finally looked up and spoke. There was no laughter at the table now.

'Sorry, mate, I wasn't thinking. No offence intended.'

Jimmy looked at his watch and stood up.

'None taken lads, none taken, but the way I look at it, it's best to let the past alone. Then maybe it will let you alone. See you.'

He left the table, put the bottle and glass on the bar, nodded to the barman and walked out. The barman didn't respond but gave Jimmy's back a half-angry look as he left. Then he looked at the glass and bottle. Why did the Englishman do that? Collecting glasses, clearing tables, was his job. What was the reason? What was he trying to do, avoid giving a tip? But it couldn't be that because he did leave tips. The suspicion natural to the Roman mind lasted as long as it took for Jimmy to leave the bar. Then the barman went back to his paper, pointedly leaving the bottle and glass where they were.

'God Almighty, that was a bloody gash thing to come out with. I tell you, mate, I felt like the floor should just open up and swallow the pair of us. I'll have to do better than that.'

'We both will.' There was silence for a moment. 'I tell you what, Ron, I didn't think it would be so hard.'

'Hard?'

'Not the study, the book stuff, I expected that. And it's not the discipline. It's what you have to become, the person you have to try and be, for others. I don't know if I can do that.'

Ron's natural cheerfulness reasserted itself.

'Come on, sure you can, we all can. You've just got to give it time. The main thing is to learn, that's why we're here. You learn by your mistakes and you get better. That's the way you get where you're going.'

'Maybe so, but those mistakes hurt people, like we hurt Jimmy just now. And sometimes the damage done is a lot worse and whoever gets hurt can't just get up and walk away. There's a price for everything, Ron, I found that out a long time ago, and I don't want other people having to pay too high a price just so I can do my learning.'

Ron thought about it.

'But it can't be helped, can it? Other people always pay the price one way or another.'

'I suppose so.'

Ron finished his beer.

'Another coffee?'

Danny pushed his cup away.

'God, no, I'm getting so I hate the filthy stuff. One is plenty.'

'Why not have a beer then?'

Danny looked at him, somehow it had suddenly turned into that sort of day.

'Because it wouldn't be a beer and it wouldn't stop at one, and the price could be more than I would want anyone to pay.' The emphasis in the words was not lost on Ron.

'Bloody hell, it's a day for finding out about people, I'll say that. Jimmy's lost a wife and you...' He let the rest of it hang in the air.

'So I drink tea when I can get it and coffee when I can't.' The big smile came back. 'And I try to learn from my mistakes.'

They got up. Ron put his hand in his pocket, pulled out some coins and put the payment with a small tip on the table. They walked out together. The barman looked up from his newspaper. They had left everything on the table for him to clear away. He nodded to them as they left. They were okay, they were regulars. Outside on the cobbles they stood for a moment. The afternoon was free of study or lectures, it was theirs with no calls on their time. By unspoken consent they turned away from the busy Corso traffic and went towards the spring sunshine at the bottom end of the street. They would walk down to the Tiber where it would be warm and bright and Rome would be looking its best.

'I wonder what the rector wanted to see Jimmy about?'

'Who knows?'

And they left the street, not tourists but certainly not Romans, an odd couple.

Jimmy had also walked towards the Tiber. He could have used the Corso Emanuele which led directly to the Vatican, but it was too busy for the walk to be pleasant. Instead, he made his way through the side streets to the Ponte Mazzini, crossed over and walked along the quiet, tree-lined road above the river. As he walked he wondered what the rector wanted to see him about. It wasn't time for the routine monthly meeting and he couldn't think of anything that had happened which would require a meeting.

He put the question out of his mind. He would be told soon enough. He busied himself with thoughts on a different matter, one with which he was familiar – pain. It was hard to believe the way some chance remark, like the one Ron had made in the bar, could suddenly rip open an emotional wound and make it as if all the hard work of healing had never happened. The pain had just flooded back. He dealt with it in the only way he could, the way the kind old Mayo priest had shown him. He accepted it. He knew he deserved it, so he didn't try to fight it. A few short years ago the pain of loss and guilt could combine so that he came close to madness and self-destruction. Now a humble acceptance kept the worst of its demons at bay. Jimmy's mind strayed to his studies, he let it, it helped.

All his life he had heard the stories at Sunday Mass of how Jesus cured people possessed by evil spirits. He had always found them vaguely annoying when read out on Sundays alongside the eternal truths enshrined in the Gospels. He had sometimes wondered how the Church could mix a real Jesus and real miracles with such long-dead crap.

Now he no longer wondered. Now he knew it wasn't crap. The demons of self-destruction were very real. One of his first New Testament essays had been on the miracles of Jesus and he had drawn high praise for his understanding of the destructive power of inner demons. For a brief period he was regarded as a possible scholar. He had even been asked out for a drink by a Roman-based English Dominican. But that drink and subsequent essays quickly put him back where he belonged, among the plodders.

The pain that Ron's remark had brought flooding back was infinitely worse than any physical pain. As a child he had learned that it was possible to stand outside physical pain, to feel it but to find a place deep inside yourself where it could not touch you. He had used that lesson many times in his life as a policeman. Too many times. He had tried to use it with this pain but he could find no place inside himself that was free of it. Pain. You never got to the bottom of pain. However bad it was you knew it could always get worse. Of one thing he was certain, this pain, real pain, wasn't something you could overcome. The best that could be hoped for was acceptance and, ultimately, forgiveness. If forgiveness ever came.

Suddenly he smiled. What the hell did it matter? He was who he was, what his past had made him. Now he had to make the best of it. A pretty young woman smiled back at him as she passed, mistakenly thinking the smile had been meant for her. That was nice, thought Jimmy, a fortuitous piece of uncomplicated human contact. The young woman's smile lifted him.

Jimmy arrived at a bridge which carried a wide, busy main road across the Tiber. He turned left, headed for a big tunnel which swallowed the road's four lanes. Inside the tunnel the traffic noise bounced about so much that thinking became impossible. Leaving the tunnel, he went down a pedestrian underpass and came out into the bright sunshine on a wide piazza facing St Peter's Basilica. One side of the piazza was lined with people sitting at tables talking and drinking. On the opposite side the Vatican began with the Palazzo del Sant'Uffizio, home to the Congregation of the Doctrine of the Faith. An innocent sounding name until you were told it used to be called the Holy Office, and before that, the Inquisition.

Between the Palazzo and St Peter's was a modern, steel security fence which jarred with everything around it. Jimmy walked through the people crossing the piazza towards a gateway at the end of the fence where two Swiss Guards were on duty. Even after eight months in Rome he still thought they looked ridiculous. Their striped red, blue and yellow uniforms, dark floppy berets and knee-length pantaloons were more suited to a carnival. As he approached the gateway an American couple, talking loudly, pushed past him and suddenly he remembered it was even more crowded than usual because it was Wednesday, the day of the public papal audience. The day the pope would be out and about in his popemobile. Sod it. He hated crowds, in fact he hated Rome. But then again, where did he like?

At the gate he gave his name and the name of his rector. At the office inside the gate his name was checked against a list. After being swept for concealed weapons he was signed in and given his pass. The guards' uniforms might be quaint but the security certainly wasn't. He walked up the wide, cobbled road towards the complex of Renaissance buildings. This was the Vatican no tourists saw, where the work got done and where the lives of over a billion Catholics were influenced and guided.

So why did the rector want to see him? Not a slap on the wrist. He hadn't put a foot wrong since he came to Rome and he was sure that the rector couldn't have found out anything about… at least he was almost sure. He was being careful, but these days he knew he made mistakes. He had made one back in the bar with Ron and Danny. He had told them something about himself and they had laughed and the pain had come again. Pain, why did it always come back to pain?

Jimmy stopped outside a side entrance to one of the big old buildings. Here an office was made available to the Duns College rector when a student was in Rome.

I can't put any of it right, he thought. I can't bring any of them back and I can't change what I was or what I did. So what the fuck am I doing here? But he didn't stand and think for long, because he knew exactly why he was here.

This was the place he had finally come to when he had learned from the kindly old Mayo priest that a certain kind of pain cannot be hidden from or managed. The kind of pain that had been crucifying him for five years. He had learned that only deep contrition and a firm purpose of amendment could hold it in check. Only the giving up of his whole life might one day take it away. He had found himself driven to a simple choice: take his own life, or give it. No choice at all really. For Bernie's sake, he had chosen to give it. For Bernie's sake, how could it be otherwise?

Chapter 2

NO ONE HAD expected Pauline McBride to take any pleasure in her appointment to Duns College when it had been announced, no rector ever did. When a rare Duns student was accepted for training, the College – which was one temporary office and some headed notepaper – was given a rector. The post, though honorary, wasn't regarded as an honour. Her colleagues assumed that she would resent what had been done to her. She wasn't on the staff of one of the national Colleges in Rome. She was, when not wasting her time on Duns business, on the staff of the Collegio Principe, founded in 1519 by Cesare Borgia, Machiavelli's prince. Its purpose was the study of the relationship between religion, politics and power. The Collegio Principe was not on the traditional rota and that meant she had been made rector for a special reason. It was widely believed that Professor McBride had been turned into a statistic. The Vatican could now point to a black, female College rector seconded to its lists of appointments. Progress, equality and gender justice with the minimum of nuisance. The Vatican way.

The office was small with most of the space occupied by a large, ugly desk. The bulb hanging from the ceiling had no shade and glowed weakly, adding despondency as well as light to the room. The small window was grimy and closed. There was no carpet on the floorboards and the walls and ceiling had been painted a bilious green. It was where the most lowly servants would have been housed in the glory days of the building. The rector liked the room, it suited her mood when she had to come and make use of it.

Professor McBride was working on her laptop when Jimmy entered and she barely acknowledged his presence. He was glad to be able to stand for a few minutes and get his breath back after climbing the several flights of stairs which took you from the grand and very cold downstairs rooms up to these garrets in the roof. The rector finally closed the laptop. She nodded to two chairs in front of the desk with their backs almost touching the wall.

'Sit down, please.'

From their first meeting she had reminded Jimmy of the headmistress of his primary school who he remembered as a most unpleasant woman. The resemblance was particularly pronounced today. Jimmy sat down. The rector busied herself putting her laptop into a carrying bag which she pushed to one side of the desk, then smiled a false greeting.

'It is bad enough that each month I must be dragged away from important and relevant work to waste my time discussing your supposed progress. I do not blame you, you understand, I merely point it out. I always think honesty by far the best policy in relationships, be they personal, political or whatever.' The accent was American, so was the air of superiority. 'Do you know what this meeting is about?'

Jimmy shook his head. 'No idea.'

'Really?'

Her silent look gave Jimmy the impression that she didn't believe him.

'I was asked to arrange for you to come here for a meeting at two o'clock.'

So, thought Jimmy, the meeting was not with her but it was going to take place in the rector's office. Strange.

Professor McBride looked across the desk at Jimmy. There was a definite air about him of, if not criminality, something that justified mistrust.

'Has anyone questioned you about your papers recently, Mr Costello? In fact have you been questioned by anybody official about anything?'

Jimmy shook his head.

'Nobody's questioned me about anything.'

'I have to tell you that if I had had a decisive role in your selection you would not be here. You do not strike me as at all suitable for the priesthood, not even the diocesan priesthood.' She spoke as if being a diocesan priest had the same standing as being an inmate of San Quentin. 'I know that Duns students are given more latitude in their general oversight because they are men of sufficient independent means to serve the Church without requiring financial support of any kind. Yet if I read your file aright…'

Aright! thought Jimmy. What a bloody poser.

'…you have only a policeman's pension to live on. I must say I find that a most unusual and questionable circumstance.' She waited for Jimmy to explain. Jimmy disliked the woman as much as she obviously disliked him. But he didn't want her as his enemy, so he obliged.

'My late wife and I bought our house in London when we first married. After she died I moved away and the house was sold. It was just a small house but it fetched what I thought was an almost ridiculous price. That, with my savings and two investments made many years ago, gave me the finance to take up a Duns College place.'

Professor McBride sniffed and looked angrily at her watch.

'Your time may be of no value but mine certainly is so I intend...'

But Jimmy never found out what Professor McBride intended because her mobile rang. She answered it, then put it away and looked at Jimmy.

'Apparently you are about to be interviewed by a detective from the Rome police. An Inspector Ricci is on his way up. I am to confirm his identity and then leave him here to interview you.'

What the hell did the police want, thought Jimmy, making sure that his surprise didn't register on his face.

They sat in silence looking at one another until there was a knock at the door.

'Come in.'

The man who came in looked very sharp. Around six feet tall, well groomed, thirtyish, with the physique and good looks of an Italian footballer. He wore a light grey jacket with a strong pinstripe and jeans. The jacket should have looked wrong, the top half of a city suit, but on him it looked just right. The three buttons at the end of each sleeve were undone and the cuffs slightly flared to show a glimpse of silk lining. The dark shirt was open at the neck showing a very slim silver chain. The watch was white metal too. Light kit to set off his dark skin and short, black hair. Designer sunglasses rounded it all off.

Suit jacket and jeans, thought Jimmy, a man of two halves. He decided he didn't like either of them. If this was a copper he was either bent or on a bloody clothes allowance. The inspector took off his sunglasses and gave the office a brief once-over as if he feared for the wellbeing of his rig-out. Then he closed the door and switched on a smile, his Roman charm bringing more light into the room than the window and bulb combined. 'Good afternoon, Professor. I am Inspector Ricci, you were expecting me?'

They shook hands.

'Actually, Inspector, I was not told the reason for this meeting.' But she couldn't get the same acid tone into her voice for this charming officer that she had managed so easily when talking to Jimmy. Having made her point she let it go. 'I have been asked to verify your identity and then leave you with Mr Costello.' The rector indicated Jimmy. The policeman smiled at him, he had a nice smile. Jimmy made a mental note to be careful of this man when he smiled. It looked very practised but would work better with his sunglasses on because it didn't quite make it into his eyes.

The inspector took out a leather warrant-card holder and handed it to the rector. While she examined it he turned round to shake Jimmy's hand. Jimmy stood up, but he waited just long enough before shaking the offered hand for the smile to melt and another look to come into the policeman's face. Make someone dislike you and you're halfway to knowing where you'll stand with him, thought Jimmy.

'I suppose you would have known I was a policeman as soon as you saw me, Mr Costello? After all, you were one yourself for many years in London before you decided to give it all up and come here to be a priest.'

Ricci's English was excellent, the Italian accent allowed to remain just right for his suave image. But Jimmy didn't believe in fairies and he didn't believe in charming police inspectors, no matter how Italian they were. So he made another mental note. If this smarmy bugger needed handling he would almost certainly have to be handled very carefully.

'No, since you ask, I wouldn't have taken you for a policeman. You look far too expensive.'

Professor McBride held out the warrant-card holder.

'Do you want me to wait, Inspector?'

'Thank you, but that will not be necessary. I would not wish to waste your valuable time.'

Considering the views she had expressed earlier about how precious her time was, Professor McBride seemed strangely annoyed that she was being, albeit charmingly, dismissed.

After the door had closed behind her the inspector went and sat in the rector's chair. It was funny, thought Jimmy, the number of people who thought authority lay in locating your bum in the right chair.

'First, Signor Costello…' there was the briefest of pauses, but Jimmy left it at Signor Costello. He didn't want this guy thinking they could get to be friendly. He had made sure they started off on the wrong foot and that's where he wanted it to stay. 'You were a policeman in London, yes?'

Jimmy waited long enough for the inspector to be on the point of asking his question again and then answered.

'Don't I get to be told what this is all about?' Jimmy looked at the eyes. They registered. Annoyance – that was good.

'Certainly, Mr Costello, as soon as I confirm the information I have about you is accurate I will explain everything. I assure you, there is nothing to worry about.'

No, thought Jimmy, of course there isn't. Why would being pulled in and questioned by a detective inspector worry anybody?

'You were a policeman in London?'

'Yes.'

'What was your department and rank?'

'CID and I was a sergeant.'

'You took early retirement?'

'Yes.'

'Why was that?'

'It was offered to me.'

'Why was it offered?'

'My superiors thought it best.'

'And why was that?'

'Ask them, it was their decision. I didn't say I agreed with them.'

'Would you have agreed with them?'

'They never asked.'

'But if they had?'

'They didn't.'

'Is there something about your retirement you are unwilling to tell me, Signor Costello? I assure you, these questions are purely routine.'

'Of course they are. If you say they are, then they must be. I retired, what else is there to tell? Don't policemen ever retire in Italy?'

'Why are you being so unhelpful, Signor Costello? I merely wish to confirm the information I have been given about you. Your reasons for retirement were not at all problematic, were they?'

'I don't know.'

The inspector registered mock surprise.

'You don't know! How can you say you don't know?'

'I just open my mouth and let the words come out.'

'You know very well what I mean, Mr Costello.'

Signor when he's okay, Mister when he's pissed off, Jimmy noted. A small thing, but every little helped in this kind of game.

'The way I look at it, to decide if anything about me is problematic I would need to know who it was that felt it worthwhile to poke their noses into my past, what it was they were interested in, and why. If I knew that, I might be able to work out whether why I retired would be in any way problematic for them. Although even if I knew all that, it doesn't mean I would tell them what they wanted to know, or anybody they sent sniffing around to get their information for them.'

The inspector abandoned the chair and stood by the window with his back to Jimmy. The sun was trying its best to shine in but losing the battle. Even so, Ricci took out his sunglasses and put them on. Maybe they helped him to stare at the grime. Or maybe they helped him think. Then he took them off, put them away, came back to the desk and sat down.

'Alright, let's say your retirement is your own affair.'

Jimmy almost smiled. The Italian accent had gone.

'The accent comes and goes doesn't it? When the rector was here you definitely sounded Italian.'

The inspector didn't try his smile. That was progress.

'I was born in Glasgow. I lived there until I was twelve, then my family moved to Rome. At university here I studied Modern English Literature and I did a year at Leicester University as part of the Erasmus exchange scheme. The accent is just for window dressing when I think the occasion benefits from it. It helps put people at their ease if they're being questioned in English by an Italian copper. That okay, Jimmy? Does that answer your question?'

Jimmy didn't answer. He hadn't asked any question.

'Look, I don't want us to get off on the wrong foot and for some reason it seems you do. So how would it be if we stop pissing around and I tell you what this is all about?'

But Jimmy wasn't ready for an olive branch. He wanted to be in the driving seat before he...

Then suddenly everything changed. What the hell was he doing? Why was he putting a wall between himself and this man? Why was he still clinging to the old rules? This was

Rome, not London. He was in the rector's office, not some bloody north London nick. This wasn't about trust no one, like no one, let no one get close or know what you're thinking and always be ready to kick the shit out of them before they kick the shit out of you. He had to have changed. For Bernie's sake, for Michael's sake.

'Alright, I'm listening.'

It hadn't come out at all friendly, but it was the best he could do. A priest in training should want to help, he told himself. There was no reason to worry if the police came into his life. He should try to co-operate if he could. That was what he told himself. Unfortunately he didn't believe himself.

Chapter 3

'I HAVE BEEN asked to look into the death of an archbishop here in Rome. The death may or may not be suspicious. Let's say that at the moment it's being treated as an open question. I'll be working independently and I'll be working off the record.' He paused. 'Ask away, Jimmy, this isn't meant to be a monologue.'

Jimmy was angry with himself. Five years out of it and you get sloppy. You sit at a table with people you hardly know, having a few beers, and you tell them your fucking life story. A copper you've never seen before, with no reason that you know of for talking to you, tells you some archbishop may have been murdered, and as soon as he opens his mouth there's a question for him to see written all over your bloody face.

But what the hell. Ask the man, it doesn't matter. The Jimmy Costello who would care is dead. He died more than five years ago at a London hospital bedside.

So he asked his question.

'If the police are interested why isn't it official?'

'I didn't say the police were interested. I said I had been asked to look into it. As far as the local police or anybody else is concerned I'm on leave pending medical reports.' Ricci grinned. 'But don't worry, whatever the report says I might be suffering from will have to be serious, but I'm sure it won't be catching.'

Jimmy smiled back. Being like other people wasn't so hard, you just had to make the effort.

'Okay, you're a policeman who, at the moment, isn't a policeman. Either way I'm getting interviewed. So what's it all about?'

'I don't know much, just what I've been told and what I could figure out for myself. Not long ago a high-powered but unofficial request got made to the Minister to have the police look into this death and do it off the record. I was sent to the Ministry and got handed the job. Someone arranged for me to be able to drop everything and get on with it. They also created a phoney medical report which says I need to be given indefinite leave because I might have something terminal. Whoever it is has enough clout to keep the whole thing on a need-to-know basis within the police community. All of which means the original request came from a very powerful source.'

'Like who? The Vatican?'

'I'm not in a position to say. But this is Rome. Who else could tell the Minister to jump through a hoop like that?'

'If you say so.'

'As for the death, as far as the world is concerned Archbishop Francis Xavier Cheng died of natural causes, and that's how it will stay. Even if it turns out otherwise. There will never be any official police involvement in this, that much has been made clear to me.'

Jimmy tried to smile to soften his words, to make them as friendly as he could, but it died at birth. He would have to work on his smile. 'Okay, it's high-level and getting done on a need-to-know basis so you just naturally arrange to spill the whole thing to a complete outsider – me. I don't understand, but at this point I guess that's how you mean it to be, so keep going.'

The policeman kept going.

'Archbishop Cheng was seventy-three years old and, of the last thirty years, had spent twenty-two in one Chinese prison or another. He was released five years ago and placed under house arrest for a year, after which he was allowed to resume his ministry. Just over two years ago he was given permission to come to Rome to see the pope. He had been here about three weeks when he became ill and died.'

'So why wait two years and then decide the death needs looking into?'

The inspector shrugged.

'Who can say? The Vatican does things in their own way and their own time. Maybe they know something now they didn't know then.'

'There was an autopsy?'

'There had to be.'

'And it turned up something?'

'Yes and no. Death was caused by asphyxia, suffocation brought on by respiratory depression. That sort of thing happens to frail old men. I've read the autopsy report. It was unusually thorough.'

'Because?'

'My guess is the Vatican thought the Chinese would want to know exactly why he had died. It seems they looked after him during his house arrest, made sure he got back to being as physically okay as was possible after what he'd been through. For whatever inscrutable reason they wanted him as fit as he could be and back at work. It looks like they were beginning to trust him, perhaps even getting ready to work with him in some way. Whatever their motives, they had got as far as trusting him enough to let him come to Rome. For the Chinese, that's trusting a Catholic archbishop a lot.'

'You're an expert on China?'

'I got it all from someone who's a serious China-watcher. He says maybe Cheng was a try-out as a secure, unofficial contact between Beijing, the underground Catholic Church in China and the Vatican. He had never been a member of the government-approved Catholic Church and his time in prison proved his loyalty to the pope. He would have been ideal for a go-between sort of role.'

Jimmy set it out in his mind. It was unofficial which was bad and it was high-level which made it worse. Unofficial meant the rules didn't apply. With the rules you got some sort of protection and although rules could get broken, which he knew better than most, they couldn't be totally ignored. And anything involving the real high-ups meant the people pulling the strings and giving the orders were fireproof. It would be the foot soldiers who'd get their balls crushed and never get to know the reason why. Jimmy felt his instincts going into red zone, telling him he should have nothing to do with it. But he wasn't letting himself listen. Those instincts belonged to a copper, a north London DS with a family to protect and provide for, who did what had to be done by whatever means came to hand. A man who, please God, didn't exist any more. A man who had finally disappeared in the far west of Ireland. He wasn't a copper now, he was a priest in training. He was trying to become someone people could turn to for help. Someone who knew good from evil and did the right thing and did it willingly. Oh shit, he thought, stop sniffing at the fucking thing and get on with it.

'Did the autopsy turn up anything?'

'They found a trace of some sort of opioid.' The inspector

pulled out a small notebook which he flicked open. 'The nearest they could get was buprenorphine, an opioid analgesic which can bring on respiratory depression. To kill anyone who was fit and healthy, the dose would have to be massive.'

'But a frail old man like the archbishop?'

Ricci nodded.

'Yes. If you had it in a form you could administer without the victim knowing, in a drink or in his food. It's not conclusive. The trace was faint and he may well have been given a morphine-related drug for pain shortly before coming to Rome. The autopsy showed he'd been gone over more than a few times in prison. He would almost certainly have had enough residual pain to need some sort of medication.'

'Alright, it's not much, but if something new has come up I can see why someone might think his death would bear looking into. Now do we get to where I fit in?'

'Now we get to you. I don't think the Vatican trusts me. It's nothing personal, you understand, it's not even professional. It's just that the Vatican doesn't trust anyone. I report directly to the Minister's Office via his senior aide and the Minister passes anything I give him to whoever made the original request. My guess is that everyone wants to be sure that the Minister passes on everything he gets. More than that, they want to be sure that I give the Minister everything I get. They want me watched every step of the way by somebody they can trust. In short, they want their own trained detective watching me. They must have looked around at what was available here in Rome and come up with you. Either they were very lucky or I've been underestimating the power of prayer all these years. Just when they need it they can put their hands on a detective sergeant from the Metropolitan Police who's training for the priesthood. What would you say, luck or divine intervention?' Ricci grinned, it wasn't the charm-laden smile, it was genuine, it reached his eyes. 'Either way, you're going to be my watchdog. What's it feel like to be on the staff of the Vatican already? Unofficial and unacknowledged, but fast work for a new boy.'

Jimmy shrugged his shoulders. He didn't find the situation humorous.

'If I agree.'

Ricci's grin faded to a smile, his 'nice' smile.

'I strongly advise you to agree. I get the feeling you wouldn't like what would happen if you didn't.'

The delivery was slow, clear and flat. The point was taken.

'Do you want to explain that, or is the threat just from you?'

Ricci stiffened slightly. He'd known plenty of dangerous, violent men, men you were wise to be frightened of. He recognised one of them sitting opposite him now. He hadn't seen it before. But now, suddenly, there it was. Christ, how did someone like that turn up in a priests' training college?

Jimmy sat looking straight at the inspector's eyes. No one could have guessed that inside his head there was a voice screaming at him, Told you so you stupid bastard. Get out of this or do you actually want to be fucked?

With an almighty effort Jimmy switched it off. He tried to relax. Then the voice in his head came back, but this time different. God in your mercy, help me, a sinner. Bernadette, pray for me. Michael, pray for me. Jimmy's eyes became weak and slightly unfocused. His voice when he spoke was quiet, almost defeated.

'I'm sorry, Inspector, that came out wrong. What I meant was, will you please explain to me what you mean?'

Ricci didn't answer. Opposite him was a man saying sorry. An ordinary sort of man whose face and body looked crumpled, like his clothes. A tired man with sad eyes. Yet seconds ago something had looked out from those same eyes. Something which had frightened him, something savage, capable of great harm. Then it was gone, and here was this... this what?

Then it dawned. Here was a penitent, someone trying to atone for sins. A man with a burden almost too great to bear. He had been told to expect a retired detective sergeant from the London Metropolitan CID, a man with a clean record who had been given early retirement due to ill-health. A man who probably drove a desk for his last few years' service. Someone the Vatican could push around, bully and browbeat if he didn't get into line quickly enough and do what he was told. But this was some sort of Jekyll and Hyde. Ricci didn't understand who this man was, but he understood very clearly he didn't want anything to do with him. He didn't want him anywhere near him while he was working. In fact he didn't want him anywhere near him at all.

He got up.

'I'm sorry if you thought I was threatening you, Signor Costello. My words were perhaps ill-chosen. All I meant was that a refusal would upset whoever put your name forward. I felt that you, as a priest in training, would regret disappointing anyone in the Vatican. However,' the Italian accent was back and so was the smile, 'I can see that you are unhappy about this.' He moved round the desk to Jimmy. 'I will inform the Minister's Office that you do not wish to be further involved.' He put out his hand. 'Thank you for your time.'

Jimmy got up.

'I didn't say...'

'It's quite alright. I understand completely.'

They shook hands.

'*Buongiorno.*'

The inspector left the office. He didn't close the door and

Jimmy heard him whistling as he walked down the stairs.

Well, he had tried and he had failed, but nobody ever said it was going to be easy. He should just get used to the failure. Jimmy looked into the future, then said to no one and to everyone, 'Oh, shit.' He left the office and followed the inspector down the stairs, past the cold, grand rooms, out of the door and into the warm sunshine. Soon he was back among the crowds where everything was just as it should be and everyone had a spring in their step.

A week later Rome held one of its glittering evenings. Old men looked their wealthiest and young men their most beautiful. Women of all ages and none sparkled and shimmered. Power, wealth and beauty mingled easily. The setting had all the magnificence that the occasion deserved. Only innocence was absent, neither wanted nor missed. All that was best and brightest in Rome was telling itself it was having an extravagantly good time. In one of the bright, crowded rooms, with his back to the wall in all senses of that phrase, the Minister listened sullenly, his face that of a naughty boy caught out by his mother in some more than usually humiliating practice.

'My dear Minister...'

The Minister looked down at the champagne glass in his hand. He loathed the stuff, why did he continue to drink it? Once, about a million years ago, when he knew what happiness was, or at least how to enjoy himself, he had liked good champagne. But then he had also liked sex with amusing women and passionate men. He had liked driving fast, expensive cars and eating fine food at the best restaurants. How and why had he let it all go? How had it all come to this? He looked up and tried to assert himself.

'Really, Monsignor, as the Minister I hardly think...'

The sleek man wearing a Roman collar, black suit and the red accessories of his rank, fell silent and waited with an exaggerated air of respect. But the words had petered out so the sleek Monsignor resumed.

'The inspector has already told the Englishman most of what he knows. He may not want him in the investigation but what the inspector wants is not the issue. To allow the Englishman to be left out now is not a viable option.' He made a deprecating gesture with the hand not holding his champagne. 'I defer, of course, to your judgement. If, having received the inspector's report, you have accepted his advice to dispense with the Englishman, I will convey that decision to...'

The Minister jerked to life, splashing a small amount of warmish champagne from his glass onto one of his highly polished black shoes.

'No, no, Monsignor, that will not be necessary, I can see that you are right. It's just that...'

He looked despairingly past the prelate for the help he knew would not come. The Monsignor waited, refusing to end his misery. Having pulled the wings off the fly, he denied it an easy end by stepping on it. He was a cruel man by nature, but in this case his cruelty had motive. The Minister had to be reminded that he couldn't make decisions as if this matter rested in his hands. He was free to run Italy in whatever way he and his cohorts saw fit. But in certain matters he was a man under authority, like everyone else. The words of the New Testament were as true today as they ever were – 'those who are not with us are against us'. For Holy Mother Church there were no neutrals, no middle ground for anyone to occupy. The Minister finally looked at him and smiled the weak smile that was the white flag of surrender.

'Why don't you go and fuck yourself you pious piece of useless dog shit?'

His whole being was crying out to shout those words, to shout them out so loudly that the whole circus would be brought to a stunned silence. He knew that once, long ago, when he was still a man with balls and not a political eunuch, he might have actually done it. But now his words, when they came, continued in the hushed tones they had both been using and were heard only by himself and the priest.

'Of course, Monsignor, you are right as always. I will see to it.'

'Tomorrow?'

The last turn of the screw.

'Of course.'

'Thank you, Minister. Now, if you'll excuse me. I am rather busy tonight.'

The priest turned and left, moving on to other business. From across the room the Minister's closest aide began to hurry through the throng to see if he could breathe any life back into the corpse which was standing, still with its back to the wall.

Chapter 4

THEY SAT AT the same table in the same bar. Jimmy and Ron had beer in front of them, Danny had his cup of coffee.

'Danny, I just don't see the problem. Jesus was human and divine at the same time, sort of half and half.'

'A mild and bitter God.'

Ron looked at Jimmy, puzzled.

'Come again?'

'Mild and bitter, it was a drink years ago. You mixed half a pint of mild beer with a half of bitter beer. I don't suppose mild ever got to Oz.'

'It never got to Jamaica either. I thought you were quoting from some poem, 'a mild and bitter God'. Sounds like it might be Milton or George Herbert, someone like that.'

Jimmy tried out his smile. He was getting better at it.

'Your trouble is you think too much, always looking for more meanings.' He took a drink. 'Sometimes it's all just about the beer.'

Danny looked at Ron. Ron took his cue.

'I wish it was always just about the beer. I reckon life would be okay if all you had to worry about was where your next pint was coming from.'

Danny grinned. Well done Ron, the mild and bitter thing hadn't been much of a joke, but from Jimmy any joke was a good sign and deserved encouragement.

'If we take Jimmy's metaphor of a mild and bitter God, my problem, Ron, is that the words of the Mass say that He came to share in our humanity. We'll be the mild beer.'

'So?'

'So does that mean that prior to his birth on earth Jesus was all bitter beer? No mild, in no way human? His humanity, the mild, only began at the Incarnation, His birth?'

Ron thought about it for a minute.

'I suppose so. No, hang on, that's not right, at least I don't think that's right.'

Danny laughed.

'See what I mean now?'

'Not really, I like to keep things simple so I don't ask the awkward questions. The way I look at it, if you're never likely to get asked the question why bother to find out the answer?'

'But what if you ask yourself the question?'

Ron was stumped and fell silent.

'You know what your trouble is?'

'What's my trouble, Jimmy?'

'You're cursed with an enquiring mind. Maybe it comes from having been a copper.'

'You were a copper too, so how come you don't have one?'

'I was a lot of things, but now I'm just a student. I keep my head down, do as I'm told and don't ask any questions.'

Danny took a sip of his espresso.

'Let the dead past bury its dead, eh? Well it's not a bad rule when you get to our age. None of us is without a few things we'd rather leave behind, and with some of us maybe it's more than a few.'

Ron decided it was time to change the subject.

'Do you miss the wife, Jimmy?'

Jimmy looked at him. What sort of a bloody question was that? But he kept any hint of anger out of his voice. Ron might be stupid, but he meant no harm.

'Every day, Ron, only every day.'

'You know, you've opened up more in the past three weeks than you did in the previous eight months. Ever since you got hauled in to see your rector, it's as if you're a different bloke. It must have been a real heart-to-hearter, that meeting.'

Ron wasn't really stupid thought Jimmy, he was just a simple soul. He'd probably be a good priest because he was too thoughtless to notice what havoc a few careless words could do. He just got on with it and said whatever came into his mind.

'It was an interesting meeting in a way. I finally found out I should try and see things differently, let myself go a bit. Let people know who I am, who I want to be.'

Danny looked at him with serious eyes.

'Ron's right, you're more open now, more trusting. I think that must have been a big thing for you to take on. I hope it works for you, Jimmy, I really hope it does.' He took another sip of his coffee, but the unspoken doubt in Danny's words brought a period of silence. Then a fashion-plate of a man walked into the bar and came over to their table. He took off his designer sunglasses and slipped them into the top pocket of his short-sleeved silk shirt, and smiled. He had a nice smile. The three men looked at him but he looked only at Jimmy.

'Hello, Jimmy. Got a minute, outside?'

There was no accent today. Jimmy paused. Let Danny and Ron know this was a copper, or leave it as just an English bloke who wanted a word? Leave it.

'Sure.' Jimmy stood up. 'Be seeing you, lads.' He finished

the beer in his glass and pushed the half-full bottle across to Ron. 'There you are, Ron, a bonus for you.' He took his glass to the bar and nodded to the barman. The barman gave his back another suspicious look as Jimmy walked to the door where Adonis in a silk shirt and chinos waited.

Outside the bar Ricci put on his sunglasses and they began walking.

'Tell me something, are you protected by God Almighty or does it just look that way?'

'Where are we going, to your nick?'

'No, I'm on sick leave, remember. I'm supposed to be getting ready to be told I'm dying. I can't swan in and out of nicks. We're going somewhere to talk, a bar, not far away but not one like that dump back there. Somewhere comfortable and quiet where you're going to tell me all about yourself.'

'Fine, if you want to be bored to death that's alright by me, just so long as you pick up the tab. The way you look I would guess we're going somewhere expensive.'

'That shouldn't worry a Duns student, not a real Duns student. And that's what we're going to talk about. Not Jimmy Costello the priest in training but another Jimmy Costello, the one who peeped out at me in the rector's office. My guess is, that's the one who gets himself looked after by God Almighty.' Ricci paused and took a sideways glance at the man walking beside him. 'Or maybe it's the Prince of Darkness. Either way, we'll talk about that Jimmy Costello.'

Jimmy didn't like it. This was where it was going to get messy. Co-operate, be the new Jimmy, tell the truth and take the consequences. Or do the sensible thing and pull down the shutters? What was it Danny had said in the bar? Let the dead past bury its dead. It must be a quote. He's a clever bugger, Danny, probably reads a lot. Jimmy decided not to think about it. Time enough to decide what to do when he found out what Ricci knew, what he wanted and what he wanted it for. So they walked on, a crumpled, middle-aged man and a smart, youthful one. Another odd couple.

The Campo del Fiori wasn't the Piazza Navona. There were no film stars, Seria A footballers or big-time celebrities. The Campo was a busy square full of covered market stalls. There was a statue of some long-ago Dominican friar who had been burned to death for being right at the wrong time. Giving him a statue on the spot where he went up in flames was the Catholic Church's way of making amends. Around the sides of the square were smart bars and restaurants where local money hung out. Market stalls next to serious money was very much the way Roman style put on display, but only for its own amusement. Ricci was welcomed as a valued customer when they went inside his bar. Jimmy looked around. It obviously wasn't the sort of place that got crowded during the day so it must be more of a night-time place. Or maybe it was the sun. Drinking inside on a sunny day, no one saw you and you saw no one. Ricci went to a quiet table and ordered a Campari Soda. Jimmy asked for a beer, any beer. The look he got from the waiter was very much like one a magistrate might give to a bag-snatcher as he handed out the sentence. They sat in silence until the drinks arrived and when they came he noticed the beer was imported, Tuborg. Ricci picked up his glass.

'I'm going tell you a mystery story, Jimmy, then you're going make sense of it all for me. Cheers.' He took a drink. 'When I met you last time I didn't like you, you were not what I had been led to expect. I was told I'd meet an ex-London CID sergeant. Someone who had taken early retirement after his wife died of cancer. Someone who had come to Rome to train to be a priest. What I got was you, and like I said, the you I got I didn't like. More important, I really didn't want you to work with me. So I went to the Minister's aide and told him you were not suitable, that you were not what I had been expecting and not what the investigation wanted or needed. I also told him I strongly suspected you were not what you seemed, that your background would almost certainly bear further looking into. Everything seemed fine. The aide agreed that this investigation was too sensitive for any chances to be taken. I could drop you and the Minister would arrange that we find a new man. So I got on with things. Then, one week later, I get pulled in by the Minister himself and slapped on the wrist very hard and told that you're as pure as the driven snow and that you're on this case whether I liked it or not. All I had to do was follow orders and do the job I had been given. And under no circumstances was I ever to mention to anyone my concerns over you.' He took another drink. 'Okay, so far?' Jimmy took a drink and nodded. The beer was good.

'Now comes the interesting part. Remember I told you I did a year at Leicester University on the Erasmus programme when I was a student? Well, while I was there I met another student called Billy Campbell who was from Glasgow, like me. It turned out that Billy had lived near where I grew up. I never knew him as a kid because he wasn't a Catholic – with a name like William Campbell he wouldn't be – so we went to different schools. But both coming from the same place we started to meet and we talked quite a lot. He was doing Art History. He was a good artist, could have gone to Art School, but he knew he wasn't good enough to be a professional so he chose university. We became real friends, in fact I went to more Art History lectures than I went to English ones. We found out we were both interested in going into the police when we graduated. As it turned out, we both did. We've kept in touch ever since, even visited each other, and he's been as successful in the Met as I have here.' He took another drink. 'Well I phoned him after I'd been hauled over the coals by the Minister. I didn't like what had happened. Someone wanted to put you next to me even if that was the last place I wanted you to be. Why was that? What was so special about Jimmy Costello? So I asked my mate Billy to nose about the Met records and maybe ask around and see what he could find out about you. But I told him to keep it very off the record and very low key.' He took another sip of his Campari Soda. He liked to make a drink last, thought Jimmy. Was that being mean or being careful, or maybe both?

'And he found out what?'

'Not much. He told me your file was thin, too thin for a DS working north London for the years you did. He spoke to a couple of blokes who said they remembered you but that's all they'd say, they remembered you. Billy said it looked like you must have been a pretty anonymous copper who didn't do very much.'

'I told you, there's nothing to find. That's no big deal. We can't all be high-flying young crimebusters. Somebody has to be Mr Plod and do the routine stuff.'

'Now that may be true, but I doubt it because of two things. One, your record wasn't just thin, it had been filleted. And two, he'd just asked a few questions about you when he suddenly got told he was being sent to America. A special request had been made for him to give a short series of seminars on scams involving twentieth century modern greats to the top bods of some big art museums. That was his speciality, Modern Greats.'

'So?'

'So all he could think of was that he'd been chosen to go to America and show some art-world big hitters how good he was at his job. He was too busy getting ready to be a star to find out any more about an ex-copper as a favour for a friend.'

'And all this means what?'

'That I didn't do as I was told and keep my nose out of your past, and I got caught looking. So now I think somebody, maybe God Almighty himself, might have my balls in a vice and, unless I get help, could be about to turn the screw. I think I need your help.'

'What makes you think I can help you?'

'Because your record had been doctored, officially doctored. A thorough job, not just a few sheets pulled. That's not something anyone low level could do or get done. Also, instead of pulling in Billy and giving him a bollocking for nosing about into Detective Sergeant James Costello, he got taken out of the frame by someone important enough to get quick favours from across the pond.' Ricci let things sink in for a minute. 'Look, I'm good at what I do. I'm a good copper. Don't let all the trinkets and Armani shit fool you, that's just window dressing.'

'Like the accent?'

'Just like the accent. I've been around and I know the score. Maybe I know it better than most. I think you are, or were, a dangerous man. And I would guess you've always been a man of few, if any, friends. That means the people who look after you and see to it that no one gets a look at your past are doing it because you paid them or because they're afraid of you, of what you know or what you might do.'

Jimmy took a drink of his beer.

'And which do you think, money or the frighteners?'

'It has to be the frighteners doesn't it?'

'Does it?'

'Look, you're a Duns student which means you've got

44

plenty of money, but you were only ever a DS, so where did all the money come from?'

'I sold my house.'

'Do you seriously want me to believe that out of the proceeds you were able to buy the kind of protection you're getting and still have enough left to be self-financing for the rest of your life. Your house sale wouldn't stretch round all of that, would it? And even if it did, someone who pays big money to buy a clean past and protection doesn't come to Rome and sign up for the priesthood. They go and live the high life on the Costas or somewhere like that. What else is loot for, if not the good life? So that leaves it with, either you know enough to make some very important people feel very worried or you're such a dangerous bastard they don't want you coming after them. Or maybe both. Remember, Jimmy, I know people don't have to look dangerous to be dangerous, so the quiet, scruffy look cuts nothing with me.'

Jimmy could feel the old times seeping back into his life and he didn't know how he could stop it.

'Okay, for the sake of argument I'm a dangerous bastard. What would you want a dangerous bastard to do?'

The policeman pushed his glass away and leaned closer.

'If God Almighty wants to punish me then I want the Prince of Darkness looking out for my arse. Tell me the truth the way you see it. Am I right or wrong? Am I in deep shit here, and if I am do I need your help?' Ricci sat back.

Christ, thought Jimmy, why is this happening to me? I want to bury the London copper and do the right thing. I want to change, be the man I should be, the man Bernie and Michael deserve. And here I am being asked to help this bloke, who may very well be in the deep shit he thinks he is, and the only way to do that is to go back to what I was. That can't fucking well be right.

Jimmy made an effort. He wasn't going to slide back without a fight.

'Look, you got a slap on the wrist, your mate got bumped across to the States and I've got a thin record. A few coincidences.'

'If you say so. But would you call it a coincidence that my uncle's ice-cream factory just outside Glasgow suffered a fire four days ago and he got a call telling him it wouldn't be just a fire next time.'

'Who told you?'

'My cousin phoned. I'm the only policeman in the family, he wanted to ask me what they should do. He said my uncle was treating it like it was nothing, just yobs, but my cousin thinks someone's been told to put the arm on him.'

'It happens.'

'Wouldn't you say it's more like someone's decided to put pressure on me through my uncle? Or do you see it as just another coincidence?'

Jimmy didn't see it as a coincidence. It was a message alright. But was it just for Ricci or was it for both of them? Either way it was a very carefully delivered, very clear message, and that made it serious.

'Shit!'

'Yeah, Jimmy, and like I said very deep shit. And if it means the Minister and the Vatican don't get what they want, I think I'm the one right in it.' They both sat in silence. The waiter came over and asked if they wanted more drinks. Ricci looked at Jimmy, who nodded, so he ordered two more.

'So what help am I supposed to give you?'

'First, you agree to work alongside me. Second, you use your contacts from the old days to see that my uncle is left alone. And third, you tell me why I should be frightened of you. If we're going to work together I need to know who I'm working with.'

'All of which is fine for you. What do I get?'

The new Jimmy wouldn't have asked, but for the old Jimmy it was always the first question to get asked. So it got asked.

'I suppose all you get is a chance to do the right thing. You get to help me and my uncle.' Ricci finally finished his drink. If another was coming there was no point in making it last. 'And you get to try and find out if Cheng was murdered. Maybe you even get to find out why, and who was responsible. There's no money in this that I can see, Jimmy, just doing the job and doing it right.'

'That's fuck all and I never worked for...' Jimmy didn't finish the sentence. Don't go back, Jimmy, at least don't go all the way back. Go only as far as they make you go. The drinks came. They both waited until the waiter was gone.

'Being on the side of the angels never turned a profit, Jimmy. The real pay-offs are always on the other side of the street, but I guess you know that better than me. I suppose it all comes down to whether you really are taking this priest thing seriously.'

Jimmy knew he was right. If he did take being a priest seriously he would have to help because that was the right thing to do. But that would mean resurrecting a Jimmy Costello he hoped he had buried for good. And that was definitely the wrong thing to do unless he was certain, absolutely certain, he could stay in control. And if there was one thing he knew about this situation it was that he would be far from in control. So the answer should be 'no'. That way he didn't risk losing the new Jimmy. But the new Jimmy wasn't so easily satisfied. He took it one stage further. He looked at it from another viewpoint. It shouldn't be about what Jimmy Costello wanted. If he walked away from this it meant he was putting himself first, last and always, the only one that mattered. If he did that it would mean he hadn't really changed at all. If he took it on he had to go back to being the old Jimmy Costello. If he walked away and just thought about himself then he still was the old Jimmy. The only difference was that this time there was no wife and kids to hide behind and tell yourself it's all for them. Christ, what a mess, you're wrong if you do and you're wrong if you don't. The Catholic Church, it gets you coming and it gets you going. No wonder they said Catholics were always the experts on guilt.

'Well, Jimmy, are you in or out?'

Jimmy took a drink.

'So what do we do? Do you go and see the Minister's aide or what?'

Ricci's smile reached his eyes and didn't look at all practised. Relief usually doesn't.

'I'll see to this end. You get on with the Glasgow business. I want to be sure my uncle's not going to be part of this.' He picked up his drink, 'Cheers, you made the right decision.' He took a long pull at his Campari Soda, he wasn't being careful any more. Jimmy watched him. Like hell I made the right decision. I didn't make any bloody decision at all. He took a long drink of his Tuborg. Neither of us did.

Chapter 5

THE BUDGET FLIGHT had left Ciampino in bright sunshine and it was clear skies all the way until the North Sea. The final descent took the plane through thick cloud into a dark, wet afternoon. Going down the steps which had been wheeled to the plane's doors, Jimmy turned up his coat collar against the squally rain. Once on the tarmac he didn't hurry as some passengers did. His legs felt stiff and the weather made him feel even more dispirited than he already was. It was all very well for Ricci to say, 'use your old contacts'. What Ricci didn't understand was that if he got in touch with any of the old contacts, the ones who had fixed his file and kept him buried, he would be a dead man very quickly. His safety lay in staying well away from those contacts.

By the time he got out of the rain, his hair and coat were wet. He thought of the Rome sunshine he had left just two hours ago. He ran his fingers through his hair and began to climb the wide, carpeted staircase up to the Arrivals terminal.

'Bloody weather,' he said out loud.

'Get used to it, pal, this is Scotland.'

The Glasgow voice belonged to a smiling young man in

49

a smart, black crombie overcoat, carrying a small suitcase. Jimmy stood still against the stainless steel handrail and watched the man's back. It was nothing, it couldn't be. Why would anyone be put on the plane? Anyway no one knew which plane he would be on. He continued up the steps. I'm getting paranoid, he thought. Then he remembered the old joke, 'just because you're paranoid doesn't mean they're not out to get you!' He smiled to himself. Don't be frightened of shadows, stay sharp. Crossing the Arrivals hall he tried to make his mind find the rails of the old routine.

Be careful but not so careful that you're slow. See what's there but only take notice of what matters. Don't get noticed, don't… don't… He heaved a heavy sigh then said, 'I'm getting too bloody old and tired for this crap.' He was passing an elderly lady in tweeds. She looked at him and moved quickly away. He tried again. Don't make mistakes but know when mistakes have been made, your own or anybody else's…

Because he had only brought hand luggage, a holdall, he was through the terminus building in ten minutes. Just outside Arrivals he boarded an airport bus and asked the driver to let him off at the railway station.

The bus was nearly empty. Jimmy put his holdall on the seat beside him. He had looked out for the Glasgow accent wearing the crombie as he went through the terminal and spotted him at the carousel waiting for the luggage to come from the plane. He was no one, just a coincidence. Sitting in the bus looking at the window, watching the raindrops running down, Jimmy went over things. After his meeting with Ricci in his fancy bar he had gone back to his apartment in the Prati district. He had got out a battered old notebook and looked up the number of a pub in London. He knew he should have thrown the notebook away years ago, it was part of a past he had turned his back on. But somehow he always put it off. Now, when he needed it, there it was. Was that luck or divine intervention? He had rung the pub at about UK lunchtime and when it was answered had asked, 'My name's Jimmy Costello. Can I still contact Bridie MacDonald through this number?'

'Bridie who?'

'MacDonald. Bridie MacDonald from Glasgow. I want to talk to her.'

'You must have a wrong number, there's no one of that name here. What number did you dial?'

Jimmy gave his own Rome phone number.

'No, mate, nothing like. You're miles off,' and the phone was put down.

Two days later his apartment phone had rung and when he answered it a London voice said, 'Ten o'clock Mass Tuesday week, St Peter the Apostle,' and rung off.

When he had told Ricci he was ready to go to Glasgow, Ricci got angry because he wouldn't tell him any more. Ricci thought it meant he didn't trust him. The truth was he wasn't sure how to handle the thing.

Now he had arrived he still wasn't sure.

Another couple of passengers got on the bus, showed their tickets to the driver, stowed their big cases in the luggage racks and sat down. Jimmy looked at his watch, it was three o'clock. He looked out of the window. Everything was blurred by the rain. The driver closed the doors and the bus moved away out of the bus stand. Tomorrow was Tuesday. He should have plenty of time when he got to Glasgow to find out where the church was and give it a walk-by. That way he would get the meeting sorted in his mind. In so far as he could, which wouldn't be by much. The bus stopped right outside Haymarket Station. Jimmy bought a single to Glasgow.

St Peter the Apostle was a big church in a leafy outpost of

privilege and wealth. The Catholic money in this parish was new money. When there were enough Catholics to justify a permanent church the parishioners of St Peter's wanted to make sure that what they got looked good enough to be a symbol of their right to be there. St Peter's had taken its lead from Westminster Cathedral. It had a tower, not a spire, and stone flourishes among the elaborate Italianate brickwork. You might like it or you might hate it, but you couldn't ignore it. Most importantly, you certainly couldn't mistake it for something Protestant. It couldn't have been more Catholic if you had flown a Celtic flag from the top of it.

Jimmy had found a place where he could look at the front of the church without being noticed. The heavy main double doors were shut and the few people who had gone in to Mass had used a side door. He had seen Bridie arrive in a black Mercedes driven by a middle-aged woman. The car had gone into the car park behind the church. A few minutes later they had both reappeared, talking. Just a couple of pious, Catholic biddies going to weekday morning Mass, except they weren't dressed like biddies. The driver was smart and sombre in a well-cut suit. Bridie was expensively brassy. Both affected old-style black mantilla lace head-coverings and carried thick prayer books. Jimmy waited until the Mass was under way then walked across the road and into the car park. The Mercedes was there with a few other cars. He went and stood beside it. Morning Mass, unless the priest was a real zealot, would last no more than half an hour and he wanted to be by the car when Bridie and her driver came out. Also he wanted to try and calm himself and go over things one last time. He leaned against the car with his hands in his coat pockets and waited. After twenty minutes a young woman came into the car park. She gave Jimmy a glare that said, What are you hanging about for, but didn't take it further.

She got into a snappy little red sports car and drove off. Soon other people began leaving and after that Bridie and her driver came round the corner. They both saw him but neither bothered to look at him and kept on talking. 'So I said to Father Leahy, Father, I've done the White Elephant stall for ten years and if you want Mrs Mac to help me you can have Mrs Mac to do the whole thing because I don't need her help or anyone else's.'

The driver pulled her door open.

'The cheek, telling you that you need help to do your stall.'

Bridie opened the passenger side door, got in and pulled it shut. The engine started and Bridie's window slid down.

'What the fuck are you standing there for, Jimmy Costello? If you came to see me, get in – unless you're thinking of running alongside.' Jimmy opened the back door and got in. 'I'll take you back to your hotel and you can tell me what you want on the way.'

'We could talk right here, Bridie. It won't take long.'

'You're getting a lift, pal. And it had better not take long. Where to?' Jimmy gave the name and address of a B&B. The car slid away across the car park and out onto the road.

'Know the way, Norah?'

'Where's it near?' The driver's question was for Jimmy. She looked at him in the mirror.

'The station.'

'Which one?'

'Is there more than one?'

Bridie turned round.

'Stop fucking about. Which station?'

'I don't know Glasgow. I just got somewhere near the station when I came in from Edinburgh.' Norah nodded and Bridie turned away. Jimmy had felt uncomfortable about this meeting ever since he knew it would have to happen. Now, with Bridie at close range, he knew he was right to be uncomfortable. He was right to be shit-scared. Norah looked at him in the mirror.

'I'll take you to Queen Street Station and drop you there.'

'Fine.'

The car headed towards the city centre. Bridie didn't turn round when she spoke. He would have to talk to the back of her head.

'Okay, Jimmy Costello, what do you want?'

'A factory out at Cumbernauld got a Molotov cocktail through the window recently. It was an ice-cream factory owned by...'

'Johnny Fabrizzi. I heard about it.'

'I need to know where the idea originated.'

'That's a fucking queer way of putting it. Why not just say you want to know who did it?'

'Because I don't want to know who did it?'

'No?'

'No. I don't care who did it, and I already know why they did it.'

Bridie paused for a moment.

'Okay, so now I know what you don't care about. What is it you do care about?'

'What sort of organisation was it that wanted it done? No names, no identification, just what sort of outfit was it?'

'Are you trying to get whoever it is off Johnny Fabrizzi's back? Is that it?'

'No. If Johnny Fabrizzi does business in this town he takes the chances that go with it same as everybody else. He'll have to look after himself, if somebody's putting the arm on him let them get on with it. It's nothing to do with me.'

'So what is to do with you?'

The driver looked in the mirror and Jimmy smiled. She would never know what that casual looking smile had cost him in effort. Thank God he had practised.

'That's new since my time, Bridie, something for nothing, free information. I didn't know the Freedom of Information Act applied to your kind of business.'

'Still a smart fucker. No one knocked that out of you yet?'

'Not yet. Look, I'm just calling in a favour. When I gave you Jamie to take home you told me to ask when I wanted something. Now I want something so I'm asking. Why I want it is my business.'

'Like fuck I told you to ask.'

'Okay, a man in a pub said the actual words. But it was the same pub I used to let you know I'd got Jamie's body and it was the same pub that set up this meet. As far as I'm concerned the words came from you. If I'm wrong stop the car and I'll get out and you won't see any more of me.'

'I can make fucking well sure I don't see any more of you any time I like, pal.'

Jimmy felt the knot of fear tighten in his stomach and knew he had to stop it creeping into his voice. If Bridie got a whiff of fear he was dead. She didn't work with weaklings, she stamped on them. All the old fear was right back with him now. He remembered how he had ridden with her in her Mercedes those years ago in London. When he had got out she had told him to kneel down. Then her man Colin had shot him in the back of the head. This time, if the same thing happened, it really would be the gun at the back of his head that went off, not some other gun. This time he wouldn't wake up with only his trousers soiled. He wouldn't wake up at all because what would be left of his face would land in bits of his own brains.

'Well, Bridie, what's it to be?' were the words he said. Oh

God of mercy keep my bloody voice calm, was what he was praying. Bridie turned and looked at him.

'If I can do anything you'll have it tomorrow at the latest.' Then she turned to the driver. 'What stall did Mrs Mac do last year?'

'The bottle stall, remember? She helped Mrs Anderson. It didn't make nearly as much as it usually does. Mrs Anderson couldn't understand it, she said it seemed to go as well as she expected.'

Bridie laughed.

'The devious young bugger. He wants her on my stall because he knows I'll spot her if she dips into the takings. Well, Norah, maybe young Fr Leahy's not as green as he's cabbage-looking after all.'

'What do you think, take her on and see what happens?'

'No, what's the point? If she lifts some cash and I catch her he won't do anything. Her husband does the parish accounts so he can't risk offending him by accusing his wife of being a thief. And I can hardly have her legs broken, can I? If she's light-fingered let her get on with it somewhere else.'

'If her husband's a successful accountant why does she do it? She can't need the money. Is it an illness do you think?'

'If stealing's an illness, then Glasgow's been in an epidemic for as long as I can remember.' They both laughed.

Jimmy sat back and stopped listening. I'm no bloody good at this any more, he thought. It's got to be done properly or not all. A half-hard bastard is no bastard at all. If I get by with Bridie this time it will be on the back of old times not on any talent that's left. I'm just too fucking old and tired. He thought about what Ricci had said in the bar, 'Use your contacts from the old days to see that my uncle is left alone.' Who the hell does he think I am, James bloody Bond. If his uncle's in trouble let him sort it out himself. I'm going to have my hands full just staying alive.

The car turned into George Square and pulled up in front of the station. Jimmy leaned forward. 'I'll hear from you then?'

'Fuck off.'

Jimmy got out and the car pulled away. He went into the first bar he came to and ordered a double whisky. He didn't like whisky but just now beer wouldn't do what was needed.

He drank the whisky as soon as it came and ordered another. With the second one he took his time. What was this really all about? Everything that had happened only made sense if the archbishop really had been murdered. But could it be about more than just a holy old man popping his clogs, even if someone popped them for him? He shook his head. No, because if it was it involved the Italians, the Chinese and the Vatican. And those were only the ones that he knew about, for Christ's sake. And whatever was going on why was he part of it? That was the bit that made no sense at all. What sort of Alice in Wonderland scenario put Jimmy Costello alongside a possible diplomatic incident? And who ordered the ice-cream factory torched? The Chinese, the Vatican or the Italian Secret bloody Service? He grinned as the whisky took effect. Maybe he was James Bond after all. Maybe, without noticing it, instead of signing up for the Catholic priesthood the papers had got mixed up and he was now part of MI fucking 99. He finished his whisky and felt better. Whatever this was all about it certainly wasn't James Bond, because it wasn't some drama, it wasn't even comedy. It was pure bloody farce. He got off his stool, left the bar and headed to his hotel which was nowhere near the B&B whose name and address he had given to Bridie. At least he'd managed to stay careful.

Chapter 6

IT WAS ABOUT eight o'clock that night when the phone rang in his room. The message was brief. There was no introduction, no preamble of any sort.

'It was organised through Special Branch and they didn't use local talent. The local police don't want to know so they're writing it off as hooligans. It was nothing to do with anything in Glasgow. That's it. Understood?'

'Yeah.'

Whoever it was rang off. Jimmy slowly put the phone down.

'Shit.'

It wasn't bad news. It was very bad news. The fire was exactly what he didn't want it to be and Bridie knew where he was staying. Did that matter? She'd come across with the information so maybe it didn't, but with Bridie you never could tell. He should have stayed in Rome. This wasn't his sort of business any more. He couldn't deal with people like Bridie, he just wasn't up to it. The phone rang again.

'Your lift to the airport is here, Mr Costello. I'm afraid I'll have to charge you for the two nights even though you'll not be staying tonight after all. Your bill is ready at Reception.'

'Thanks, I'll be down in a few minutes.'

Jimmy began to gather his things and stuff them into his holdall. He hadn't ordered a car so it had to be Bridie's people waiting for him downstairs. There was no point in running. Even if he got past whoever was downstairs, how long would he last in Glasgow with Bridie looking for him? It was her turf and she knew it like she knew the inside of her handbag. What choices had he got? He didn't want to finish up as a permanent Glasgow resident, maybe in the same cemetery as two of Bridie's sons. What the hell, it was just possible the car would actually take him to the airport.

Bridie's driver was waiting for him at Reception. She was still wearing her Mass clothes, only the mantilla and prayer book were missing. Jimmy paid his bill and followed her out of the hotel. It was the black Mercedes and there was no one in it. Jimmy looked around. What was there to see, why look? What's the point of being careful at the wrong time?

'Get in.'

He threw his holdall onto the back seat and got in beside the driver. It wasn't a long journey and it wasn't to the airport. She took him to Queen Street Station.

'I thought you were taking me to the airport?'

'The airport is over thirty miles away at Prestwick. If you want to fly somewhere go to Edinburgh and fly from there, I'm not your taxi. I just deliver you here and give you your message.'

'Then why is it called Glasgow airport if it's bloody miles away from Glasgow?'

If the driver was annoyed she wasn't about to show it. Jimmy liked her, whatever it was she did besides driving for Bridie he guessed she would be good at it.

'Finished being funny?'

He nodded. Now he knew he was safe the tension had

eased and he didn't need to hear his own voice to know he was still alive.

'Okay, here's your message. There's no more favours for you here, Costello. If you're still in Scotland, anywhere in Scotland, tomorrow morning your stay will be permanent. And if Bridie ever hears you're back you'll wind up like Jamie, and you know how Jamie wound up.'

He knew.

'Now get out.'

Jimmy watched the black Merc pull away then looked around.

'What the hell am I looking for? This is a railway station, who am I going to see?'

He bought a ticket then went to the platform where an Edinburgh train was in. While he sat in the train waiting for it to pull away Jimmy thought about Bridie. He knew that running most of Glasgow's serious crime over the years had cost her a husband and two of her sons and God knows what else. But she was still at the top of the pile and still had the guts and muscle to do just about anything she wanted. But what she actually did was go to morning Mass and help at the parish bazaar. How the hell do you figure a woman like Bridie? A violent, Mass-going biddy who runs serious crime and a parish bazaar stall. He wondered what she thought about it all, her life, her family, her business and her Church. If she ever thought about it. He specially wondered why she went to Mass in the morning. But then he thought, I suppose she's got a lot to pray about, we all have. The train pulled away from the station out into the night and Jimmy switched off his brain. Time to rest. Later on, when he was safely back in Rome he would do the thinking.

At Edinburgh airport Jimmy walked to the nearest departures screen. There was no flight to Rome but there was the last KLM Cityhopper going to Schiphol. From there it wouldn't be a problem to get to Rome. He went to the KLM desk and bought a ticket, checked in and went through the security checks into the departure lounge. In one of the bars he looked at the beers and ordered a Tuborg. He took his drink to a table and sat down. It wasn't very busy, the rush of the day was over. All that was left were people who had to take a late flight, tired, quiet people. He looked around. Just people on their way to different places passing the time among the glass, chrome and bright lights of the duty-free shops. Ordinary people who, if they looked at him at all, would see just another ordinary person waiting for his flight and having a beer. And that's what he was, just an ordinary person, waiting for his flight. He was going home. He grinned. 'Never touched me, Bridie. Never bloody touched me.' And he took a drink.

His flight landed at Schiphol just after midnight local time. There he had a choice, a flight to Florence which would get him on his way within the hour or he could wait two and a half hours for a direct Rome flight. He was out of Scotland so there was no hurry, but the idea of hanging round an airport for a couple of hours didn't appeal so he opted for Florence. At Florence airport he had the same choice, hang around and catch the first Rome flight just before seven. That would get him into Fiumicino at seven fifty-five. Or he could go to Florence station and catch the five thirty train which would also get him into Rome at seven fifty-five. He was knackered, he didn't want to hang about in another airport. He decided to go to the station, get a bit of breakfast and take the first train to Rome so he could rest, stretch his legs and sleep maybe. The train would put him directly into central Rome, not out at the airport. The train made sense.

The taxi from the station dropped him off outside his apartment. The tree-lined street where he lived was well into another beautiful morning and people were on the move. He had made it back, he was home and dry. He went up to his apartment. Once inside he drew the bedroom curtains, shutting out the morning sun, undressed and went to bed. He hadn't been able to sleep on the train and his body was crying out for rest. Four hours later he woke, showered and shaved, then dressed and made himself some coffee. He took his coffee to the phone and dialled Ricci's mobile. Ricci was quick to answer.

'Yeah?'

'I'm back, it's sorted.'

'He'll be left alone?'

'I did what I could.'

'But he'll be left alone?'

'I told you, I did what I could.'

And he put the phone down. It wasn't a lie, he had done what he could. He had done what he went to do. He just hadn't done what Ricci wanted him to do, that's all. The phone rang again. He picked it up.

'Tell me he's alright.'

The voice was angry.

'He's okay. I did what I could.'

There was a silence.

'You did what you could?'

'That's what I said.'

There was another pause.

'Okay. Thanks.'

Jimmy put the phone down. If Ricci let his personal feelings screw up his thinking he would make more mistakes. He'd already made one, quite a bad one, and what made it worse was he didn't even know it. But it's not my job to tell him, thought Jimmy, just like it's not my job to tell him that maybe he's not as shit-hot as he thinks he is. It's not my job to tell him bugger all, not unless I need to. Only if and when I need to.

Jimmy made himself another coffee.

The fire had only closed one part of the factory and only for one day. A look at the Glasgow *Herald* website before he had left Rome had told him that. The important thing was that now he was sure that it was a message and he knew what sort of outfit had sent it. And that meant he knew what the message was supposed to do. Which showed it didn't just mean, keep your nose out of Jimmy Costello's past, Inspector Ricci. It meant a lot more than that.

He looked at his watch. It was just after one and he felt hungry. He would go out, walk in the sunshine for a bit to get rid of the damp, depressed feeling he'd picked up in Scotland and brought back with him. Then he'd get a plate of pasta. After that he would come back and think. There was a lot to think about. He smiled and finished his coffee.

Never touched me, Bridie, never fucking touched me, and he got his jacket and went out.

When Jimmy woke he was in bed with a clear plastic bag hanging from a stand at his bedside feeding fluid to his left arm. He felt no pain. He didn't feel much of anything. He guessed that was because he was shot full of stuff. He lay there trying to remember. He remembered leaving his apartment. Then it all went blank. The door of the room opened slightly and a nurse put her head round. She smiled at him and disappeared and the door closed. Jimmy just lay there. There was nothing to think about, so he didn't think. He went back to sleep. When he next opened his eyes Ricci was sitting by the bed looking at him. He wore a light sports coat and an open neck blue shirt with his sunglasses in the top pocket.

'Hello Jimmy, welcome back.'

'How bad is it?'

'Pretty bad. They certainly messed you up, a few ribs broken and the doctors were worried about your spleen for a while. The biggest worry was whether your head injuries had done some real damage. But you're a tough old bird. It seems you'll make a full recovery.'

'How long have I been out?'

'You were out for two days after they brought you in, then you sort of came round and rambled for a bit. You were trying to tell me about someone touching you or not touching you. You didn't make much sense. Then you seemed to start sleeping properly. You slept for two whole days. Now the doctors say you'll be okay.'

'I don't remember talking to you.'

'I don't suppose you'll remember anything for a while. But it will come back, just give it time.'

Jimmy looked at the ceiling. He felt tired again.

'Your wallet was gone and your watch and mobile.'

'I don't have a mobile. I don't use one.'

'Just your watch and wallet then.' There was silence for a moment. 'Was this a random mugging, Jimmy, or was it something else? You live in a classy neighbourhood. Not many people from the Prati get mugged inside their entrance lobby.'

Jimmy tried to shrug but stopped as the pain shot through him. He grimaced. Ricci put a gentle hand on him. 'Stay still. Any moving will hurt. They kicked you about quite a lot. Maybe they were Roma fans and thought you supported Lazio.' He was lightening things up.

Jimmy smiled. Smiling didn't hurt.

'I wasn't wearing a Lazio shirt.'

'Maybe you look like a Lazio supporter.'

'What's a Lazio supporter supposed to look like?'

'I don't know, ask a Roma fan. Football isn't something I'm interested in.'

Jimmy felt better for talking. He guessed Ricci knew that, or maybe the doctor had told him to get him talking to wake him up a bit.

'Where was I found?'

'In the lobby of your apartments, beside the stairway. A neighbour found you.'

'They were waiting for me?'

'Must have been. You've got a very good address, Jimmy, and good security goes with a good address. If they were inside the building then they weren't muggers hanging about on the off-chance. Was it anything to do with the trip to Glasgow?'

'Maybe. Maybe somebody wanted to remind me of a message.'

'A message? One that went with the fire at my uncle's place?'

'No, another message. One I was given at the station before I left.'

'Quite a message. It nearly killed you. Couldn't your old contacts have protected you?'

'You don't understand, do you? The message came from one of my old contacts. That's the sort of relationship we have. If I try and talk to them, they try to kill me.'

Ricci started to laugh but it died away.

'You're not joking are you?'

'Look at me. Do I look like I'm fucking well joking? This was from one of them who owed me a favour. That's why I'm in here and not in the morgue.'

Ricci thought about it.

'Sorry. With what I found out and what I guessed I naturally thought you had contacts, people who could protect you.'

'They're only interested in protecting themselves. I know too much and if, for one second, they think I might tell anyone what I know I really will be a dead man.'

'I see.'

'No you don't.'

'You're right, I don't. If you're such a threat why aren't you dead already?'

'Because they tried and they found out I'm hard to kill.'

'They tried?'

'In London, a few years ago. The one who ordered it is dead, so is the one he sent to do the job. So are a few other people. But I'm still alive and if they're sure I'll keep my mouth shut they'll leave me alone. After the London business I deposited some papers, life insurance. They'll have guessed I'd do that, so now it's important that I stay alive or die in the right way.'

'The right way being only after they've got their hands on your life insurance.'

'That's right. Now you know.'

'Now I know.'

Jimmy felt totally used up. He closed his eyes and as he fell asleep his last thoughts were, dear god, let it all end here. I've had enough.

After a while a doctor came in and checked his pulse.

'He's doing fine. He'll be up in a couple of days and out of here in a week.'

'Thanks, that's good news. I know he'll be glad to hear that when he wakes up.' Ricci got up and looked at Jimmy. 'Get well, there's work to do. And we're the ones who are going to do it.'

He left. Jimmy slept. His body was busy getting well.

Chapter 7

DOCTORS MAKE MISTAKES, but in Jimmy's case their diagnosis confirmed Ricci's assessment. He was a tough old bird and mending quickly. Ricci was his only visitor and came at the end of most days. He would bring Jimmy up to date and they would discuss progress. At this stage it was all that Jimmy could do. Ricci did the paperwork. He wrote up notes, cross-referenced, checked and then wrote up more notes. Jimmy hadn't shared the Glasgow information with him. Time enough for that when he knew where it fitted. Bridie's information gave him Special Branch and that put UK Intelligence in the picture. They were the only ones who could have got Special Branch involved. The whole thing was growing before his eyes, growing a damn sight too fast, and it only made sense if Cheng had been murdered, and the murder was the tip of a very big iceberg.

After three days of checking and re-checking they still had nothing except Cheng.

'Okay, let's get a better picture of him. There's got to be plenty of paper on him, files, archived articles, official memos. See the people he met, anyone who knew anything about him. Give it the works.'

Ricci had the full support of the Minister so he used it. For four days he never stopped digging and each evening visited Jimmy to go over what he had found.

Cheng had been born in Guandong Province in southern China but the family moved to Portuguese Macau in 1945 during the civil war and Cheng was educated by the Jesuits. When he left school he applied to join the order, was accepted and sent to Rome for training. In Rome he was a star student, tipped for a top-flight career, but after ordination he asked to go back into Mao's People's Republic as a parish priest. He dug his heels in and in the end got what he wanted. He went and China simply swallowed him up. Ricci's paper trail dried up until 1971 when his release was officially announced. He'd served five years of re-education through hard labour under the careful direction of the Red Guards, just another victim of the Cultural Revolution. The only reason his release was noticed was that the Fr Cheng who had gone into prison was Bishop Cheng on release. He'd been elevated by the Vatican while he was being 're-educated'. Not that they'd thought to tell anyone. Then nothing until 1978, when he was re-arrested at the tail end of the Cultural Revolution for anti-patriotic behaviour and acting as a spy for a foreign power, official code for any Catholic priest loyal to the Vatican. This time the sentence he served was ten years. His refusal to sign up to the government-sponsored Official Catholic Church meant that he spent a further seven years in prison at one time or another. But one more Catholic bishop being arrested or released wasn't news except to the handful of China-watchers. To them, which members of the Catholic hierarchy were in favour and which were in prison was as good a barometer as any to the power struggles within the ruling Communist Party. As a simple rule of thumb Bishop Cheng was invaluable. If he was in prison, the hardliners were on top. If he was out the reformers were calling the shots.

By the end of the century China was changing fast and ready to play its part as an economic superpower. In 1999 they got back Macau from the Portuguese and during the official celebrations it was noted by the government-controlled press that a senior Catholic cleric who had grown up in Macau but had served all his priestly life in the People's Republic was visiting his family. That was Beijing's way of saying that any member of the Catholic Church, even the unofficial Catholic Church, had the same freedom of action and movement as any other citizen who had served the Chinese people loyally and for so long. The now Archbishop Cheng was photographed with his family and local Communist officials.

Ricci showed Jimmy a copy of a newspaper photo, a small, smiling man who looked shy and insignificant in clerical black but who, even in the news photo, gave an impression of deep inner peace and strength.

The trip to Macau was a success and was the beginning of his official rehabilitation during which neither he nor the government ever referred to his years in prison. To the Vatican and to the Chinese government, Cheng was a small piece in a long and hard-fought political chess game. After Macau the game had moved into a new phase and Cheng's role changed accordingly.

His visit to Rome figured widely in the national Chinese media, a signal to the people of China and to the West that a new tolerance was growing which could even encompass unofficial Catholic prelates. His return to Rome should have been the crowning moment of his rehabilitation but it didn't turn out that way. He died suddenly and in what could now appear to be suspicious circumstances.

Ricci was sitting on the bed. He put down his notes. Jimmy was in his pyjamas sitting on the chair beside his bed.

He looked at the notes. A man's life in a few pages.

'Poor old sod.'

'Wouldn't you think, Jimmy, that this shows that if there is a God he is at best indifferent to human suffering or at worst using humanity as a plaything to service a rather nasty sense of humour? Or, being a good Catholic, don't you allow yourself to dwell on such things too much?'

'I don't dwell on them at all. We die. God or no God it's the same for everyone. You've got all you're going to get on him and now we know him as well as we're ever going to. So who would want him dead?'

Ricci shook his head.

'I've tried them all. Diplomats, bureaucrats, people with contacts in the underground Catholic Church in China, they all come up the same. Archbishop Cheng was universally loved and respected as a priest and as a man. There's nothing I can find that might make him a target.'

They sat in silence for a minute. Ricci reached down, ran his fingers through his pages of notes and then looked back to Jimmy.

'Maybe it is just a case of natural causes.'

'It's all a load of fucking bollocks, that's what it is.'

There was no doubt in Ricci's mind that Jimmy was ready to be discharged. Inactivity may have left him irritable and angry but Ricci wholeheartedly agreed with his assessment. 'And if it's a murder, it's the best one I've come across. No suspects, motives or clues, and no reason for it to have happened. Nothing. What are we supposed to be looking into and why am I here? That's what sticks in my throat. Why drag me into this?'

'To keep an eye on me?'

'That doesn't stand up. You get told to bring me in on things. But when we meet, you don't like me...'

Ricci smiled, a real smile.

'I didn't know you then.'

'You don't know me now. You only think you know me.'

'Have it your own way.'

'As I said, you don't want me on the case and you say so. What happens?'

'I get stuck with you anyway and I get smacked on the wrist and warned off.'

'Then there's your mate from university suddenly getting sent to America. They probably expected you to get someone to sniff about, an inter-plod favour, one copper to another, off the record. They would have had that covered, you would have got what they wanted you to have. But you came at it your own way. They didn't know about Billy so they weren't ready for him. When he turned up they had to move quickly, which they did, and it had to be good, which it was, which means resources and contacts, which they have. All of which makes them official. Which is exactly what I got told in Glasgow.'

Ricci was looking at him.

'You never told me that it was something official. I thought it was just local muscle being told to put the arm on my uncle to get at me. You told me you'd straightened it out.'

'Wrong. I told you I did what I could. What you thought I meant was your affair. I didn't go to Glasgow to help your uncle. What the hell would I go to Glasgow to help your uncle for? I'm not with Age Concern. I'm supposed to be acting and thinking like a copper, not a bloody care worker.'

'You're a tricky bastard, Jimmy. Why didn't you tell me?'

'Why should I? It was your mistake. If you let personal feelings queer your judgement it's not my job to nursemaid you. Our job is to try and make sense of this shit. After that my only priority is to look out for me and up to now I've not done so well on either score.' He could see that Ricci was pissed off at him, but he didn't care. 'It was Special Branch who organised the fire in Glasgow.'

'Special Branch!'

'So my guess is that Special Branch also arranged for your mate's trip to America.'

Ricci rejoined the team. There would be time later to think about Jimmy and Glasgow. Now he needed to think about the job in hand.

'There's only one outfit that could use Special Branch for stuff like that, British Intelligence.'

'I know.'

'Why would they be involved?'

'God knows. But they are, they have to be. All I can think is there's some firm out there watching all this who can get British Intelligence to do their dirty work for them while they stay invisible.'

'Okay, let's say someone who can pull some very powerful strings is watching us. Where does that get us?'

'It makes me ask why they drew attention to themselves? Why set up the Glasgow thing? They must have known we'd look into it and that there was a good chance we'd come up with Special Branch.'

Jimmy was right. Why show yourself if you've invested so much effort in staying invisible? Ricci thought about it and came up with the only answer that made any sense to him.

'Because once they got rid of Billy to America they knew they couldn't stay invisible, that we'd work out the fix was in, so they decided they wanted us to know we were being watched. The fire at my uncle's factory was their way of saying, we know who you are, we know what you're doing and we can reach you any time we want so make sure you come to the right conclusion.'

Jimmy nodded his head in a tired way, it made some sort of sense and he had nothing better to offer.

'Maybe I should have told you before but I'm not up to this sort of thing anymore. I have my hands full just looking after me. Look, don't expect too much. I'll do my best but I can't promise my best will be good enough.'

Ricci sat forward.

'It's okay, you were right. I didn't think it through, you did. I thought family, you thought copper. I guess I'm more Italian than I thought I was. Maybe there's not much of the Glaswegian left in me.'

'Thank God for that if the Glaswegians I've met are anything to go by. And don't worry you made a mistake, it was your family they targeted not mine. If it had been my daughter or her kids in Australia you'd have had to be the one doing the thinking for both of us.'

But Ricci knew Jimmy was just saying words. You didn't help anybody by being sloppy. Being sloppy got people hurt.

'Look Jimmy, if Cheng's death is clean why is Billy going to America and why the fire? If the key to this isn't Cheng then all that's left is you and me and it's not about me. Whatever's going on you're a part of it. Are you sure there's nothing in your past that could link you to any...'

'Nothing.'

'There's got to be something, something or someone you know. You have to be connected to Cheng or the Vatican somehow.' Jimmy shook his head. He had gone down that road as far as it went. There was nothing. 'Then it's a brick wall. We've got Cheng and that's all we've got.'

It was that time any detective hates to arrive at in a case. Nowhere to go.

'No it's not.' Jimmy was sitting up, he had an angry look about him.

'What's up?'

'If this is about me we need to know, don't we?'

'Yes.'

'So why don't we just fucking well ask? Why piss about wasting our time trying to work it out? If we're working for the good guys, let's ask them. If they won't tell us, we'll tell them to go and fuck themselves and their investigation.'

Ricci grinned.

'They've got you mad at them now, haven't they? You look like you could be a bit of a handful when you're mad.'

The anger went out of Jimmy's eyes.

'Maybe once, back when Moses was in the fire brigade and Pontius was a pilot. Now I just want to ask the tricky bastards what's going on. Either we're on the same side and we help each other or we're not.'

'You and me are supposed to be on the same side but you didn't tell me about Glasgow.'

'I told you when you needed to know.'

'And now we need to know if this is anything to do with you?'

'Yes. What have we got so far.'

'On Cheng's death? Nothing.'

'That's right. Nothing was what we were always going to get even if we went all over Cheng like a cheap suit. If it's a murder and it's fireproof it means it was done by people who can kill an archbishop in Rome and leave the body lying about and still be sure of total immunity. They know there's nothing to find. There's nothing, and we found it.'

'You're saying this is political?'

'It's got to be, what else can it be? An Intelligence Service is out there watching us, but why does it have to be British Intelligence? The Glasgow thing got organised by Special Branch but if the CIA asked for it to be done they'd do it, they'd do it for any friendly agency if the story they got told was okay. This has to be political. And that, my friend, puts it well out of our league. We're not official so we don't have official resources which means instead of looking we need to be told. Like I said, up until now we didn't need to know, but now we do. I think the Vatican wanted to watch us, to be sure we could cut it.'

'And if we came up with nothing...'

'Which is what we were supposed to come up with...'

'But still wanted to go on because now we know we're looking for something...'

'Then we'll get told. We'll get told what we need to know and be able to move on.'

The room door opened and a nurse came in. Ricci turned to her.

'It's okay, nurse, I'm about to go. Just give me a few more minutes.'

'Signor Costello needs his rest.'

'Gone in a couple of minutes, promise.'

Ricci's charm bounced off and hit the floor with a thud.

'Two minutes.'

Then she left.

'No sale for your good looks there.'

'Jimmy, there's a problem.'

'Just one?'

'Look, maybe you're right but how do we do this? You can barge in and say, "Tell us what we want or I quit." That's fine for you, you get to go back to being a student priest. But what about me? I go back to what? If I say go fuck yourselves to the Minister then whoever put me into this will see to it that I'll be lucky to go back to work as a traffic cop.' He paused. 'You can see what I mean can't you? Your career as a copper is over, mine's just taking off. It's a big ask for me to go along with it your way, a very big ask.'

Jimmy smiled. His smile was getting better, he'd been practising it while he was stuck in hospital. Now it nearly went all across his mouth.

'Being on the side of the angels always is a big ask, isn't it? Wasn't that something you told me?'

Ricci took the point.

'Okay, it's easy to tell someone else to do the right thing. It's not so easy to do it when you have to pay the price yourself. Maybe right and wrong never look quite so clear cut when you're at the sharp end.'

'Don't worry, I don't need you to do much, you won't get any crap on your record. I'll see to it that you stay as clean as your nice, sharp clothes.'

'And you, will you stay clean?'

'Me? Who the hell would notice or care if Jimmy Costello picked up another bit of crap. I stopped smelling of roses long ago when...'

'Moses was in the fire brigade and Pontius was a pilot.'

They both grinned.

'I get out of here tomorrow morning. Set up a meeting to talk to that Minister's aide for as soon as you can. Now piss off. I'm tired and like the nurse said, I need my rest.'

Ricci got off the bed and Jimmy climbed in but Ricci didn't leave.

'About Glasgow, will my uncle be okay?'

Jimmy's eyes were closed.

'How the hell would I know? Your uncle's nothing to do with the case so it's nothing to me one way or the other.' Jimmy turned over. 'Close the door on your way out.'

Ricci left closing the door quietly behind him. He had no doubts that Jimmy was on the right track. He must have been something special as a detective. He had a mind like a steel trap on wheels, and it only ran in one direction when he was working. Maybe that's why they wanted him on this case. Will I turn out like him if I get to be as good as he was, as good as he still is? And if I turn out like him, will it have been worth it?

He would set up the meeting, but from now on he would trust Jimmy about as much as he trusted the Minister's aide, which was only as far as he had to. By the time he was out of the hospital he had made a decision. He had been right the first time. He didn't like Jimmy Costello after all.

Chapter 8

JIMMY WAS BACK home, having a cup of coffee. His body was aching after the journey from the hospital, reminding him that he wasn't quite ready yet to go ballroom dancing. There was a buzz from the street door. He went to the intercom. It was Danny.

'Come up. Top floor.' There was no glad to see you in Jimmy's invitation. Nobody had visited him in hospital except Ricci. It wasn't that he had wanted visitors, if he'd been asked he would have told the nurses to turn away any that came. But that wasn't the point. Nobody had come to be turned away, not Danny, not Ron, not anybody.

Danny appeared at the door and Jimmy took him into the living room where he motioned him to an easy chair. They sat down.

'What's been going on, Jimmy?'

'I was in hospital, that's what's been going on. If you'd bothered to ask you'd have known.'

Danny laughed his deep West Indian laugh.

'Oh I asked. When you suddenly dropped out of sight I asked. You'd been given permission to make a short trip back to the UK on urgent family business. Which sounds a bit

78

thin seeing as how you told us not so long ago that you got no family in the UK. When you get back the first thing that happens is you get mugged and put into hospital. Ron and I came to see you but we got told you weren't having any visitors. No one. You were off-limits.'

It must have been Ricci's idea, though God knows why he did it.

'I just thought I didn't have any visitors.'

'And I phoned every morning. Didn't anyone say? Today they said they'd discharged you so I came round. I just want to know if you're okay.'

'Thanks, Danny. I'm a bit fragile still, but like the bloke said, I'm a tough old bird. I'll be fine. How are things going with you?'

'Not so well.'

Jimmy could tell it was going to be something serious. Danny paused before going on, getting himself ready.

'I'm giving up at the end of this term. It's just not for me. I wanted to tell you before anyone else because…' he paused again, looking for the right words, 'because I think we might have become friends. Because I think there's something I recognise in you that I know is in me.'

'About being a copper?'

'No, something about living with who we are, about accepting the person we find we've become. I think we're both looking for something. Not a new start, there's never a completely new start. The past doesn't let you go that easily. But trying to change, trying to make sure the future is different. I thought becoming a priest might be a part of building a future I could be happy to live with. Maybe you did as well. In my case I was wrong.'

'Do you want to talk about it?'

'No. It won't help to drag it out and show it about.' Danny

grimaced. 'It's no big deal. I'll survive. I'll go back to Jamaica and get myself a place. Nothing fancy. I didn't stash away a pile from turning a blind eye while my hand was out or anything like that. I got by on my salary. I wasn't married so it wasn't hard. I'll get by on my pension and go back to being just another old sinner. One more bad Catholic in need of God's love and mercy.'

They sat in silence.

'Coffee?'

'No, I hate the muck.'

'That's right, I forgot. You say it whenever we go to the bar. Why do you drink it if you don't like it?'

'It's a penance.' They both laughed. The seriousness had gone. Now they were just talking. 'Each day I have to say three Hail Marys, and drink filthy coffee.'

'It must have been a real serious sin.'

'A Jamaican who hates coffee – that's not just serious, it should be mortal. But there's no mortals these days, Jimmy. Nobody's sin sends them to Hell any more. Everything's venial now. The days of big sins and big sinners are over. Everybody gets forgiven. Ever since somebody discovered that God's love is unconditional. You can't deserve it, you can't earn it, you get it whether you like it or not.'

'Like fluoride in the water.'

Danny laughed loudly.

'Spot on. And if God's love is unconditional his forgiveness has to be as well. So we all get forgiven whether we ask for it or not. Like fluoride in the water.' Then the laughter died away. 'Except that it isn't like that, is it? Most people don't want to think about whether they need forgiveness or not because they never look at themselves too closely. If they did they might not like what they saw.'

'Listen, it was nice of you to call but I'm a bit weary.'

Danny got up.

'Sure. I just popped round. I can see you're needing your beauty sleep.'

Jimmy got up and put out his hand.

'Thanks, Danny. I'm sorry you're packing it in.'

After Danny left Jimmy picked up the phone and dialled Ricci's number.

'You get that meeting with the Minister's aide? Good, when is it? Pick me up. Never mind that, let me deal with it. I said I would. Don't worry, I know what I'm doing. And we'll skip our meeting tomorrow. I want to be ready for your man when I see him. Just get me there, I'll do the rest.'

Jimmy put the phone down. Two days to rest up and then it was back to work. He went into the bedroom, drew the curtains and lay down on the bed. In a few minutes he was asleep.

'They won't let you in. You can't just walk into a government office and see whoever you like.'

'We'll see.'

Ricci had picked Jimmy up at nine thirty and was now driving through the mad Roman traffic. A passing car swerved in front of him. Ricci pumped the horn a couple of times, a reflex reaction. Everybody pumped the horn.

'Just being with me won't get you in. I haven't got that kind of pull.'

'Let's just wait and see.'

Ricci drove on. If Jimmy wasn't going to tell him he wasn't going to tell him.

'I hope you know what you're doing, that's all.'

'Like you had it your way so I got no visitors?'

'That was just a simple precaution. You were rambling. If you had visitors you might have said something.'

Jimmy knew Ricci was right but it didn't make him like being managed.

All the bloody scooters in the world seemed to be on Rome's roads, thought Jimmy. And on cue a powerful scooter, ridden by a woman wearing a smart business suit and a bright yellow crash helmet, cut up a leather-clad Suzuki rider. He retaliated by revving up his big bike and roaring past her, causing shockwaves of braking, swerving and hooting. Meanwhile, a Barbie babe in a tight white top, sunglasses and jeans, with masses of curly black hair spilling from under her helmet calmly slid her scooter into the openings the manoeuvring caused. Then everything subsided back into the usual horn-laden chaos.

Jimmy wondered why there were so few accidents. One day of this madness in London and the roads would be strewn with crash-helmeted corpses. But for Rome it was pure routine.

Ricci pulled across the traffic and turned into a back street behind a big government building. It was like all the other streets to the rear of the fine buildings. On one side were the unlovely backs of offices and on the other, high, blank brick walls.

They came to one of the entrances in the high walls. Originally designed for coach and horses, it was big enough for a car or van to get in but nothing bigger. Ricci turned the car into the entrance and stopped at a barrier where a female guard stood at the window, watching them. Another guard, wearing army fatigues and with an automatic rifle slung round his neck came out of the hut carrying a clipboard. Ricci slid the window down, showed his ID and gave his name. The guard took the ID, checked the photo and checked Ricci. Then he checked his list. He gave Ricci back his ID and looked at Jimmy. Ricci looked at Jimmy.

'Okay, now what? Do you get us shot or what?'

'Tell this guy who you're here to see. Tell him you have a visitor with you, give him my name and ask him to okay it with your man inside. Tell him to tell your man you have to bring me to the meeting and apologise for not being able to give him any notice. Do it all slow and easy.'

If the guard understood what Jimmy had said, he didn't register any response. His companion emerged from the hut and positioned herself where she had a clear field of fire at the car. Ricci spoke to the guard with the clipboard, who disappeared into the hut. The female guard just stood in the same place but now she wasn't holding her rifle quite so casually. After a few minutes the first guard returned and once more asked for Jimmy's name. After he had added it to his clipboard list, he told Ricci to pick up two temporary passes at the reception desk.

The barrier was raised and they drove into a courtyard with a few cars parked and three bulk waste bins against a wall. As Jimmy got out of the car he wondered how they got emptied. The back of the building was several storeys of grimed-over brickwork with lots of small windows. It was festooned with drain pipes of all sizes. This was the side of the building where it got rid of its waste, the arse end. They walked away from the car. The guard holding the rifle watched them all the way and the muzzle of her gun tracked them until they went into the building through a heavy door.

They walked down a corridor with no covering on the stone floor, went through another door and found themselves in the reception area. This was front-of-house, where the people who mattered came and went, all was style and elegance; the floor, now marble and inlaid with patterns, the ceiling domed and elaborately decorated.

Once Jimmy and Ricci had been electronically swept Ricci collected his pass and began the business of explaining Jimmy to the official behind the desk. Phone calls were made while two immaculately uniformed guards looked on, nursing highly polished weapons. Finally Jimmy's pass was handed over and they crossed the hall to the lift.

Their man was on the third floor, which made him important. His office was high enough to be out of the noise of the street but not so high that the rooms had become small. They walked down a carpeted corridor and stopped at a door. Ricci knocked and they waited.

'Knock again.'

'He heard. He'll tell us to come in when he's ready. He's probably pissed off for having to okay you without notice.'

After a short while a voice called them in.

It was a big, baroque room with large windows letting in plenty of light. The furniture was contemporary and stylish, in sharp contrast to the room itself, which was from an age when office chic hadn't existed and art was never abstract. On the ceiling, surrounded by fancy plasterwork, a group of naked young ladies were about to get up to naughty things with some men who had pointed ears, pointed beards and goats' legs. The floor was covered in an immaculate light, neutral-coloured carpet. The sort not intended to be trodden by feet that saw a lot of street work.

Jimmy liked it all. Something appealed to him about the sight of the naked cherubs smiling down from the plasterwork at the sleek, glass-topped desk with its thick chromium legs. It was all vaguely ridiculous, and the cherubs saw the funny side. The man behind the desk obviously didn't. Either he was sucking a wasp or he was angry and about to let them know it.

He rapped out something in Italian.

Ricci's voice was humble. 'Signor Costello speaks very poor Italian.'

The Minister's aide turned his stare on Jimmy.

The wasp gave him trouble again. He really should stop sucking it, Jimmy thought as he sat down next to Ricci.

'Perhaps you can explain, Inspector, why Mister Costello has to be present, and without any notice?'

It was Jimmy who answered.

'Because I phoned him this morning and told him to pick me up and bring me. I told him if he didn't I was out of this and for good. So he brought me.'

The expensive cut of the aide's dark suit did its best to hide his chubbiness. He had a full face and curly fair hair. Pure *cinquecento*, real ceiling material. A bad-tempered cherub in a city suit, Jimmy thought.

The aide kept his eyes on Ricci.

'I am not satisfied, Inspector...' Jimmy cut in. 'I want you to arrange a direct contact between me and a representative of whoever originated this investigation. If I am to continue as part of all this,' he paused to be sure he created the right effect, 'there are certain questions I need to ask and they can't be asked through intermediaries... or functionaries.'

Ricci looked down at the backs of his hands, which suddenly seemed to have developed a fascination for him.

The choice of words couldn't have been worse.

The aide looked at Jimmy with cold fury in his eyes. Before he could speak Jimmy stood up.

'Good, now that's done I'll go. Thank you, Inspector, for bringing me. Goodbye Mister...?'

But the aide didn't volunteer a name. On his face, anger and loathing were nicely blended with pure amazement. A well-dressed cherub who'd bitten into a bad oyster. Well, at least the wasp was gone.

Jimmy went down in the lift to reception where he handed back his pass and left the building through the front door, the one people who mattered used.

Outside, in the sunshine, Jimmy realised he hadn't felt this good for a very long time indeed. His smile became a grin. Forgotten games of the past: Squashing the Snotty Bastard.

They met up at Ricci's restaurant where Ricci ignored the welcome, he wasn't in a mood to be polite to waiters.

'You did well to just walk out.'

'He took it badly, did he?'

'What do you think? Intermediaries or functionaries, for God's sake. Nobody must have talked to him like that since...' Ricci paused, trying to find the right words. He failed. '... for a very long time. You couldn't have offended him more if you'd punched him on the nose.'

'I couldn't do that, it might spoil his looks.'

Ricci looked at Jimmy. He said odd things at times, he was a hard man to figure. They sat down at a table and Ricci ordered two coffees. Jimmy watched the waiter go. It was the same one and he had given him the look again.

'I see I'm still a bag-snatcher.'

There it was again.

'And what the hell is that supposed to mean?'

'Why do we have to come here? Why can't we go somewhere else, somewhere, well somewhere that's...'

'Cheap and dirty, like your bar? Because I like it here and it's on expenses. I need to be a regular in a few places like this, to blend in.'

'So what is it you do exactly? When you're not busy dying from something terminal and running unofficial investigations for the Vatican, that is.'

'I suppose there's no harm in you knowing. I work in the... what might get called in London, the Glitz Squad.'

Jimmy laughed. 'The Glitz Squad. What's that?'

'It's what it says. I operate on any case where there is or

might be a Beautiful People involvement.'

'What, celebrities and the like?'

The coffees came. They waited until the waiter had gone.

'You don't know Rome, Jimmy. It's not London, it's a different world. High fashion sits at the same table with low life and you can't always tell the difference from the way they dress. Crime follows the money and if the money wears glitz, so does crime. Underneath all the glamour and gushing the usual nasty things go on, maybe even more so. The rich are always targets and the super-rich are bigger targets. They didn't get or keep their money by being kind and gentle. I get plenty of work, I earn my pay.'

Jimmy thought he probably did.

'So how rich is super-rich?'

'With you it's the haves and have-nots. With me it's the haves and have-yachts.'

Jimmy grinned.

'That's good.'

'I got it out of an English newspaper.'

'And does all your gear come on expenses?'

Ricci nodded.

'Has to, I couldn't afford the shirts never mind the rest of it. But it's more than just dressing up. The way I dress, anyone who knows about clothes and stuff will know that there's no way on God's earth I could do it on a policeman's pay. If I'm a self-serving, dishonest bastard who gets what he wants any way he can, I just naturally fit right on in.'

'So how about politics and politicians. Are you used to dealing with people like Charlie the Cherub?'

'Charlie the Cherub?'

'Your man from this morning.'

Now it was Ricci's turn to grin.

'Yeah, it fits. I meet them socially sometimes. I don't

usually deal with them though, politicos are normally off my patch. Charlie the Cherub, what made you think of it?'

'The office.'

'You know, up to now I took him seriously, senior personal aide to the Minister and all that. I thought of him as a big hitter. I don't think I can any more. From now on he'll always be Charlie the Cherub.'

'Believe me, whatever he is he's not a big hitter.'

'How do you know?'

'Because I got in.'

'And what does that mean?'

'If he was half the man he thinks he is we'd have been turned back at the barrier. He would have sent us packing.'

'If he hadn't okayed you we might have got shot at the barrier, not just sent packing. Those guards aren't for show. They'd use their guns if they thought they had to and leave any questions until afterwards, for somebody else to deal with.'

'I should hope so. Armed guards who ask questions when they should be shooting would be no bloody good at all.'

'What would you have done if he had sent us packing?'

'Gone away and tried something else. As it was I got in, and that means either he's not very hot on security...'

'Which he is.'

'Of course. Or he knows I have to be on board, that I'm important to whatever's going on. He was being careful. He let me in to see why I was there. He wanted to be sure that whatever I was up to he would be in a position to cover his back.'

'And that's it, you betted on him being careful?'

'I've met his sort a hundred times and more, they all run true to form. They're successful. They get to go right on up but never right to the top. They get to be the deputy this or principal assistant that. They're usually cleverer than the people they work for, often quite a bit cleverer, but they're always second-raters. The bottom line for them is, always make sure you have a way out from under if things go pear-shaped. They never carry the can, they're never the one to blame. And that means they won't commit, not fully. They haven't got the bottle to match the brains. So you'll always find one of them in the kitchen but they never get to be the chef. And if things get too hot they don't take the heat or help put out the fire, they put all their talents into getting out clean. When you need them most, they'll not be there.'

'And you guessed he'd be like that?'

'No, but it was worth a try and as it turned out I was right. Once I was in I knew what I was dealing with, so I just let him have it between the eyes and walked away. No sense in overdoing it, overdoing it spoils it. It's like making a hit. Keep it simple, keep it clean and walk away. Put the muzzle against the head, pull the trigger and it's done.'

'You sound as if you speak from personal experience. Is that one of the things that got filleted out of your record?'

It was a genuine enquiry.

'You don't have to have done something like that to know how it's done.'

It was an evasive answer.

Each took a drink of their tiny espressos.

'Okay, you did what you did and I took the flak.'

'Did it amount to anything?'

'Not really. Huffing and puffing, threats of reports to my superiors.'

'But you got out clean, you put it down to me like we agreed? You got my ultimatum with no warning just like he did and you both did what you thought was for the best?' Ricci nodded. 'Good, because if you were wrong to bring me he has to be wrong to have let me in and, believe me, the way he will tell it he won't be wrong.'

Ricci nodded again. He had come out clean.

'After he'd let off steam at me he chewed you up but it'll come out okay.'

'I told you it would.'

'So what happens now?'

'We wait until we get contacted. When we get the meeting with our man from the Vatican we ask our questions. If we find there's anything to chase, we're off and running.'

'What do we do till we get the call?'

'See your China-watcher again. I want to know if there's still something we might not know about Cheng.'

'Like what?'

'He went into prison first time as a priest and came out as a bishop. How and why did that happen? When he surfaces in Macau in 1999 he's an archbishop. Again, when and why did it happen? Was it support for someone under the cosh, was it for services rendered or was it part of some sort of diplomatic game? If it was, then were the moves all over once he got rehabilitated or could he have been part of some new game?'

'So exactly what is it I'm looking for?'

'How should I know? Ask your China-watcher. One thing you could ask, was he still an archbishop when he died?'

Of course. Bishop in secret, archbishop in secret, so why not cardinal in secret? Of course. Ricci saw the question had to be asked.

'If the answer's 'yes', is it important?'

'How the hell would I know? I don't even know why I'm doing this. But if I'm only going to be allowed to know diddley-squat about what's going on, I want all the diddley-squat. We'll sort out if any of it's important later.'

'Okay, I'll look into it. What are you going to do?'

'I'm going to rest. I mend quick but not as quick as I used to. I'll arrange some leave of absence with my rector, make up some sort of cover story. Now that there's a chance we might actually be getting started I can't do this and my studies. My not being where I should be will already have been noticed. I'll need to fix it so it's not going to be a problem.'

'Will she kick?'

'I doubt it. She doesn't like me, doesn't consider me a suitable candidate for the priesthood. She hates any time of hers that I take up, so if I drop out for the rest of this year that'll be like an early Christmas present for her.'

Jimmy stood up.

'You'll pay if it's on expenses?'

'Sure.'

Jimmy left and Ricci watched him go.

How the hell did a man who could talk with easy familiarity about blowing someone's brains out get into a priests' training course?

But he stopped himself thinking along those lines. It served no useful purpose to speculate about how Jimmy had turned up in Rome. If his record had been fixed and he got vouched for by the right kind of people it could happen easily enough. What mattered now was whether he brought something special to the inquiry, and he did. He got in to see the Minister's aide and almost certainly got them a Vatican contact. And he'd done it like he said, with no mud sticking on anybody but himself. Ricci smiled. He used his nice smile even though there was no one there to see it. Watch out, Jimmy, if that aide gets a chance to do you some harm he'll jump at it. You made him look bad this morning and he's going to have to do some very fancy talking not to come out of things with a black mark against him. You were bang on about his sort. Their greatest duty was their greatest joy, the delegation of blame. When someone dropped them in it, that was the unforgivable sin, one they never forgot. Take care, Jimmy, because if he turns up the heat on you don't look to me for help. Like you said, I'll be well out of the kitchen.

Ricci looked at his watch. Time to get moving. He would set up a meeting with his China-watcher and ask about that cardinal business. It was obvious when you thought about it. So why hadn't he? He was going to have to get up to speed. That was the second time Jimmy had got it right and he had been nowhere. If this case ever came to something there could be a lot of top brass saying 'well done', and he wanted those thanks pointed in his direction, not at some retired has-been from London. He put some money on the table, pushed the bill into his pocket and got up. He nodded to the waiter as he left. He definitely needed to get up some speed.

Chapter 9

'CALL AT MY office at three tomorrow afternoon. He said nothing else?'

Ricci turned the car into the narrow entrance behind the fine Ministry building.

'How many times do you need telling?'

They stopped at the barrier, the guard came out of the hut with his clip-board. There were no problems, both names were there. They drove in and parked the car in the same place as last time. Jimmy got out and noticed that the three bulk waste bins were open and had been emptied. How did they do that? he wondered. They went through the back door and on into the reception area where they picked up their passes, went up in the lift, and knocked at the aide's door.

'Come in.'

It was a woman's voice. Inside there were the two chairs in front of the desk and sitting behind it was Professor McBride. She gave them a steady look.

'Come in, please, and close the door.'

Ricci closed the door and they sat down. McBride didn't speak, she waited. Jimmy broke the silence.

'Professor, what are you doing here? What we're here for

is nothing to do with Duns College.'

'Only very indirectly, Mr Costello. You are currently assisting Inspector Ricci, who is officially on sick leave, in an unofficial inquiry. You are doing this at the request of the Minister who, in turn, is responding to a request made of him. But you are also currently a Duns student, so in that respect but in that respect only, it could be said to be Duns College business. And since you have brought the matter up I think I should point out that for a Duns student to become involved in such a bizarre course of action without seeking the necessary permissions is irregular in the extreme. Not to mention how incompatible with your studies involvement in such an inquiry would be. As to whether it is at all fitting for one training for the priesthood...'

'Excuse me, Professor.'

'Yes, Inspector?'

'We were told the Minister's aide wanted to see us. If you could please explain...'

'There you're wrong, Inspector. All you were told was to be here at three. You were not told that the Minister's aide would be whom you would see.'

'I naturally assumed...'

'Then I'm afraid you assumed wrongly.'

Jimmy asked the question.

'Why are you here?'

'Because, Mr Costello, you asked to talk to someone in authority in this matter. Apparently you have questions you wish answered. I will answer them in so far as it is in my power so to do.'

So to do! Still a prat, whatever hat she was wearing this time.

'Professor, I don't like being pissed about, not by you, not by the Vatican, not by anybody.' Jimmy noticed Ricci stiffen slightly in his chair but he didn't care. 'I'm here because somebody, I thought the Vatican, wanted my help. So far all that's happened is that I've been pissed about.'

'Does being savagely beaten and put into hospital come under your heading of being "pissed about"? I would have thought it rather more serious.' She was smiling, she was enjoying herself. Jimmy relaxed, he smiled as well.

'No, that wasn't being pissed around. But it wasn't the Vatican who had me put in hospital, was it?'

'No. The Vatican is not in the habit of putting people in hospital.'

This time it was Ricci who moved things on.

'Professor, will you please explain?'

'Certainly. Mr Costello made it clear that unless he received more active co-operation he would withdraw from the inquiry. It has been decided at the highest level that his services should be retained, so I have been asked to liaise in this matter.'

'You, Professor?'

'Does that surprise you, Inspector? I wonder why? Is it, perhaps, because I'm a woman?'

Ricci became confused.

'Not at all. I just expected that, well, from the Vatican I expected…'

'You expected a man, a priest, probably a Monsignor at the very least. Someone with a touch of red about them to lend authority. Well I'm afraid all you've got is me and not a touch of red to be seen anywhere. So what can I do for you?'

Jimmy cut straight to the chase.

'Why me? Why am I so important?'

Professor McBride looked at Jimmy then at Ricci, then back at Jimmy.

'I am happy to answer that question, Mr Costello, but I have been asked to give my fullest co-operation. My answers will be quite forthright. I will hold back nothing. Are you both happy that I speak about you in front of each other?'

Ricci didn't mind. He was as clean as a Sunday in white socks.

'It's okay with me.'

'And you, Mr Costello, is it okay with you?'

Jimmy hesitated. It wasn't okay with him, but what could he do? His past was no business of Ricci's, and he was pretty sure Ricci would use anything he heard if ever he felt he needed to. The question was, would he ever need to? The next question, a very big question, was how much did she know? If she knew... The new Jimmy took over. For God's sake, what does it matter? he told himself. Let Ricci know. Just get on with it, you were the one who wanted to know why you're in this. Let the woman tell you.

'Sure, go ahead.'

'Very well. The investigation you are carrying out is a highly sensitive one and might have far-reaching consequences...'

'If it shows that Cheng's death was not due to natural causes.'

The sharpness of Jimmy's interruption surprised Ricci but that wasn't what Professor McBride took exception to. He could ask all the questions he wanted in whatever manner he chose. What she did take exception to was the way Jimmy used the name.

'Archbishop Cheng.' She paused but Jimmy left it alone, so she continued, 'And it is not quite that simple, Mr Costello. Even if there was only a suspicion of foul play credibly established in the minds of various interested parties, the repercussions could be considerable. In fact, were your investigations to leave the death as an open question, that might be far more damaging than a confirmation that Archbishop Cheng's death was a deliberate act.' Jimmy noticed she didn't say 'murder'. He was listening as carefully to her as she was to him. 'When it became apparent that Archbishop Cheng's death might have to be investigated, the first concern was to ensure that full control was retained over the investigation, especially its outcome. Seeing as there was no way of knowing what might be the result of any enquiry, it was essential that nothing was begun until it was certain the outcome could be handled in whatever way was deemed best.'

'Handled?'

'Yes, Inspector, handled?'

'In what way "handled"?'

'Presented to any interested parties in a way that satisfied all interested parties.'

'You mean manipulated?'

'If you prefer. The circumstances of the Archbishop's death will be presented, if and when they are presented, in a way that ensures that the repercussions, should there be any, will do as little damage as possible or as much good as possible to those most interested in the matter. Surely you as a policeman are not unused to such things. For the police to manipulate, or handle, information in the way it is released is, I am sure, not something new to you.' Ricci nodded, he didn't like it but he couldn't argue with it. 'And you, Mr Costello, are an essential ingredient of the future management of the outcome of the enquiry, if it should prove necessary to...' she smiled at Ricci, 'handle it, as you are also, Inspector.' She looked from one to the other. 'You are a matched pair.'

'Never mind what sort of pair we are. Why me in particular, why am I so special?'

'As the result of any enquiry into Archbishop Cheng's death was unpredictable we needed to be in a position to endorse or to reject the outcome as we saw fit. The enquiry had to be as thorough and professional as the sensitive nature of the case would allow, which meant two detectives with proven abilities. However, our requirements went beyond professional skill. One of the detectives had to be above suspicion, with no trace of corruption attached to him. If we wished to endorse the findings we wanted to be able to point out that the investigation had been led by an officer of experience and integrity and that its findings were above suspicion with no question of any failure of method or thoroughness, nor of any tampering with or distortion of the evidence.' Jimmy began to feel uncomfortable. He knew what was coming. 'The other detective had to be someone whose presence as part of the enquiry would render any findings unreliable. Someone whose record, when properly looked into, would show him to have been a thoroughly corrupt officer.'

She let it sink in.

'We began our search for a suitable candidate in Rome, but the few officers drawn to our attention were not up to the job as detectives. We widened our field of search but how true we found the old saying, that you can never find a really corrupt policeman when you want one.' She looked at Jimmy and smiled. 'Then you turned up, Mr Costello. Your application had come to Rome and my attention was drawn to the fact that you had been a Detective Sergeant in the London Metropolitan Police. I thought it worth following up because you were a Catholic and therefore more traceable for us. Also you had been given early retirement, which might or might not mean something. When I was told your official file was remarkably slim and uninformative about your career, I realised we might at last have what we were looking for.'

She paused. If she was going to hang him she wanted to give him the chance of saying a few last words.

'Nobody objected to you nosing about in police personnel files?'

'Good heavens, no. The questions were asked by people who thought they were making genuine enquiries on behalf of Rome about someone applying for the priesthood. It was the sort of thing the Metropolitan Police would bend over backwards to facilitate. The friends who had fixed your records were, for once, quite out of their depth and unable to intervene. You cannot take the Catholic Church down an alley and just kick it into submission. Well, actually you can, and in certain parts of the world people have and still do. But not in London. In London we get co-operation.'

'Okay, so you got told about my record. That it wasn't anything special.'

'How true. According to your official record, what was left of it, you hardly existed as a policeman. Considering how long you had served that was very encouraging, so further enquiries were made through your old parish in Kilburn. Those enquiries revealed the sort of man you had been. Serving and retired policemen who remembered you confirmed the extent to which you were feared. We got a very clear picture of you, Mr Costello. You can hide your past from officialdom in many ways but you cannot erase the memories of ordinary people. A picture was drawn from the memories of people you probably never noticed but who noticed you because you were a man to be avoided, a man to fear. You were just the man we were looking for because whatever else you were, everyone who had any knowledge of you professionally agreed that you were an excellent detective, probably one of the best in London. And there you were, suddenly dropped into our lap in our time of need. Good luck or divine intervention? Which would you say it was?'

Jimmy knew the answer to that one.

'I wouldn't say.'

'So we brought you here and gave you a preliminary interview. That interview confirmed that you were not suitable priestly material, but you were just what we needed for our investigation when it began. So you were given a placement at the end of which you received from...' She was trying to remember a name. Jimmy helped her out.

'Sister Philomena.'

'Yes, Sister Philomena. Sister Philomena gave you an excellent report.'

'Was that placement a fix?'

'A fix?'

'Was it some sort of set-up?'

'Good heavens, no. Our resources do not run to setting up false placements, real ones are hard enough to find. It was a perfectly normal Duns student initial placement. It was a fix, as you call it, only in so far as it kept you in the system so that you would be in Rome when we needed you. It was fortunate that you did so well. Had anything gone wrong it would have been a nuisance for us here. But when we were ready we teamed you with Inspector Ricci. This is why you were brought to Rome. Why you are necessary.'

There was an uncomfortable silence. Even the aide's chic wall clock ticked in what seemed a shocked manner.

When it was clear that neither Jimmy nor Ricci were inclined to say anything, Professor McBride went on. 'I hope that answers your question, Mr Costello. I don't think I left anything out.'

Nothing much, thought Jimmy. Only a few dead and broken bodies in London. Nothing that would spoil a placement report and upset your plans.

'No, I think you covered the ground. Would you answer two more questions?'

'Of course, it's why I'm here.'

'If we find Cheng's death…'

'Archbishop Cheng's death.'

'…is suspicious, how serious is that likely to be?'

'Serious enough to justify all we have done and are prepared to do in the future. And we are prepared to do a great deal. I cannot exaggerate how serious this matter could become. Your second question?'

'Is Inspector Ricci any good as a detective and is he really as squeaky clean as you say he is?'

Ricci looked uncomfortable. He had recognised in Professor McBride a heavyweight. A hard case and as clever as they come. She would know him as well as she obviously knew Jimmy and, though he knew he had nothing to hide professionally, somehow that didn't fill him with confidence.

'Oh, yes. Inspector Ricci has his eye on considerable advancement and wouldn't dream of jeopardising his promotion chances by getting his hands dirty. And although he hasn't your skills as a detective I think you will find him a useful assistant in the inquiry.'

Ricci's attitude changed in a flash, she had touched him in a sensitive place.

'What do you mean, assistant?'

'Oh come now, Inspector, you have been assistant to Mr Costello's lead in this from the moment you started to work together. That we are in this room together having this meeting is down to Mr Costello's judgement, experience and strength of purpose. You were both carefully chosen not only for the reasons I have given but to complement each other in your work. I realise that you are a serving inspector, albeit on temporary leave, and that Mr Costello, before retirement, never rose above sergeant, but rank in this matter is immaterial. Mr Costello leads. That's final.'

Ricci was out of his seat.

'If he leads, I quit. You've just been telling me what sort of policeman he is, corrupt and dangerous, and now you want me to...'

'Was, Inspector. I have told you what he was, not what he is.'

'Was, is, what's the difference?'

'All the difference in the world I should have thought. Please, Inspector, sit down.' Ricci sat down, his anger had run out of steam and reason was seeping back. This woman had clout, she would make a bad enemy.

'When this investigation is over, whatever the outcome, particular thanks will be expressed to the Minister for his co-operation in setting up this inquiry. He in turn will express his thanks to whoever in the police assisted him. For obvious reasons, you will be the one whom they will be told led the inquiry. Officially, Mr Costello's role will be entirely subordinate to yourself.'

Reason was fully back in the driving seat.

'What if you need to use what you know about him to discredit the findings?'

'That will be your affair to manage as you see fit. You will need to arrange it so that Mr Costello's involvement, though a minor one compared to your own, was sufficient to severely prejudice the outcome. You will also need to explain how and why you became suspicious of him. But all that can be arranged if it becomes necessary. I'm sure you will deal with it perfectly well, if it has to be done at all.'

Jimmy sat there listening as they talked about him. It was funny, he didn't mind, he didn't mind what Ricci knew or what he thought. It was all true and as bad as it sounded. It was because it was true that it didn't matter.

Ricci was all reasonableness now.

'Okay. If it's all unofficial anyway, which of us actually leads doesn't matter one way or the other.'

'How sensible of you. Now, are there any more questions?'

Jimmy put away from him all that she had said about him. It was as it was, it couldn't be made different, so it was irrelevant, just as what Ricci thought of him was irrelevant. Now he knew why he was here. He would do what he had to do as best he could, not because it was what anybody wanted, but because a good and possibly holy old man deserved the truth about his death to be known. It was something he could do for Bernie and Michael. His priest training could wait. It would get sorted out afterwards. Now he had to be a detective and a bloody good one. So he got down to business.

'If Cheng was murdered it was done by people who were certain they could get away with it. There's no real evidence, no motive, nothing. If they exist they're invisible.'

'I would have thought that narrows the field considerably.'

'Not at all,' Ricci cut in. One invisible man is no easier to see than a crowd of invisible men.'

Jimmy liked it. 'He's right. So what we need is a way in. Something that we can see, something that is Cheng-related.'

Professor McBride sat back.

'You have looked into his life as fully as you can?'

'Yes.'

'And studied all the available evidence regarding his death?'

'Which is just the autopsy report, yes.'

'Which is not just the autopsy report.'

'What else is there?'

'Did you look into his funeral?'

No, they hadn't looked into his funeral. The body had been flown back to China as soon as the autopsy had been done.

'If we had, what would we have seen?'

'Hardly anything, Inspector. You would have seen almost nothing.'

'If there was nothing to see how can…'

'Wait a minute.'

'Yes, Mr Costello?'

'It was a small affair?'

'Almost non-existent. Immediate family from Macau and a few officials from Beijing.'

'From Beijing?' Ricci was getting up to speed.

'Yes Inspector, three officials from Beijing.'

'And it took place – where?'

'Not in his cathedral. It took place in a small parish church belonging to the Official Catholic Church. One of their priests presided at the funeral Mass. After that the archbishop's body was taken to his cathedral, where he was quietly buried. No one, not even family, was present at the interment.'

If she was taking them somewhere, why pussyfoot around? Why not just say what she wanted them to know?

'Make your point, Professor. I've told you, I don't want to be pissed about any more.'

If the words and the way they were said bothered her she didn't show it.

'He came to Rome as a recognised figure in the Chinese media, a glowing symbol of their new openness and tolerance. He was buried in a silence that was almost deafening. There was no media coverage beyond the death notice.'

'So what does that mean?'

'Ah, now that question I cannot answer.'

'Can't, or won't?'

'Can't, and before you speak again, Mr Costello, I assure you that I am not in any way "pissing you about". I cannot tell you why Archbishop Cheng's funeral was such a low-key affair...' she made the point by pausing, 'but still had three senior officials from Beijing in attendance.'

Whatever she was getting at, it was passing Jimmy by.

But Ricci picked it up.

'So Cheng was a cardinal when he was buried.' He turned to Jimmy. 'You were right.'

'I never said he had been made a cardinal, Inspector. That is your assumption.'

Jimmy looked at Ricci. First a bishop in secret, then an archbishop the same way, then a cardinal. Did it matter and why was Ricci so sure?

'What makes you sure he was a cardinal?'

'Because the Professor has just made it very clear that Beijing sent three senior officials. Why three? Why any at all if it was such a hole and corner affair?'

Now Jimmy was sure.

'Because he was a cardinal.' He turned to McBride.

'This looks like a need-to-know, Professor. Either you're willing to help or you're not.'

'I cannot tell you what I do not know, and I do not know whether Archbishop Cheng had been given the red hat.'

'Then find us someone who does.'

'Would you both step outside for a moment while I make a phone call?'

They left the office and stood outside in the corridor.

'Well?'

Ricci pretended not to know what Jimmy meant.

'Well what?'

'You know what.'

Ricci knew.

'Listen, you were a bent copper, you were a dangerous man, and now it's caught up with you and it's being used. But I don't care what sort of copper you were and I already guessed you could be a dangerous man, so nothing's changed. I just hope you were as good a detective as she thinks you were so we can get a result on this one.'

'And you'll get your brownie points?'

'Yes, she's right, I want to go all the way. And if this helps, fine. I'll follow your lead so long as your lead takes us where I want to go.'

'And then, at her say-so, you'll drop me in it?'

'With the greatest of pleasure, Jimmy. It's where you deserve to be after all, not swanning about playing at becoming a priest or doing the Vatican's detective work.'

'Ah, the moral high ground. I bet you spend a fortnight there each year just to remind yourself how nice the neighbours will be when you get to be there permanently.'

'Fuck you.'

Jimmy didn't care about Ricci. But that was the point, he should care. Any normal person would. If he wanted to be a normal person he had to try to care.

'Look, we have to work together. We don't have to like each other but we have to get on with each other. So what say we just do this like it's a roster thing? The list's gone up and we've been put on a case together. Let's just do it.'

Ricci saw it was the only sensible way. They'd been put together as a team to do a job and it was in his best interests to see it done well. He'd worked with men he hadn't liked and with some crooked enough to hide behind a spiral staircase. It could be done.

'Okay, what's past is past. Get on with the job.'

'That was good, by the way, about him being a cardinal because of the boys from Beijing. I should have seen it.'

'Not really, you'd already guessed it, remember? You were past it and looking for something else.'

He's right, thought Jimmy, I'd half guessed it.

'The thing I want to know now is why Cheng being a cardinal made him worth killing. And why he had had to die in Rome.

The office door opened.

'Come in, please.'

They went back in and sat down.

When Professor McBride spoke, it was very deliberately.

'I have asked your question and I have been given a response. The Vatican can neither confirm nor deny that the late Archbishop Cheng had been given a red hat by his Holiness.' She relaxed, the words were fine. They did the job.

Ricci repeated some of them.

'Neither confirm nor deny?'

'Neither confirm nor deny.'

'The Vatican?'

'The Vatican.'

'I see.'

Jimmy didn't.

'Well I bloody don't. I thought we were going to get answers, straight answers.'

Professor McBride repeated it for him.

'Leave it, Jimmy.'

There was something in Ricci's voice that made Jimmy leave it. He didn't like it but he left it.

Ricci got up.

'Is there anything else about Archbishop Cheng you can tell us?'

Professor McBride turned the question over in her mind. The truth was always tricky. Anything else she could, or anything else she would?

'Nothing that I can think of.'

'In that case we'll be going. Goodbye, Professor, and thank you.'

Jimmy got up. He didn't know what was going on but obviously Ricci did.

'Goodbye, gentlemen. Just tell the Minister's aide if you need my help again.'

As Ricci went out Jimmy paused.

'You'll sort out leave of absence for me?'

'It's already done, Mr Costello.'

Jimmy nodded, of course it was.

'But we should discuss the arrangements. You should be fully aware of what they involve. Could you come to the rector's office tomorrow at ten?'

'Sure.'

Jimmy caught Ricci up in the corridor.

'What did it mean, the "Vatican can neither confirm nor deny" stuff?'

'That means he was a cardinal. It's Vaticanese, their way of saying yes when they can't say yes. It explains the funeral. If he'd been made a cardinal he'd have been entitled to have his cardinal's red hat and his coat of arms on his coffin. For whatever reason, the Chinese didn't want it known. In the new détente the Vatican was prepared to go along with that. What I think happened was that the Chinese let him have his funeral as a cardinal in the presence of his family, and sent officials of the proper seniority as a nod to Rome. As for everybody else, Archbishop Cheng was dead and buried and there was nothing more to know.'

'I see, so is that all we've got that's new?'

'There's nothing else unless you're prepared to go to China and start digging.'

They came to the lift and waited.

'You did well in there, you put things together neatly.'

'Yeah, and I learned a lot as well, in fact I learned too bloody much.'

They took the lift down, went back to the car and the guards checked them out. Soon they were back in the Roman traffic. Ricci picked it up again.

'So now we know he was a cardinal. I don't see how that gets us anywhere.'

Jimmy was looking out of the window watching Roman drivers playing at trying to kill each other. He answered absently.

'It has to.' He turned to Ricci. 'We know the Chinese wanted it kept quiet. Maybe that's something.'

'Great, all we have to do is go to China and interview some senior government officials in Beijing.'

Jimmy shook his head.

'It's not the Chinese. Why build him up, then kill him? And why kill Cheng in Rome? It makes no sense.'

He thought about it. Murder for him had always been simple, either an act of impulse or follow the trail until you found out who benefited most, which usually meant follow the money. But this wasn't an impulse killing... it was planned and it wasn't going to be about money. He had no idea how the cardinal thing could even get them started, never mind where it might lead.

Ricci did some horn pumping as a white van cut him up then got back to the subject in hand.

'It's all we've got so let's fill in what we can and see if anything comes out of it.'

'Like what?'

'Well, he must have got his red hat here in Rome before he died. That means only Cheng and the pope knew he was a cardinal. And maybe a few top bods in the Vatican.'

'So?'

'So if no one knows, it can't be part of the reason he died, can it?' There was a pause while they both weighed this statement in their minds. 'Unless…' Ricci left it hanging. But Jimmy wanted it. Anything was better than nothing.

'Unless what?'

'No, it's nothing, it can't be.'

'Try it, we're not exactly dripping with places to go on this.'

'Well, you figured it out first, Jimmy.'

'Me?'

'Remember, you said first a secret bishop, then a secret archbishop, so what else might have happened that nobody knew about? You asked me to ask my China-watcher, why not a secret cardinal? Well, now we know. He was a secret cardinal.'

'But if no one knew…'

'You guessed. Why shouldn't somebody else guess? Why couldn't someone else work out it would happen.'

'What? And killed him because he might be a cardinal?'

'I told you it was nothing. It can't be.'

Jimmy was in new waters but he still used the old methods, the only ones he knew: was this an isolated killing, was it just Cheng? Use your experience, he urged himself, do the same things, follow the same routines, ask the same questions. Forget it's the Vatican, forget it's Rome, forget it's political. Just ask the same questions. It's not a normal killing, so have there been others like it? Is it related to anything?

'How many others?'

'How many others what?'

'Cardinals who've died suddenly. How many other unexpected deaths in, say, the last two years?'

Ricci gave a low whistle and braked slightly as a Fiat sports car cut in, apparently intent on suicide on his front bumper. Jimmy's question had made him forget to pump the horn.

'It's a bit rich isn't it, murdering cardinals?'

'If we're right, one's been done, so why not ask if there's any more?'

'Alright, if you think it's a question worth asking. You lead in this, remember.'

'I'm seeing McBride tomorrow to sort out my leave of absence. I'll ask her who I need to see to get the information.'

'She going to arrange something terminal for you, like me?'

Jimmy gave a small laugh.

'The way things are going I think I may already have something terminal.'

The car pulled into the Via Ovidio and stopped outside the Café Mozart next door to Jimmy's apartment block. He got out and realised he was tired again. No, not tired, weary.

'I'll let you know how I get on.'

Ricci nodded and drove off.

Jimmy went through the main entrance and started to go up the stairs by which he had so recently been deposited, a piece of broken rubbish.

'Do it right next time, you bastards. Do it right and finish the fucking job.'

Chapter 10

'SIT DOWN, MR Costello.' Jimmy sat down. 'I'm afraid I have been guilty of a little subterfuge.'

'Oh yes?'

'I didn't ask you here to talk about your leave of absence.' The little room was stuffy. It was high up in the building and there was no air-conditioning so any warm air rose, and as the window didn't open, it stuck, stale and oppressive. Jimmy began to feel not just crumpled but tainted somehow. Professor McBride obviously wasn't affected by the room. She was wearing a smart dark blue jacket and skirt and a plain white blouse with an open collar. In the lapel of her jacket was pinned a small cross. To tourists she could have been a Roman businesswoman. To a Catholic she looked like a nun. To Jimmy she looked like a judge about to hand down a stiff sentence.

'I asked you here to tell you something. Something about yourself.'

'I know all I want to know about myself, Professor. There's nothing I want to hear from you.'

'That's true. It's not something you'll want to hear but you do need to hear it.'

'If you say so.'

He didn't care. It was going to be nasty and it was going to be true and there was nothing he could do about it. Saying it out loud wouldn't change any of it.

'Yesterday I explained why you are here in Rome. What I didn't explain was that I was not in favour of using you.' Fastidious bitch, thought Jimmy, set me up in this shit then distance yourself from the smell. 'I thought you unsuited for the role.'

'Not bad enough? Or too bad?'

'Not well enough, Mr Costello, not nearly well enough.' He wasn't ready for that. It had come at him from nowhere. 'That my opinion was overruled in your selection is obvious from your presence here.'

He wasn't sick, what was she on about? It was true he didn't bother with check-ups, but that was because he didn't care if there was something nasty there. He had watched Bernie die from something nasty that hadn't shown until it was too late and Michael had died from something nasty that killed as soon as it showed. You died, that was all, the way didn't matter. What was the point in getting formally introduced to what was going to kill you? But he wasn't sick right now. He knew that for certain because he had just come out of hospital and he had been cleared as okay to leave. If there was anything they would have spotted it.

'What's supposed to be the matter with me?'

'In my opinion you would do well to seek psychiatric help.'

He couldn't fault her for being different. Given what she knew about him or had guessed, she could have accused him of being many things but he hadn't expected it would be that he was a nutter.

'I'm mad, is that it?'

'Mr Costello, I have no medical training whatsoever, but I have spent most of my working life studying people who operate the levers of power. The men and women who decide the fate of others. My special field of study has become those who have great power but whose behaviour and motivation could be classed as abnormal.'

'For instance?'

'Dictators, those who lead totalitarian regimes, heads of terrorist organisations, all the ones you would expect. But also presidents, prime ministers and, sadly, religious leaders. I study people who perpetrate injustice. I study people with power.'

'And power corrupts?'

'Absolutely. No one who has real power can ever be sure they will not succumb to the misuse of that power or that their power will not influence their mental state.'

'What's that got to do with me? You don't think I ever had any real power, do you?'

'No, I don't think that. Let me explain what I mean by using as an example, Saddam Hussein. Saddam in his political life was utterly ruthless and devoid of pity or remorse. He had to care for no one nor trust anyone. In fact he had to be a monster. But he was a loving husband and father, kind, trusting, and caring. A father to be relied upon, that his family could turn to. In order to be able to live such conflicting lives he had to be two different people. He had to live a schizoid-inducing duality sustained in one case by an unshakable and fanatical belief in the rightness of his actions, and in the other by a profound love for and commitment to his family. Saddam the dictator was able to believe in his love for the Iraqi people yet still do terrible things to them – to individuals, groups and whole communities. To anyone he saw as a threat. I'm afraid it is not uncommon for those who have a fanatical love of abstract humanity to inflict great cruelty on real people.'

'Is that what you spend your time doing, watching mad dictators trying to conquer the world? Why not just watch old James Bond movies?'

'Semyon Frank predicted the terrible cruelty of Bolshevism long before the October Revolution. George Bush's famous, or infamous if you prefer, War on Terror could be said to be the same thing in different clothes. The justification of evil acts is often some greater good.'

'Well I'm not Saddam and thank God I'm not bloody George Bush. And I was never fanatical about my work as a copper. Corrupt, yes, I give you that. But fanatical, no.'

'No indeed. You were never fanatical as a policeman. Just as you say, corrupt. Your fanaticism lay in your effort to be a good Catholic, to be a good husband and father, to be a good parishioner. You had to be obsessive about that to sustain the duality you had imposed on your life. The Good Catholic in your private life, the Corrupt Policeman in your working life. Those mutually incompatible personalities were only possible so long as you took the template of your police life from a small group of highly successful but deeply dishonest officers. They were corrupt and, to some extent, they were allowed to be corrupt. So you chose to go the same way and, so long as an official blind eye was turned, you could believe it was an acceptable part of an imperfect system. That there was some form of greater good which justified your individual acts of violence and dishonesty.'

He waited. She had been spot on so far and he didn't want to know where this was going. But it was something he knew he had to hear.

'And my home life? My life as a good Catholic?'

'I know nothing of your wife, Mr Costello, but I am pretty certain she was the one you looked to for the validation of your image of yourself as a good Catholic. Not the Church itself and certainly not any priest. I would guess she was all that you believed a good Catholic should be: devout, believing, loving, loyal. That she stayed with you, loved you, accepted you, was the endorsement your private life needed for you to sustain it. Once she was gone, your world simply fell apart. My guess is that before she died, maybe during her illness, you glimpsed what being your loving and faithful wife had cost her, knowing as she did what sort of man you were as a policeman. That tipped you over the edge and after she died you suffered the inevitable psychotic episode. You almost killed two men whom you thought represented all that had gone wrong in your life. You were acting out a psychotic fantasy in which you had cast yourself as Nemesis. Those two men you so savagely attacked were a message to all the others that they could be reached by justice, even if they were beyond the reach of the law. That one of them was a powerful criminal who would have done you great harm after he came out hospital was what gave you your honourable early retirement. Where you should have gone, of course, was to prison.'

'Prison would have been a death sentence.'

'You aren't suggesting early retirement and a pension, to save the Metropolitan Police embarrassment, was justice for what you did?'

No, he wasn't saying anything about justice. He didn't want to say or hear anything more, because she was right. He was hearing the truth about himself and it gave him almost unbearable pain to be confronted by what he had always known since he sat at Bernie's hospital bedside when she had died. What he had buried so deep that he could pretend he didn't know. Now McBride had calmly shredded his emotional defences and told him that the only two things his life had achieved were making his wife suffer so much and for so long, and turning himself into some sort of sick monster.

'Are you saying that what I did to those animals was because I was sick, mentally sick?'

'I told you, I have no medical training. I am making an interpretation of what happened on the basis of years of study. I couldn't say whether your condition made you clinically insane but I doubt it. You thought you were acting rationally and you carefully planned what you did. I'm sure you would have been found, for criminal prosecution purposes, quite sane. But what you did was the action of a very disturbed mind, a mind I think, which is still very disturbed.'

She had to be wrong, please God, make her wrong.

'So how come I'm here, how come you got overruled?'

'My field is the politics of power, not psychiatry. There were two people on the panel which conducted your extended interview who were specialists in the field of mental health. Their view was that your going to Ireland after you left London and living quietly, going to Mass and choosing a kind old priest as the person you talked to, showed remorse, a willingness to repent, to confront what you had done. Your decision to make amends for your life by applying to become a priest meant that you were no longer a danger to yourself or others and open to recovery.'

'But you disagreed.'

'I know how well a condition like I have described can be camouflaged. The world I study is increasingly peopled by those who achieve great power but whose evilness remains hidden until it is too late to restrain them. Sadly I sometimes think that our world today owes more to the Book of

Revelation than to the Gospels. I am quite sure you could appear to have begun your recovery and yet be someone who is still motivated by something that might not be fanaticism but is certainly sufficiently obsessive to be dangerous.'

'You think I might still be a fanatical Catholic then? That applying to become a priest was part of some obsession?'

'No, I think the goal you now pursue with such a single-mindedness, a single-mindedness that could become dangerous, is to make your life right.'

'Right?'

'Right in a way you think your late wife would accept. I think you are determined to become a good man and you are prepared to do whatever it takes to become that good man. If you pursue that goal without regard for the consequences either for yourself or others you will recreate your old duality. You will try to embody the old saying, that out of evil cometh good. It is a good thing for you to want to be a different person, one your wife could have been proud of. It is a bad thing to destroy yourself and possibly others in the attempt.'

She was right, of course. She knew him better than he knew himself. But suddenly the anguish which had been filling his mind left him. She knew and she had made him face it. It was no longer denied, buried deep within him, festering. It was out in the open. Please God it could now be dealt with, and not in his way, but in a way Bernie would have wanted it.

'So what can I do?'

'You need a friend, Mr Costello. You have tried to go on living your life in your head with yourself as judge and jury on what you are doing and how you are doing it. You are trying to fight the good and evil in your life entirely on your own. If you continue you may well break down and suffer a more severe, psychotic episode. This time if you try to kill someone you may very well succeed. If so then you will spend the rest of your life heavily sedated in an asylum or be tried for murder and serve the rest of your life in a secure establishment for the criminally insane. There will be no question of a recovery.'

It was the way she said it that made a cold hand clutch at Jimmy's heart. She was so certain, so matter of fact. He knew she was speaking no more than the simple truth but that only increased the horror at how far he had continued to travel the road to his own destruction.

'You need a friend, someone to take the role of your late wife, to support you and help you. But this time someone with whom you share your thoughts and feelings, someone you do not close out of one half of your life. You must learn to live one life and to live it outside your head, and live it with others.'

He thought about it.

'Will it be you? Will you be my friend?'

'Good heavens, no. As I said before, I didn't want you for this work. I thought you unfit and I still think you unfit. Also, to be quite frank, I don't like you. You are not a nice man, Mr Costello, not at all nice. But putting that to one side, I can't help you because I am far too busy. I've already said I resented the time our monthly meetings took up and kept me from my work. The meetings were necessary of course. I wanted to monitor you. Your progress or otherwise as a student was, as you now know, irrelevant. But your mental state concerned me so I had to give up the time.'

She had put him on the floor and now she was busy kicking the shit out of him. Oh well, what she was doing with her words he had done often enough with fists and feet. If you're going to put someone down make sure they stay down. That was a universal rule. It obviously applied as much to people who worked for Rome as it did to corrupt coppers or north

London gangsters.

'So that's it. That's what I have to do, find a friend?'

'I can only advise you. The way you take that forward is your own affair. How is the enquiry going, by the way? Any progress?'

Her voice hadn't changed. It was still coldly matter of fact. But she'd finished with the dangerous head-case who was on the way to becoming criminally insane and now she was talking to the clever detective who was supposed to be good at getting results.

'Maybe. We're checking out if any other cardinals have died over the last two years, unexpectedly but apparently of natural causes.'

'I'll send you someone who can give you all the details you need. Anything else?'

'What about Ricci?'

'What about Inspector Ricci?'

'As a friend.'

'I will give you a word of warning about Inspector Ricci. He has a talent for the kind of work he does. He moves among people whose lives are built around show and display. False, constructed lives for false, constructed people. He can see through their show with an almost amazing insight. He can see the real person behind the façade. He can pass as one of them without becoming one of them. He cultivates the right friends. He will go far, but he will not go as far as he expects. I told you, he has a spotless record. When he gets to the top he wants no skeletons in his cupboard to hamper him in enjoying his power and authority. He may even have political ambitions. If and when you find yourself in circumstances where you need Inspector Ricci to commit unconditionally, be careful. He may very well not be there. I tell you this because you must work together, and work well. Yesterday he found out about you. Today you find out about him. Now, if there is nothing else I must conclude our meeting.'

She stood up. He was dismissed. Jimmy stood up.

'Thank you, Professor.'

'Not at all, I have been asked to give you my full co-operation. I hope you feel you are getting it.'

'Oh, yes, I appreciate that you're holding nothing back. Goodbye, and once again, thank you.'

'Goodbye.'

Jimmy left feeling numb and shell-shocked. No, he thought as he descended the cold stone stairs, she was holding nothing back. No one could accuse her of that.

Chapter 11

THE SMALL LIBRARY had once been part of the residence of a minor Borgia whose name had made him a bishop at sixteen but whose lack of talent or holiness ensured that when he died, aged thirty-four, he was still only a bishop. A good man, for a Borgia, he had left his second Rome residence to the Church on the understanding that his soul would be prayed out of Purgatory and into Heaven in no more than a year. The Church had accepted the gift on the grounds that, for a Borgia, he had been quite a good man.

The residence had eventually been turned into a college and the room in which the China-watcher sat had become the college library. The China-watcher loved the room. He loved the rich plaster decoration of its ceiling and the dark wooden shelves filled with handsomely bound books. He especially loved being alone in this room, which he frequently was when he visited. One day it would be taken over for some other use and the volumes archived out of sight, their contents digitised and databased. But until then he would use this place to sit, think and pray.

He was sitting beside a small table in a leather club chair. Opposite him sat Inspector Ricci waiting for an answer.

Finally it came.

'Definitely.'

'He was a cardinal?'

'Certainly.' He paused for a moment. 'In my opinion.'

'Are you sure?'

'Certainly.'

'Thank you.'

'In so far as it is possible.'

Ricci fidgeted. He didn't want to press the old man but he wanted a straight answer.

The China-watcher was a tiny, delicate, oriental man in a shiny black suit with a Roman collar and wispy grey hair. The club chair made him seem even smaller than he was. He looked very old, except for his eyes which shone with either mischief or delight. Or maybe it was both. Ricci got the feeling that if handled in the least bit roughly, he might break, like some porcelain trinket.

Ricci tried another tack.

'What makes you so sure he was a cardinal?'

'Because he came to Rome.'

'But you told me that he was probably sent to Rome by the Chinese to see if he could be a link between them, the Vatican and the Underground Church.'

'Yes, that is so.'

'Then how does coming to Rome make you sure he was a cardinal, if it was the Chinese who wanted him here?'

'Archbishop Cheng was sent to Rome by the Chinese. I have given you what I think is their reason.'

There was another pause.

'And?'

'You never asked me why Archbishop Cheng was summoned to Rome.'

'Summoned to Rome?'

'By the Vatican. You never asked me why the Vatican wanted him here.'

'And should I have?'

'That is not for me to say. Your reasons are your own. I have been asked to answer your questions which I have done to the best of my ability.'

Ricci sighed, it was tough going. The old priest watched him. His wrinkled face was creased with a grin. He was enjoying himself.

'Please tell me, Fr Phan, why was Archbishop Cheng summoned to Rome?'

'To be given his red hat by the pope in person.'

'So he was sent by the Chinese for one reason and summoned by the Vatican for another.'

'If both parties had not wanted Archbishop Cheng in Rome he could not have come. His visit was arranged by a joint agreement.'

'So Archbishop Cheng was summoned here to be made a cardinal when he was sent here on behalf of the Chinese government?'

'No.'

'No?'

'No.'

Ricci sighed again.

'No he wasn't made a cardinal or no he wasn't here on behalf of the Chinese government?'

'Both.'

'Neither?'

'Yes.'

'Yes?'

'Yes. No is the answer to both questions.'

The grin widened. Fr Phan hadn't had so much fun since the time a rather silly CIA agent had tried to pump information from him about a high Chinese government official rumoured to have become a secret Catholic.

'I give up, Father. You've defeated me.'

Ricci sat back into the comfortable chair and smiled at the old Vietnamese priest. He would help when he was ready. He just wasn't ready yet.

'How did you become a China-watcher?'

'When I was eighteen I was sent from Vietnam to Hong Kong to represent a French business based in what was then French Indo-China. While I was in Hong Kong, Dien Bien Phu happened. The French were kicked out and I was left stranded. My family came from what became the Communist North. I couldn't go back so I decided to do what I had, for a time, been thinking about. I applied to be sent to Rome and trained for the priesthood. I was accepted and after six years I was ordained and went back to Hong Kong. My family were not among the million or so North Vietnamese Catholics who had managed to go south and I had lost touch with them. China was playing Big Brother to the North Vietnamese government, so watching China and Vietnam was one small way of feeling that I was keeping in touch with my family. I kept on watching until I was told by a refugee from my home town, who had got out in the mess that was the end of the American war in Vietnam, that my family were dead. I stopped watching Vietnam but kept on watching China. It was something I was good at and the Church wanted me to do it. So I did it.'

'And you're still doing it?'

The old priest nodded. He had wanted his bit of fun and now he was ready to tell the inspector what he wanted to know. 'Archbishop Cheng would have been made a cardinal *in pectore* when he was last imprisoned.'

'*In pectore?*'

'Latin. Literally, "in the breast". It means Archbishop Cheng was created a cardinal in secret. When that happens it is known only to the pope. Not even the cardinal so named is necessarily aware of his elevation. In any case he cannot function as a cardinal while his appointment is *in pectore* because it is only used in situations where the individual or their congregation need to be protected from any reprisals the elevation might cause. It is used when the individual is functioning in a dangerous situation.'

'So Cheng was already a cardinal when he came to Rome, but he may not have known it?'

'No, he would have known. He would have been told as soon as his position in China began to be regularised, as soon as there was no danger to him or his people. The Chinese government, however, would not have known. It was a move in the game that Rome was saving.'

'Why?'

The little priest shrugged.

'I don't know. I watch China, not the Vatican.'

'But others in the Vatican would definitely have known?'

'Oh yes, at that stage there would have had to be others to arrange for Archbishop Cheng to be told but in such a way that the Chinese would not get to know.'

'So it was still secret?'

'Secret, yes, but no longer known only to the pope.'

Ricci nodded. 'I see.'

'And although Archbishop Cheng was sent by the Chinese, he was not really here on their behalf. He was sent as a sign to show Rome that Beijing was prepared to trust him. If Rome chose to use him as a contact in some way, the Chinese were showing they were open to negotiations. When he arrived in Rome he was seen by the pope. What they talked about is known only to them.'

'And the Chinese, if in some way they could have found out he was a cardinal, might they have wanted him dead and wanted it to happen in Rome not China?'

'No, they very much wanted him alive and I would think it mattered little to them whether he was an archbishop or a cardinal. If they cared at all they would probably have favoured it.'

'So why the ultra low-key funeral?'

'They didn't want anyone else to know that they hadn't known. It was a matter of face-saving, both domestic and international. They had begun to build up Archbishop Cheng as some sort of symbol of the new China, a China that encouraged individuals with talent and flair. A China that was safe to invest in and work with. But they didn't want anyone thinking that the new China had gone soft or sloppy. The Vatican had made a move they hadn't seen or countered and that was unacceptable to Beijing. However, as Archbishop Cheng was dead and the matter was of no particular importance in the grand scheme of things, they buried it.'

The grin was back and Ricci realised Fr Phan had made a joke. 'Buried it. Yes, I see.'

The priest nodded.

'A little joke, inappropriate perhaps. We are talking about the death of one who might have been a great man, one who was undoubtedly a holy man. But I allow myself a little fun from time to time...' another pause, 'between friends, you understand.' Ricci understood alright, it was another joke. They'd only met twice and the priest had had a little bit of fun at his expense on both occasions, as it now turned out. 'Inspector, I have tried to tell you what you want to know. I was asked to co-operate by someone I trust. Many people seek me out and ask me things. I don't always tell them what they want to hear. I am afraid that trust, real trust, is not common currency among those who seek my knowledge. Alas, they often think that they can use me and the information I can give them.'

'Use you, how?'

'The Catholic Church is frequently in a position to know – far more accurately than the Diplomatic or Intelligence Services of most Western governments – what is the reality of the situation on the ground in certain volatile or hostile parts of the world. We often have people and resources in the places where it would be very dangerous for the personnel of Western governments to go. So their undercover emissaries come to the Church and ask it to give, or get, information for them. The Church is seen as a reliable source. I have many contacts in Intelligence in China and in the West, and I am happy to act as a source to both, provided my action promotes the common good. I share my information only if I can be sure, in so far as anyone can ever be sure, that it will not be used to do harm, but to inform and thereby improve relationships, to do good. Mine is a world of trust based on experience, favours asked and favours given. It is all off the record, as have been our conversations, Inspector. I must hope you will do no harm with the information I have given you. It seems of no particular importance to me but I have learned over many years that the value of information is not necessarily apparent to the one who provides it. Its value is known more accurately by the one who requests it.'

The old man smiled, the speech was over, it was time to go. Ricci got up. He went and put his hand out to the old man who took it. It was like holding an incredibly delicate figurine. Was it because he was Vietnamese or was he really as old as he looked?

'Thank you, Fr Phan, you have been most helpful.'

The priest nodded and smiled but said nothing. Ricci turned and walked away.

So, people had known about Cheng being a cardinal before he came to Rome. Jimmy had guessed but others might not have needed to guess. That meant the next step was, who knew? And after that, who might they have told? And lastly, why? Maybe things were getting going at last. He was sure the list of who knew would be very short. The shorter the better. He was beginning to get a good feeling about this inquiry. It might actually get him somewhere. Things were definitely looking up.

Danny looked around the café.

'Why did you drag me here? Why not our usual place?'

'I wanted to be somewhere different, with people who were enjoying themselves.'

The café was crowded with tourists. At the next table a party of young Germans were laughing and talking loudly.

'What's the matter, don't you like to see people happy?'

'What the hell are you up to, Jimmy? You suddenly disappear and the next thing we know someone's put you in hospital. No one's allowed to see you, then when you're out of hospital you drop out of classes. Leave of absence, we get told. Duns College business, not anybody else's. In other words, clear off. But here you are. So what's going on?'

'Is anybody else interested in me?'

'Not really. They're all too tied up with their studies.'

'What sort of copper were you, Danny?'

'Me? I was Traffic.'

'Traffic.'

'You sound disappointed. What sort of policeman did you want me to be?'

'Oh, not any particular sort, I just thought you would

have been at the more serious end.'

'Good guess. I only did the last five years in Traffic. Before that I was in Narcotics.'

'So what got you moved to Traffic?'

'Two bullets. I was damned lucky they didn't get me moved to the cemetery.'

'It's nasty work, Narcotics.'

'And dangerous, man, don't forget the dangerous.'

'So what were you?'

'A sergeant.'

'Never try for higher?'

'No. I never wanted the responsibility. Maybe that's why I'm finishing. If I became a priest I would have to be responsible for people, advise them, judge them. It's not for me.'

'Did you ever do any undercover work?'

'No, just catching the bad guys and getting convictions.'

'Getting convictions?'

'You know how it works. You know they're guilty, you just want to hear them say it. You do what you have to and make them say it. I'm a big man and not naturally violent so I got brought in sometimes. I could hurt people enough but not hurt them too much.'

'Needs a nice judgement.'

'If you've done it you'll know. With me nobody died, nobody got put into hospital. They were bad guys, we just needed to hear them say so.'

'So you got shot?'

'On a routine bust, dropped my guard. The guy using the gun was dead before he hit the floor but by the time we'd got him I was on the floor too.'

'And then?'

'Then I got better and I asked to go to Traffic. I was

finished in Narcotics. Getting shot had scared the shit out of me and I knew that if I had to go back I'd be looking out for myself when I should be looking out for someone else. And that's no good, Jimmy, is it? When you go for the bad guys you do what has to be done any way it has to be done, and you commit. If you're looking out for yourself, someone will get hurt. So I went to Traffic and no one got hurt. I served five years to get a pension, then quit, thought about what I wanted to do and finished up here.'

'No wife?'

'No, no wife. I had a partner though.'

There was a gleam in his eye.

'Oh yes?'

'A steady partner.'

'So what happened there?'

The smile widened to a grin.

'When I started thinking about coming to Rome we broke up.'

'I should bloody well think so. What did she say when you told her?'

'Nothing. Her name was Appleton and she was white rum, and when we went to bed she was the one inside me not me the one inside her.'

He laughed, so did Jimmy.

'You used to hit the bottle. Oh well, lots did and they still cut it as coppers.'

'But when you're not a copper any more and don't have to drink the day out of your mind to get to sleep, then you just become a drunk. I didn't want to end up like that so I gave up the rum and set about thinking what I did want to be. There, now you know my life story you inquisitive bastard, so answer my question. What the hell are you up to?'

Jimmy had thought hard about what Professor McBride

had told him and had come to a decision. He needed a friend. He might also need someone looking after his back if things went pear-shaped and at the moment Ricci was the only one doing the looking. But most of all he needed someone to be there if he began to lose it. Someone who could stop him if he cracked up again. He didn't want to end up banged away in some Italian psycho-bin. Danny could be his friend and watch his back. So he finally answered the question and told Danny what he was up to.

Chapter 12

THE WAITER BROUGHT the drinks and didn't give Jimmy a second look. Jimmy, he had decided, was an Act of God. Something horrible you couldn't do anything about.

'She's set up someone to tell me about any other cardinals. How did it go with you?'

Ricci took a sip of his Campari Soda.

'Good, although the guy jerked me about before he unbuttoned, but he delivered in the end.'

He ran over what Fr Phan had told him. Jimmy laughed when Ricci made the joke.

'They buried it. I like that, it's funny.'

'Thanks.' Jimmy didn't have to know it was Phan's joke.

'So, your watcher reckons that if Cheng was told when they started rehabilitating him it means somebody had to tell him. Which means a few people knew even if the Vatican was keeping it secret.'

Ricci nodded.

'That's right, we guessed, but whoever did it could have been told.'

'What about the Chinese?'

Ricci shook his head.

'My man says definitely not. They just wanted to save face, not let anyone know they hadn't known he was a cardinal. Other than that they weren't interested.'

Ricci put his hand into his pocket and pulled out a mobile phone and put it on the table in front of Jimmy.

'Take it.'

Jimmy shook his head.

'I don't want it. I had one once but I used to switch it off and forget to switch it on. I don't like the things. They go off when you don't want them to or you lose them. Anyway, I never have anyone I want to call.'

He pushed it back to Ricci. Ricci leaned forward and pushed it back to him.

'Well now you do have someone to call – me. I'm not working with a partner I can't contact. I phoned you three times this morning, where were you?'

'In the apartment.'

'Why didn't you answer?'

'I had to meet someone at lunch and it wanted thinking about so I didn't answer the phone. I didn't know who it was.'

'You have to answer the bloody thing to find out who it is. That's what phones are for. I can't hang about waiting until you've stopped thinking when we need to meet. I wasted a whole morning because I couldn't get you.'

Jimmy looked at the phone. Ricci was right but he didn't like the idea of someone being able to contact him whenever they liked.

'Nobody else will call you because nobody else knows the number. If it rings, it's me.'

Jimmy picked it up and looked at it. It was small and there were no buttons.

'How do you work it?'

Ricci leaned across and took it. He opened it and handed it back.

'Okay, you see how it works?'

Jimmy took it sullenly.

'I suppose it does everything, Makes the tea, wipes my bum, gives me access to the bloody internet and fills in my tax return.'

'Never mind what it does, it rings and you answer it. That's what it does. Here, watch.'

Ricci took out another mobile and dialled. The one in Jimmy's hand started to ring, the tone was a jingle version of the *Ride of the Valkyries*.

Jimmy looked at Ricci.

'Never mind that, we can change it. Just answer it.'

'How?'

'Press that one.'

Jimmy pressed a button and held the phone to his ear.

'Okay, you got the idea?'

'I can't hear you on the phone, your voice is too close.'

'Oh, Christ, ring off. Press that one.'

Jimmy pressed that one and watched the screen register neutral.

'Okay, I can take calls. How do I phone you?'

Ricci showed him.

'Press that.'

Jimmy pressed it.

'Now that.'

Jimmy did that.

'Now press *dial*, that one.'

Jimmy pressed that one. There was a pause and then the mobile in Ricci's hand began to ring. This time the jingle was Verdi.

Jimmy looked at him again.

'Never mind that, just ring off.'

Jimmy pressed the right button and Verdi went silent.

'What about the Wagner? I'm not having bloody Wagner going off where people can hear it.'

'Don't bother about that. I'll do it before you go.'

'I want it to just ring, like a proper phone.'

Ricci sounded doubtful.

'I'll try. It's got about fifty ring tones but I don't think it does just a ring. Look, I'll sort out something before you go.'

'If it doesn't just ring then no Verdi either.'

'Okay, I'll sort it.'

'In fact, no opera of any sort.'

'For God's sake, I said I'd sort it out before you go. Now, how do we find out who knew Cheng was a cardinal?'

Jimmy took a thoughtful drink.

'He has to be right, your China-watcher? You think he really knows?'

'If you mean, is it official, is he quoting some official record, then no, he's guessing. But it makes sense. So how do we find out who knew?'

'We don't yet.'

'Why not?'

'Because that wouldn't give us motive, and what we need is motive. Who would benefit, benefit in a big way, from Cheng's death? The best way in for us would be if he wasn't the only one. If there were others we get a connection and that might give us our reason. Either we're looking at Cheng on his own, in which case end of story, or we're looking at Cheng as one of…'

Jimmy stopped, then took a slow drink.

'Got something?'

'Listen, if Cheng is a one-off we're stuck. Even if we find out who knew he was a cardinal that won't lead us anywhere.

If one of them leaked it they're not likely to say, "Oh, yes, that was me, I told so and so all about it". You and me on our own can't take on the Vatican or any organisation big enough to do what's already been done.'

'So?'

'So we stick with what we can do.'

'Which is?'

'Which is stick with the "more than one" theory. If it's wrong, it's wrong and we say, "sorry, we got nowhere". You go back to being a copper and I get on with whatever I get on with.'

'Okay, so who would want to kill some cardinals?'

'As I understand it, cardinals do one thing no one else does: they choose the pope. They go into secret conclave where they can't be got at and they choose a pope. Right?'

'So?'

'So say a government wanted to be sure to get the right kind of pope next time round, a pope that would see things their way. To be sure that would happen you would have to get the cardinals voting the way you wanted them to.'

The right kind of pope, what was the right kind of pope? But Ricci didn't say anything. He let Jimmy go wherever he was going.

'You want to control that choice, but you can't get at the cardinals when they're actually doing the election, so before they do it you get as many as you can thinking your way and then you take out a few key players so your men on the inside can influence the likely outcome.'

'Brilliant! There's only one small flaw. It's rubbish, total bloody rubbish.'

'Go on, why is it rubbish?'

'First, it doesn't even come close to giving anyone a result worth killing for, cardinals or anyone else. Let's say you could get a few cardinals thinking your way, whichever way that might be. And it would only be a few, because Catholic cardinals are about as hard as it gets to nobble. You might have an influence on the outcome but that's all, just an influence. And if someone's killing cardinals they'll want to be pretty sure of getting exactly what they want, not just an outside chance. Then there's the timing. If you kill a few selected cardinals, and again you can't risk killing more than a few, it doesn't get you anywhere because it doesn't get you a conclave. You have to wait until the pope dies to get a conclave and that could be years. By that time there would be new cardinals, things would have changed and it would be back to square one. Like I say, it's rubbish. There's about two hundred cardinals scattered across the world so how do you get at enough of them to make your idea come even close to working? You couldn't do it. A big enough outfit might be able to buy a few and kill a few but never enough either way. You'd still not be close to getting the pope you wanted, even if the sitting tenant conveniently died so you got your conclave.' He paused. 'Or are you suggesting that they're going to kill the present pope as well?' He took a sip of his drink. 'Remember, unless you kill the pope you don't get your conclave.'

Jimmy was silent. Ricci took another sip of his drink. He hadn't meant it seriously... but killing the pope. It had been tried, a government had tried, maybe it wasn't so mad after all. They both thought about it. Ricci surfaced first. He was angry, this wasn't where they should be going.

'No, that doesn't work. I don't care who you are, you don't kill the pope. For one thing he's too well protected, ever since that bloke had a go at John Paul. But even if you did pull it off and got the conclave, that still doesn't mean you get it to go the way you want. It's still all too chancy. No, it's got more holes than a Swiss cheese. Fix some cardinals, get some others killed, then take out the pope and run a fixed conclave, and all for what, a sympathetic pope? It's fantasy. It makes *Alice in Wonderland* look like reality TV.'

'Call it fantasy if you like. But if whoever McBride sends says it may not be Cheng on his own, if there are others, it's all we've got. And if someone is trying to fix the next pope it means that the cardinals on their own aren't enough. There has to be something else, something that will not only provoke a conclave...'

'Which we know means killing the pope.'

'...but also ensures that the conclave picks the right man, or the right sort of man.'

'Come on, Jimmy, don't tell me you're serious about this, it's just wasting time.'

'If the man I get to talk to says Cheng had company, then I'm serious alright, I'm as serious as I am shit-scared. Get the waiter, will you. I think I could do with a large scotch.'

Ricci beckoned to the ever-alert waiter.

'Two whiskies, Gino, and make them doubles.' The waiter left. 'You've got to be wrong, Jimmy. It could never happen.'

'9/11 could never happen but that didn't stop it.'

God, thought Ricci, his mind just keeps on going until he makes a connection. But then why not make the connection? It's all about terrorism these days. Everyone's a player in that game one way or another and no one plays by any rules except one, do what has to be done. If international terrorism is the reason then anything became possible. They waited until the whiskies came. They both took a drink.

'I hope you're wrong, Jimmy, if you're not, well... I just hope you're wrong.'

Chapter 13

'NO, REALLY MR Costello, not pasta.' Jimmy looked at him.

Why not pasta, this was bloody Italy and they were in a restaurant for lunch, so why not pasta?

'If you will be recommended by me, try the saltimbocca. I assure you you will find it the best in Rome.'

Jimmy shrugged. He didn't care, he wasn't paying and he wasn't that hungry.

'What is it?'

The Monsignor smiled a bland smile, but though the blandness was perfectly practised you couldn't help but notice the sneer because the eyes are the traitors in the face.

'It is veal beaten very thinly with a layer of Parma ham spread over it and then fried in butter. Simple and, like all simple dishes, the outcome is primarily dependent on the quality of the ingredients rather than the talents of the chef. Like people don't you think?'

'What?'

'Like people. The outcomes individuals are capable of achieving are primarily the result of the quality of person they are, rather than of the skills they have acquired. A good man can achieve good things, a great man great things.'

'I'm not with you. I thought we were talking about what we were going to have for lunch.'

The Monsignor switched off the charm at the plug and nodded to a waiter who came to the table.

'Two saltimbocca and a bottle of the Pecorino.'

The waiter nodded, removed the menus and some redundant cutlery from the table and left. The Monsignor decided he should, as host, fill the silence while they waited.

'I hope my choice of wine is satisfactory. You musn't be put off by the name,' he held up his hand as if Jimmy was about to say something. He wasn't. 'It is indeed called Pecorino but it is *not* I assure you anything to do with the cheese. It is a little-known, rare grape variety from the Abruzzo which, under the right conditions and in the right hands, can produce a very acceptable wine. I am a personal friend of the producer and when he has a drinkable vintage he lets me know and I ask the proprietor here to buy a few cases. I find it an excellent lunchtime wine and very inexpensive. To live modestly is to live well, don't you think?'

While the Monsignor was holding forth Jimmy had noted that, as the waiter had taken the order and gone, it didn't matter a toss whether the wine was what he wanted or not.

'No, not really.'

That got in amongst you, thought Jimmy, as the bland Monsignor's eyebrows went up.

'Really! You do not think that to live modestly is to live well? I'm surprised. You didn't strike me as someone who would approve of excess.'

'Not that, the wine.'

'The Pecorino? You do not like my choice?'

'No. But not because it's got the same name as a cheese, it's because I don't like any wine much. I'll just have a beer.'

He could see that what his appearance had begun, his taste

in wine had cemented. He had now gone so far down in the opinion of the Monsignor that a dredger couldn't find him. And with blokes like him, that was the best place to be.

'I'll mention it to the waiter when he brings our order,' the Monsignor said, busying himself with his napkin. 'Is there any particular brand of beer you would prefer? Please say, I'm not a drinker of beer.'

'Just what comes to hand.'

'I see.'

The Monsignor took in the other tables and smiled to one or two of the diners. He was a see and be seen sort, a mixer, but if he moved in a gin and tonic world he was the tonic and not the gin. He was another Minister's aide type, Jimmy thought, right hand man to someone who hadn't got his brains – but hadn't lost his balls. Jimmy looked around. It was a calm and elegant place. The tables, of which there were many and all in use, were spaced so that a low voice at your table meant your conversation stayed at your table. It was all white linen, bentwood chairs and quiet money. The Monsignor, having scouted the tables, was ready to return to Jimmy.

'The only drawback here is that the Jesuits regard it as home ground. Still, it might have been worse, it might have been the Dominicans. I come here quite often. It's not far from the Gregorian and the Ministry and, on occasion, the Quirinale. Thankfully it's just too far from the Trevi Fountain to get tourists.' He was making a last ditch effort at charm so that Jimmy could acknowledge how very fortunate he felt to be sitting here.

'How do you know which ones are the Jesuits?'

The Monsignor gave up.

'So, Mr Costello, I have been asked if I would help you by giving you certain information concerning cardinals.' You weren't bloody asked mate, you were sent. You were given no choice. You were told to help me. 'I'm sorry I had to squeeze you in like this. Lunch today was my only window and I understood that what you want carries a degree of urgency.'

'This is fine.'

'Good, the people I deal with are not the sort whom you can cancel at short notice or put off until another day. Their time is extremely valuable. Mine, of course, is at the disposal of...'

'You speak very good English. You did say you were Italian didn't you?'

The Monsignor almost certainly resented the interruption, but it didn't show, not even in his eyes. He was smooth, thought Jimmy, smooth like oil.

'Yes, Mr Costello, I am Italian. Roman in fact, and I speak excellent English. I also speak excellent French and Spanish. I am only very good at Russian and Portuguese. My Serbo-Croat and Mandarin Chinese are passable but I can hold no more than polite conversation in...'

'It's okay. I only speak English so we'll stick to that.'

The Monsignor sat back. This objectionable peasant of a man had something he wanted to ask. Let him ask it. He would tell him what he wanted, then get rid of him. The waiter arrived with their food. He put it on the table and was about to leave when Jimmy spoke.

'And a beer.'

'A beer, sir?' The wine waiter had arrived with the wine in an ice bucket on a stand. He put it beside the table. 'Which brand, sir?'

'Anything local. Peroni.' The Monsignor almost winced. 'Not cold, just as it comes.'

'All our beers are chilled, sir.'

'Okay, just as it comes.'

The waiter nodded and left.

Jimmy waited. The Monsignor was praying an obvious Grace before starting his meal. When he had finished he took the bottle and poured himself a glass and put the wine back into the bucket. He took a good drink and then picked up his knife and fork and began to eat. Jimmy glanced at his plate. It looked nice, he felt sure it would taste nice. He put his elbows on the table and leaned forward.

'Over the last two years, anywhere in the world, how many cardinals have died suddenly?'

The question didn't even get a pause.

'Do you mean, died as a result of violence?'

'No, died unexpectedly, like Archbishop Cheng a couple of years ago.'

The Monsignor kept on eating and took another drink.

'Does age matter?'

'Not necessarily.'

'Five, possibly six.'

'Including Cheng?'

'You have already mentioned him.'

'Can you name them?'

'Cardinals Laurence Grimshaw, Felipe Obregon, Giovanni Stephano Capaldi, John Chiu Fa, Pius Mawinde and possibly Pietro Maria Gossa.'

'Why only possibly?'

'Because he was ninety-one and died in his sleep here in Rome. It was unexpected, in so far as a death at ninety-one can be unexpected.'

'Could the others have had anything in common?'

'Now that is an interesting question.'

The Monsignor stopped eating, put down his knife and fork, took a drink and then sat slightly forward with his elbows also on the table, his voice lowered a fraction.

'It is a question I have been half-asking myself ever since Archbishop Cheng's death.'

'Why half-asking?'

'Because of the answer.'

'A connection?'

'Leaving out Gossa on the basis of age, three of the rest have a kind of connection. Cardinals Grimshaw, Obregon, and Mawinde.'

'The connection?'

'They would have been very important if a conclave were to have been convened.'

'But not the other two?'

'Cardinal Chiu Fa was under eighty and therefore able to vote in a conclave but that is all. He would not have been an influence. Cardinal Capaldi was a Liturgist, a vital element in the changes to worship the Church is currently involved in, but that was all. In a conclave, being over eighty, he would not even have had a vote.'

'But the others, they would have been influential?'

'Grimshaw was American and Americans are always influential, they represent money. Obregon was Central American and a liberal. He could have organised the liberal wing, the modernisers. Cardinal Mawinde was a conservative, to put it mildly. He could have been a rallying point for the traditionalists.'

'And Cheng? What group did he represent?'

The Monsignor smiled.

'None, Mr Costello, no group at all.'

'So why is he connected to the other three? If he's spent most of his life in China and a good part of it in Chinese prisons how could he be...' It had clicked, and the bland Monsignor saw that it had clicked.

'Exactly, Mr Costello. He could easily have become pope

if a conclave had been called.'

'Are you sure?'

'That he would have been elected?'

Jimmy nodded.

'Absolutely not. To predict the outcome of a Papal conclave is impossible, it cannot be done. But if you mean, could he have been elected, was he the sort of man who might well get chosen? Then my answer would be, absolutely yes. He was very much papable.'

'Papable?'

'Suitable pope material. Archbishop Cheng was a man of great personal holiness and humility who had suffered tremendously for his faith. But he was also a gentle man, a man of prayer who had the capacity to forgive those who had treated him so cruelly because he put his Christian duty to the greater good before any personal feelings. I would have said he was papable, Mr Costello, wouldn't you?'

The Monsignor poured some more wine and went back to his meal. The waiter was at the table with a bottle of beer and a glass on a tray.

'Sorry about the delay, sir.'

He put the glass beside Jimmy and poured some beer, then put the bottle beside the glass.

'I took the chill off it but I'm afraid I had to use my judgement as to how you'd like it.'

Jimmy took a taste. It was just beer.

'Excellent, just right. Thanks.'

'My pleasure, sir.'

The waiter left. Jimmy took the bottle and poured some more into his glass. The Monsignor was eating, waiting for Jimmy to get going again.

'Doesn't the pope have to be a cardinal?'

'Technically, no. The pope has to be Bishop of Rome, but

so long as the candidate is in no way debarred from taking up that office anyone could be chosen. Technically you could be our next pope, Mr Costello.'

'Me!'

'Yes, you are a baptised and practising Catholic. You are not married nor, I hope, in a state of mortal sin. You are therefore eligible. If you were chosen you would be ordained priest, then consecrated bishop and then you could be pope. So could I, so could thousands, but as you said, the pope is now always chosen from among the College of Cardinals.'

'So Cheng would have to have been a cardinal to be pope?'

'Realistically, yes.'

The Monsignor pushed away his plate and refreshed his glass of wine.

'He wasn't though, was he?'

'Wasn't he?'

'He was an archbishop.'

'If you say so. I'm sure your information is more accurate than any I might have. I am, after all, but a humble Vatican functionary.'

You're something, thought Jimmy, but whatever it is it isn't humble. The waiter arrived and took the Monsignor's plate. He looked at Jimmy's untouched meal and hovered, uncertain what to do.

The Monsignor came to his assistance. 'Are you finished, Mr Costello?'

'No, I'll eat in a minute.'

'But your meal will be cold, sir.' Jimmy looked at the waiter.

'Is it any good cold?'

'Not really, sir.'

'Maybe you could re-heat it?'

'I hardly think it would be suitable re-heated, sir.'

'Mr Costello.' The Monsignor was getting annoyed. Jimmy picked up the plate and held it out to the waiter.

'Have a go anyway.'

'If you say so, sir.' The waiter took the plate. 'Will you require anything else, Monsignor?'

'No.'

The waiter left.

'If there is nothing further I can do for you, Mr Costello.'

He was ready to leave.

'There is.' The Monsignor stiffened and then relaxed. His face registered indifference but his eyes told another story. Jimmy poured the last of his beer into his glass. He took his time about it and about taking a drink. He wondered how many would die in the blast when the guy finally exploded if he got pushed any further. 'If, for the sake of argument, Cheng became pope, what effect might that have? How would a Chinese pope go down?'

'With whom?'

'With anybody?'

'The Church would welcome him as the new Holy Father, with joy and celebration as they would any new pope.'

Getting his own back is he? We'll see about that.

'Don't you know or won't you say?'

It hit home. He had been sent to co-operate, not to make a new friend nor to score points off a new enemy. His whole manner changed.

'Would you have said that John Paul II, a Polish pope, had an effect, Mr Costello?'

'Yes.'

'Indeed, yes. When he first became pope the Soviet Union looked as if not even a nuclear attack could destroy it. But it was utterly gone by the time he died. What he helped start in a shipyard in Gdansk couldn't be stopped and it brought down one of the world's two superpowers, a thing the other superpower had been trying to do for the second half of the twentieth century. And all without a shot being fired.'

'He didn't do it on his own.'

'You could argue that he didn't do it at all. That truth and justice and a desire for freedom did it from within.'

'Aided and abetted by rampant poverty and corruption, also from within.'

'Mr Costello, I am a busy man. If you really wish to discuss the fall of the Soviet Union could you do it some other time with some other person?'

'It would matter you think, a Chinese pope?'

'I think it would matter very much indeed and I think the prospect of Cardinal...' he paused, 'sorry, of Archbishop Cheng as Bishop of Rome would be something that might be opposed vigorously in certain quarters, most vigorously indeed.'

'Stop at nothing, sort of thing?'

'Perhaps.'

'Okay, I'm finished, you can go. I'll hang on and see what the... what was it called?'

The Monsignor was getting up. He was being dismissed by a crumpled, unimportant little peasant of a man. But he didn't mind, he would offer it up as a penance for the sinfulness of mankind.

'Saltimbocca, Mr Costello. I hope you find it still edible, but I doubt it. Good day.'

He forgets to say grace after meals, thought Jimmy, as the Monsignor made his way between the tables, nodding a couple of times to important-looking diners. I hope he remembers it when he next goes to confession. The waiter was back at the table.

'Do you want your meal now, sir?'

'Did he pay the bill?' The waiter looked after the Monsignor who was disappearing through the doorway into the street.

'The Monsignor has an account.'

'I see, he runs a tab.'

'Sir?'

'A tab, an account.'

The waiter smiled. He liked to pick up new English words.

'A tab, yes sir.'

'Is it a modest tab?'

'Sorry, sir?'

'A modest tab? He says he likes to live modestly. He says to live modestly is to live well.'

The waiter smiled again.

'Yes, sir, I would say the Monsignor lives well.' The smile almost became a grin, but not quite. He was talking about a good customer. 'Do you want your meal now, sir?'

'No, it won't be any good warmed up. Do you do any pasta?'

'Of course, sir. If you want pasta we can give you whatever you wish.'

'Spaghetti.'

'And how would you like it, sir?'

'Just as it comes. Ask the cook to use his judgement.'

The waiter smiled.

'Certainly, sir.'

He left. Jimmy reached out to the ice bucket. The bottle was over a third full. What sort of priest has a tab at a place like this and when he orders a bottle of wine leaves nearly half of it? He looked at the label. It said Pecorino and gave the year but otherwise it was meaningless. How much was inexpensive, he wondered. He poured a glass for himself. It was wine, just white wine.

He turned his mind back to what the Monsignor had told him. If there really was a conspiracy under way to rig the election of the next pope then the present pope had to be removed and whatever that involved was happening now. Cheng's death and the others meant it was two years into whatever was going on so he had to assume that it wouldn't be too long in coming. Leave it any length of time and things changed. All of which meant that in the near future the present pope would be dead and... and what? How do you fix a bloody conclave, for God's sake?

'Your spaghetti, sir.' The waiter put the plate on the table.

'Thanks.'

'Another beer, sir? I have one ready with the chill taken off, just in case.'

'Yes, thanks.'

Jimmy began his meal, spaghetti with a tomato sauce. How he liked it. The waiter arrived with the beer.

'You can take the wine away, it's finished with.'

'Certainly, sir.'

'Is it any good?'

'All our wines are good, sir.'

'Is it cheap?'

'We don't stock cheap wines, sir. But if you mean is it one of our less expensive wines, then yes, it is modestly priced compared to many of our others.'

'How much?'

It didn't sound modestly priced to Jimmy. It sounded damned expensive.

Jimmy went back to eating and thinking. Two hundred cardinals locked in one place with no outside contact and no way in. They had to be got at before they came to Rome or got at once they were assembled, and neither way made any sense. Before they came to Rome they were scattered across the world. Any attempt to nobble them would be too obvious. Once they were together no one could get at them except someone on the inside. Which took you back to getting at them before the conclave. It was like some stupid Agatha Christie thing. The pope will be found dead in the Vatican Library with all the doors and windows locked from the inside and a knife of oriental design stuck in his back. Then all the suspects, the cardinals, will be gathered in one room while I stand in front of them and tear off my whiskers and say: *It is I, Hawkshaw, the great detective, and I now know which one of you is the murderer.*

Jimmy ate his spaghetti. They didn't want Agatha bloody Christie on this, or a detective. What they wanted was a magician, because however it was going to be done, it was going to have to be one hell of a trick. Absolutely one hell of a trick.

Chapter 14

DANNY DIDN'T LOOK happy and when he spoke he didn't sound happy.

'I don't like this, Jimmy. I don't like what you've told me and I don't see what I can do now that you have told me.'

Jimmy signalled to the waitress. She came to the table.

'Same again?'

She was a chirpy South African.

'Just a beer, thanks, no coffee.'

She went away.

'I don't like it.'

'It gets worse.'

'I bet it does. How could it get any better?'

'I'll tell you if you want.'

Danny held up his hand. 'Too much, you've already told me too much, don't tell me any more. What I don't understand is why you told me in the first place.'

'So you could watch my back. That doesn't seem a lot to me.'

'How, watch your back? Watch for what?'

'Whatever comes.'

'I'm retired, Jimmy.' The waitress arrived and put the beer

on the table. 'If only half of what you've told me is true then it's way out of my league. This is spooks stuff, not any kind of police work that I was ever involved with.'

'Just look out for me. If you see me getting into trouble call a policeman.'

'How am I supposed to know you're in any more trouble than you've got already?'

'You'll know. I'll wear a pink carnation behind my right ear. Just keep an eye on me, and if you think I'm...'

'If I think you're what?'

'If I seem to be losing the plot... it might happen. Like you said, this is out of the frame of anything you or I ever did. I might screw up, it might screw me up. Just keep an eye on me.'

'I can do that, I suppose, but that's all I can do.'

'But you can call a copper if you think I need one.'

Danny nodded.

'If I can find one. You know what they say about coppers when you need one. And make it a sunflower behind your ear, that way I'll be sure to spot it.'

Jimmy laughed.

'Sure, a sunflower it will be.' Then he pushed his beer to one side and leaned a bit closer to Danny. He spoke quietly. 'Just for the sake of argument, how do you think someone could fix a conclave?'

Danny looked at him, stunned.

'Fix a papal conclave? That's got to be a joke? Tell me that's a joke, man.'

'Just for argument's sake, hypothetically.'

'That plot you thought you might lose? Well, my friend, you've already lost it. Shall I call a copper now?'

'Not yet. I don't need my back watched yet. At least I hope not.'

'I don't think you need anyone watching your back and I don't think it's a policeman I should get for you. I think you may need to talk to someone.'

'I'm talking to you.'

'Not me, someone who can help you.'

'Help me how?'

Danny tried to sound as serious as he knew how.

'Look, you lost your wife, that must have been bad. Then you lost your son so it gets worse. You try to get over it, you think you have and decide to become a priest. You come to Rome. You're among strangers. You decide to keep yourself to yourself, a loner, a man on the outside who doesn't mix. Then you suddenly disappear and when you come back you get put in hospital.'

'So? I explained all that.'

'You told me a story about a murdered archbishop and a conspiracy to get you here run by none other than your own College rector. Mysterious fires in Glasgow and shadowy goings on by some Intelligence outfit. Policemen suddenly getting sent to the US...'

'Fire and policeman, both singular. It was only one fire and one policeman.'

'This isn't a joke. Even if it was only one policeman or one fire, one is already too much. Archbishop Cheng died. I checked, his death wasn't suspicious. It was just an old man dying. I know that you really are a Duns student and you really do have a rector, and that's all I know for sure. Everything else is just stuff you told me.'

'I got put in hospital. That was real enough. You tried to visit me there, remember?'

'Okay, but it had all the marks of a routine mugging. Why shouldn't it be just what it looked like? The hospital bit is true but I think the rest of it is all in your head. No inspector, no fire, no Secret Services. I think you were about ready for a breakdown and when you got mugged that, on top of everything else, well, it sort of…'

'Pushed me over the edge? You think I'm nuts?'

'I think it's like a fantasy that's only going on inside your head but to you it all seems real enough. I think you need help.'

Jimmy wished Danny was right, that it was all going on in his head and the right kind of help would make it all go away. As it was, someone out there was going to assassinate the pope because they'd worked out how to fix a papal conclave, a thing everyone said couldn't be done.

'So, leaving aside me being nuts, what do you think? Would you say it was possible to fix a conclave?'

'Oh Christ, Jimmy, can't you see? That just makes me more certain that it has to be all in your head. There won't be a conclave until this pope's dead.'

'That's right.'

The realisation of what Jimmy meant stopped Danny for a second.

'Listen to me, man, you need help and you need it quick.'

The *Ride of the Valkyries* suddenly began in Jimmy's pocket. He pulled out the phone and answered it.

'It's still *Ride of the* bloody *Valkyries*, you said you'd fix that.' He listened for a moment. 'Right. I'm in a bar, La Tosca in the Piazza Colonna on the Corso. In a few minutes then.' Jimmy put the phone away. 'That was my imaginary inspector. He's coming to pick me up.'

Danny looked surprised.

'He does exist?'

'Afraid so, and he can back up everything I've told you.' Jimmy finished off his beer. 'Sorry, I shouldn't have dragged you into this but I didn't think I could do it without someone to talk to and I chose you. Sorry.'

Danny smiled a big smile.

'For God's sake, what's to be sorry for? I just got through telling you that I thought you were having a major breakdown and suffering from chronic hallucinations. That you were a mental basket-case. You don't think I wanted it to be that way do you? Jimmy, I'm glad I was wrong, but...'

'But what?'

'If what you've told me is true then you are in deep shit, man. It's going to chew you up and it won't spit you out, not alive anyway.'

'So now you're an espionage expert? I hope you're better at it than you were at making your psychiatric diagnosis.'

Jimmy was grinning but Danny wasn't.

'I don't have to be any sort of expert to know that if some stray bystander gets sucked in by that machinery they don't get left to walk away and tell the tale when it's over.'

In the distance a police siren began to be heard.

'If it's Ricci he must be in a hurry.'

'You're going to carry on with this?'

'I don't think I get a choice.'

'Well leave me out of it. I still have a choice.'

'Sorry, Danny, like you said, no one gets to just walk away.'

Danny let the words sink in.

'Okay if I'm stuck with it I'll try to look out for you but don't expect too much. And don't tell me any more.'

'I'll make sure I keep in touch.'

'And when we meet make it somewhere other than this place?'

'I like this place, I think we fit in.'

'We fit in like nuns at a strip joint.'

'Well, I like it, we're not locals. We live in Rome but we

don't belong. Why shouldn't we fit in with the tourists?'

'We came here to study. We're not tourists.'

'For God's sake look at us, two men old enough to be grandads, and you think we should fit in as students? We're freaks, something the tourists ought to have a good look at alongside the Forum and St Peter's and all the other stuff. Fools for God, that's what we are, a little Roman peep show.'

'If it's true at all it's only true about you. I'm not a freak and I'm not part of a peep show. Even if I'm leaving I'm still...'

Whatever Danny thought he still was, Jimmy didn't get to find out because a siren came down the Corso and then the black police Lancia pulled up outside and waited with its engine running and the blue light on the roof flashing.

'This your man?'

'Yeah, I'll let him come and get me. I want you to be sure he's real.'

They waited until the back door opened and a smart young man got out and came into the bar. He saw Jimmy and came to the table.

'What are you doing? Why didn't you come out?'

'Inspector Ricci, I want you to meet my friend Danny. He's a student priest like me.'

Ricci looked at Danny, then he put out a hand.

'Nice to meet you, Danny.'

Danny shook his hand.

'We've met before, Inspector, in another bar. But Jimmy didn't mention you were a policeman.'

'Have we? Sorry, I don't remember.' Ricci turned back to Jimmy. 'Okay, can we go now?' Ricci didn't wait. He walked away. Jimmy got up.

'See, real like I told you.'

'Yeah, Jimmy, just like you told me. Go careful now and remember what I said.'

'That it's all happening in my head?'

'That it will chew you up.'

'I'll remember, and I'll keep in touch. Pay the bill will you, I think my man's in a hurry.'

And Jimmy left the bar.

The police siren seemed to make no difference. It made a lot of noise but no one got out of the way, the traffic was just too heavy. The driver had to push his way through like everyone else. Ricci had been sitting in silence, sulking that he had been made to get out of the car and go into the bar, or maybe he was thinking. Jimmy broke the silence.

'How come we get a car and driver?'

'Luigi's a friend, off duty. He's doing us a favour. Don't you want to know where we're going?'

'If you want to tell me.'

'Quadraro, out of the city, down the Via Tuscolana.'

'And what will we see when we get there?'

'Two days ago the police were called to a break-in in some apartment out there. It turned out the place was empty. The young woman who lived there, Anna Bruck, was away. She couldn't be traced. No problem, just wait until she gets back. Meanwhile the scene of crime is turned over, prints get taken...'

'The usual.'

'...the usual. Pure routine and not particularly thorough. It was just a break-in. The prints got sent off and suddenly all sorts of alarm bells started to ring.'

'Was the thief someone special?'

'Not the thief, the girl who lives there. It turns out she's Anna Schwarz, the only member of the Geisller Group still at large.'

'Geisller Group?'

'A German terrorist group named after their leader, Conrad Geisller.'

'What sort of terrorists?'

'Extreme right wing.'

'New Nazis?'

'Not fascists in the traditional sense. They admired strength. Their particular creed was, "any cause that can fight its way to the top is a justified cause and any cause that wouldn't use force to achieve its aims is a weak cause and should go under". To them the law of the jungle was the natural law, the only real law.'

'Might is right?'

'Exactly, their favourite slogan translated more or less as, "it's not wrong to be strong", and their manifesto was headed, "Cause, Conviction, Action".'

'They had a manifesto?'

'Oh yes, four pages of pro-violent nonsense dressed up in socio-political jargon. Real adolescent stuff. They were a bunch of campus hard-cases. No one took any notice of them until they assassinated the Professor of History at the university where they were studying.'

'They did what?'

'Murdered him. Claimed he was perverting evolution by manipulating history to subvert natural selection. That he was a homosexual and thereby frustrating the natural law and that he was part of an atheistic liberal world conspiracy to suppress the right of the strong to assert their will and control their destiny.'

'Well you can't say fairer than that, can you?'

'They were political weirdos. They supported Israel and the US because of their use of force and Hamas and Hezbollah for the same reason. They were on the side of the tough guys regardless of what they stood for. It was all a bit incoherent. They were just stupid kids playing at being revolutionaries.'

'So naturally they topped their history teacher. Well you would, wouldn't you? And after that show of strength, what happened?'

'They went on the run. They lay low for a while then they bungled a bank raid. Nobody was hurt and they didn't get anything. Then there was a raid on a supermarket, they got away with a bundle but a security guard got shot. After that things hotted up. The media became interested and that's when they stopped being a bunch of violent young thugs and became the Geisller Group. The police turned up the gas but they managed to get away somehow.'

'How many were there in the group?'

'Four at university, five when they first went on the run, that was when Anna joined them. Her big sister Eva was supposed to be the brains of the outfit.'

'I thought you said Geisller was the leader.'

'At university he was but that didn't make him clever enough to get anywhere. He was muscle not brains. And he was good looking. At their age strong and good looking is enough to be the leader.'

'So Eva did the thinking?'

'So it seems. What little sense there was in their ideology she put there. Geisller was just a ranter and a bully.'

'And Eva's sister joined them when they went on the run after the murder?'

'Yes.'

'Why?'

Ricci shrugged.

'Who knows? Maybe she had the hots for Geisller or one of the others. Anyway, we know about them because after 9/11 US Intelligence began to turn them up. The best guess anyone came up with was that they went on the run from Germany and headed to where the real terrorists operated, Afghanistan or the Middle East. Somehow they seemed to have hooked up to someone who was al Qaeda or al Qaeda related. Whoever they were they wanted European faces who could be used for fetching and carrying, setting things up. US Intelligence was sure the Geisller Group were among those faces.'

'So what does that mean? They'd converted to Islam or what?'

'I doubt it. They were just doing their thing. Al Qaeda was a cause, it believed enough to do something, it had taken on the world's only remaining superpower. You don't get any tougher than that.'

'What happened to them? You said Anna was the only one still at large?'

'They must have wanted to break away from al Qaeda and do their own thing so they surfaced again, this time in Spain. They pulled another bank job. Probably fundraising to set up something of their own. They got away with a tidy sum but one of them was shot by a security guard. When they questioned him he spilled the works. They were on the run again but this time the police had one of them on their side. French Intelligence got them just outside of Carcassonne in a holiday let. There was a shoot out, one got killed and one got taken. Would you believe it, Geisller survived.'

'And the sisters, Anna and Eva?'

'Nowhere, and neither of the guys knew where they were.'

'Who had the money?'

'Geisller had some but the girls had most of it.'

'I see. Do you think the sisters gave them to French Intelligence?'

'No idea. I just got as much about them as I thought we needed. She's a known terrorist and seems to have been good at not getting found. She's been lying low since the Carcassonne thing and suddenly up she pops, here in Rome.'

They were free of central Rome traffic and the car was moving fast now on the Via Tuscolana.

'It was a break-in? Door forced?'

Ricci nodded.

'Yeah, but a neat job. Somebody who knew what they were doing. A neighbour in the next apartment heard some noises, knew the girl wasn't there so she called the police.'

'But the intruder was gone before they got there?' Ricci nodded. 'Don't you think that's odd?'

'Why?'

'Somebody gets in quietly, then makes so much noise that he gets heard by next door, then slips quietly away so no one sees him go. I just think it's odd.'

'What did you want the neighbour to do, stand outside the apartment and arrest him when he came out? She was frightened. She kept her door shut and waited for the police.'

'I suppose so.'

'I know so.'

With the siren going and the roads less congested they were making good time.

'Why do we have to have that thing going, we're not in a hurry?'

'We look like we're on police business. If anyone sees us at the apartments we're just cops having another look.'

'We're going to a crime scene that's two days old. Why do we need a siren? What's our big hurry?'

Ricci leaned forward and spoke to the driver. The siren fell silent. The driver lowered the window and pulled the light off the roof and stuck it under his seat. Jimmy watched him. He'd better be good at his job, buggering about like that at the speed they were going. The Lancia went on, slower now, just part of the traffic.

'Was Anna ever convicted of anything?'

'Never charged because she was never caught. They got prints, DNA and a photo from her home. Other than that they never got a smell of her.'

'What happened to big sister?'

'Gunned down outside a railway station in Austria somewhere. No one knows why it was done or who was responsible. It could even have been the sister, a falling out maybe.'

'Maybe. They interviewed Geisller?'

'Yes, he said he knew nothing about where the sisters were. He was probably telling the truth. They were all just amateurs who got to play in the big time for a while. If the real terrorists hadn't needed some innocent-looking white kids to help set up their operations they'd have tried another bank job or something like that and it would probably have ended there.'

'So Anna, late of the Geisller Group, turns up here in Rome. When did she come and what was she doing?'

'She came three weeks ago. Posed as a postgraduate student from Tübingen University in Holland called Anna Bruck doing research into Renaissance Vatican diplomacy. She requested access to certain documents in the Vatican Library. Her papers checked out which is fine until the police check again after they know who the prints belong to and find that Anna Bruck is a postgraduate student studying electronic engineering and has never left Tübingen.'

'Do we have a picture of her?'

'Not recent. The only one on file is about ten years old. It was supplied by the parents when she went on the run with her sister.'

'Did she ever go to the Vatican Library?'

'Not that anyone can remember. Her contacts with their administration were by phone and email. They thought they were dealing with someone in Holland but she could have been anywhere.'

The dual carriageway entered a busy suburb with apartment blocks all round and shops at street level. They passed a Metro station, Porta Furba.

'This is commuterland. They're packed like sardines in the morning on the Metro but it's still the only way to get to central Rome. It's too far for buses to be any good.'

Jimmy looked at the busy pavements on either side of the road. It looked a nice place to live, if you liked a view of nothing but other apartments and being treated like a sardine twice a day.

The Lancia turned left off the main road, made a couple of turns and pulled up outside a block that looked like all the others, with washing strung across balconies and slatted shutters on the windows. Here the sun was something you kept on the porch, like muddy shoes in England, even this pleasantly warm spring sunshine.

Jimmy and Ricci got out of the car.

'It's on the first floor.'

They went in and began to climb the concrete stairs.

'Her apartment gets turned over while she's away and the police find out who she is through a routine fingerprint check. Is it connected to what we're doing, Jimmy, that's the question. What do you think?'

Which was just what Jimmy was doing, thinking hard.

'Considering what else we've got in the way of solid evidence, it had better be.'

'That's what I thought. Terrorist puts it in our ball park if we're on the right track.'

'Who gave it to you, that Anna had turned up in Rome?'

'The Cherub. He phoned me yesterday evening. The Minister ordered a complete information shut-down. He doesn't want the media to get any sort of line on it. But the Cherub thought we'd want to know.'

'Good for the Cherub. Let's hope he's turned up trumps.'

They turned off the staircase and went on to Anna Bruck's apartment.

Chapter 15

IT WAS A ONE-BEDROOMED apartment. An unwashed plate, cutlery and mug were stacked neatly on the draining board by the sink. There was food in the kitchen cupboards and in the fridge. There were clothes in the wardrobe. The bedclothes were rumpled, pulled up but not straightened out. There was a four-day-old copy of *La Republica* on the settee in the living room.

It was all neat in a sloppy sort of way. Jimmy sat on the bed. Ricci stood in the doorway looking round.

'We're not going to find much, are we?'

Jimmy nodded.

'It's all been cleaned up.'

Ricci looked around the bedroom.

'The next apartment's the other side of that wall. I don't see how the thief made enough noise to get the neighbour to call the police unless he threw something against the wall.'

'What sort of noise did the neighbour say she heard?'

Ricci shrugged.

'I didn't ask.'

Jimmy reached over, pulled back the bedclothes and looked at the sheet.

'The bedclothes are rumpled but the sheets haven't been slept on.'

'So? The bed was made after the place got searched and put back together.'

They went into the living room.

'How did the woman next door know she'd gone away?'

'A note through her letterbox. "Hello, I'm your new neighbour, Anna, I have to go away for a week. Could you tell anyone who calls I'll be back next Tuesday?"'

'Why not do it in person?'

'Maybe she wanted to be seen as little as possible by as few people as she could manage.'

'So next door has never seen Anna?'

'No. No one seems to have seen her.'

'What language was the note in?'

'Italian, and I know that may be odd but it was definitely in Anna's handwriting. It got cross-checked and it matched.'

'So Anna the terrorist who is on the run sets up an alias and with this alias she comes to Rome. How did she rent the apartment?'

'All done by phone, rent paid for six months in advance. Checking references would be a formality if the money was already in the agent's account.'

'Was the money paid by a bank transfer?'

'Cash, paid into the agent's account. She used a bank in Genoa.'

'And the teller saw the photo but didn't remember her?'

Ricci nodded.

'She doesn't remember a thing, just another customer. There was nothing from the CCTV either.'

'She seems to be able to move around free as a bird and yet stay invisible.'

'She's had the practice. She had the cream of the US and

European anti-terrorist agencies looking for her and they never even got a sniff.'

Jimmy went to the window and looked out. Why was she here? There was something he didn't like about this. If it tied up with what they were looking into it was too neat and convenient. Out of nowhere, when they needed a lead, they got a known terrorist dropped in their lap.

'She does actually exist doesn't she, our invisible Anna?'

'She exists. Her parents say she contacted them twice while she was on the run, both times to tell them she and Eva were okay.'

'Contacted them how?'

'By letter. The handwriting was hers, she used a nickname she'd had when she was little and the fingerprints checked. Fingerprints and DNA taken from her home check out with here. She may be invisible but she exists and she's been here.'

'What did the two others in the group say about her?'

'Nothing, they never met her.'

'What?'

Jimmy turned away from the window.

'They never met her?'

'No, they never saw her.'

'Are you telling me she was part of a terrorist group and the rest of the group never met her? How does that work?'

'It seems she organised things through Eva. She set up the places and Eva passed on the info.'

'Explain.'

'After they'd killed the history man they were close to panicking. Spouting political bilge was one thing but killing someone was something else. Apparently Eva got them holed up somewhere and told them to stay put. She contacted her sister, who wasn't involved, and got her to set up somewhere safe. She did, and she was clever at it. She split them up,

Eva and herself, the guys into twos. She got them mobiles and email addresses. It was while they were hiding out that Geisller and the one he was with planned the bank job. With Geisller as the brains, naturally it was a cock-up. After that Anna looked after travel and hideouts. She always kept them in twos and she always kept Eva and herself together, she never had any direct contact with the men. The gang needed travelling money so Eva planned the supermarket job. It came off but a guard got shot. So now they had their travelling money but they were front-page stuff for a while. That must have been when they decided to head off. Somewhere along the line they got involved with the al Qaeda people.'

'Now three are dead and two banged up in prison for the rest of their lives and little sister has surfaced on her own.'

'Yes.'

Jimmy turned back to the window. Ricci let him think for a while but then got fed up of waiting.

'What I've told you is in a file in the car. I spent last night going through it. Reports, interviews, stuff from the past, nothing recent and certainly nothing current. So is it anything to do with us?'

Jimmy left the window and sat down on the settee.

'Maybe yes, maybe no.' He picked up the old newspaper. Then put it down. Ricci became impatient.

'Come on, Jimmy. Don't pussyfoot about. Do we follow this one?'

'Let's see if we can turn up a connection. We don't have to piss about on our own any more. Anna is a known terrorist on the run so there'll be big guns out looking for her. This flat will have been gone over by experts. Get your aide at the Ministry to give you an official hook-up to whoever is running the investigation. We'll plug into anything they get.'

'It's done already. Who do you think I got all the

background stuff from? The Cherub sent it by messenger when he told me about her.'

'Sorry, of course, I wasn't thinking.'

'Well start thinking.'

'If she's part of it she's off doing whatever she came to Rome to do. Which means we've just run out of time. The police can follow her if she leaves a trail but that's about all they can do. I doubt they can stop her. She's been too good in the past to make any stupid mistakes so my guess is she'll be too good this time. Whatever she came to do will get done.'

'Which, according to your theory, is kill the pope. But that's nuts. She's not a killer, nor even close to being one. Even if she wanted to kill him she wouldn't know how and certainly couldn't do it alone.'

'What if she'd been trained? She's been out of sight long enough.'

'Don't go silly on me, Jimmy. She's only ever moved people about. Whatever Anna was here for must have been related to what she was good at.'

'That makes sense. Maybe she was sent in to move a team. Her job is getting them in and putting them as near to the target as possible.'

'If we're right that she's gone to get her team, it's already off and running.'

Jimmy felt angry with himself. Ricci was the one doing the thinking. At least he was doing the clear thinking about Anna and where she fitted in. Why wasn't his brain working properly? What was holding him back? He made a mental effort to concentrate on the immediate job in hand and push everything else out. But he didn't like doing it. He had a vague idea he was pushing out something important.

'We need to know how she travelled when she left here, which means car rentals or travel tickets. She didn't know anyone would be looking for her so she will almost certainly use the same ID. Also, she's been away three nights if she put that note into the next door flat the day before the break-in.'

Ricci nodded.

'She did.'

'Three nights then. So we need to know if she has checked into any hotels and I need to know if your Minister will okay it for us to share some of our information with whoever is co-ordinating the search. That she's moving a team and the target is here in Rome.'

'I see. They won't have any idea why she turned up or where she's going. If we're right we can tell them where to look.' What Ricci meant was, I can tell them, but Jimmy didn't need to know that. 'Okay, anything else here?'

Jimmy gave the place a look.

'I doubt it but I'm not sure. There's something at the back of my mind, something that's pulling me away from just going straight after her.'

'What is it?'

'If I knew that I'd be the first to tell you.'

'So what are you going to do?'

'I'm going to try and work it out, it's annoying me. Either it's important, in which case I need to know what it is, or it's nothing, in which case I need to get rid of it. Either way I need to bring it up where I can see it. You get on and find out how things stand. Get what we've worked out to whoever's heading up the hunt. Then phone me when you've got anything. I need to think. I need to go over everything from where we started through to now and until you get anything from the police there's not much else for me to do but think. Can I get back from here by myself?'

'Sure, you take the Metro. It's about fifteen minutes to Termini.'

'No. I'll need more time and the Metro is too noisy, all that piped musak. What about a bus?'

'Yeah, there's a bus. But it takes about a day and a half.'

'Slow is just what I want. I'll take the bus.'

'Where will we meet if I get anything?'

'Chiesa Nuova.'

'Not a bloody church.'

'Why not? It'll be quiet, it'll be a good place to think, and maybe say a prayer. If you don't get the right sort of information we might not have anything to fall back on except prayer.'

He was smiling but he wasn't really trying to be funny. Something was happening and it was happening now, and the truth was he didn't have a clue as to what it really was. He didn't believe in a hit team, but he believed in Anna. Somehow Anna was the key, but the key to what? Anna was on the move and if she thought she was clear there was a good chance she'd leave a trail. But why had this on-the-run amateur terrorist been recruited? Why not someone trained?

'Are we going, or are you going to stand there all day? Come on, I'll drop you at the bus stop.'

They left the apartment. When the driver saw them coming he started the engine.

'Who knows?'

The question puzzled Ricci.

'Who knows what?'

'There may be a Mass on. I haven't been getting to Mass as often as I like since this started.'

'You're a bloody religious nut, that's what you are,' was what Ricci said, but what he thought as they drove away was, I am being expected to go to the Minister and tell him that a known terrorist with al Qaeda links has been sent to Rome to bring in a hit squad to assassinate the pope. This is based on what may have been the suspicious deaths of four cardinals connected by their importance should a conclave be convened. Which all means... Well, God knows what it means. It will probably mean that I'll get thrown out on my ear for wasting his time. But if the Minister thinks there's only an outside chance, he can't do nothing once he's been told. If there's any sort of chance that we're right, it will mean what? Having to move the pope, put the military into the Vatican? And then, when nothing happens, no hit squad turns up and everyone starts asking questions, I'll be the one they're asking. And what can I tell them? An ex-London copper who got early retirement due to stress and who wants to become a priest thought someone was out to kill the pope. Ricci didn't want to think about it, but it was all he could think about.

This was going to be a ball-breaker.

If Jimmy was wrong, and the odds were he was as wrong as he could be, then any career as a copper ends. It doesn't just stall, it ends. They won't even put me in Traffic. They'll kick me into the nearest gutter and jump on me before they go away and slam every door they can think of in my face. Ricci knew that if he told the Minister and Jimmy was wrong, the shit was going to hit the fan in a big way. But if Jimmy turned out to be right and the Minister hadn't been told, then the shit was also going to hit the fan. But in a much bigger way. Either way, he knew exactly who the fan was pointing at. Maybe Jimmy was right. Just at this point in time maybe prayers weren't such a bad idea.

The car pulled over and stopped. Ricci nodded to a bus stop.

'The x53 from here will take you in. When you get there say one for me, and maybe light a candle.'

'I was going to do it for both of us, we need it.'

The Lancia pulled away. The driver had put the blue light

back on the roof and the siren was on. Jimmy watched it go. Ricci was in a hurry. Of course he was. He wanted to let the Minister know what was happening as soon as possible. That's good, he thought, maybe Ricci is beginning to see our problem at last. We're following an outside chance because an outside chance is what we've turned up. But we've got to believe in it and commit to it one hundred per cent.

He looked down the dual carriageway. There was no bus in sight. He went back to his thoughts. For God's sake, why me? Why am I the one chasing shadows and telling myself they're real?

But he knew that wasn't a question he should be asking. Not if he was to give their outside chance any kind of a chance at all.

Chapter 16

JIMMY WAS LUCKY, there was a Mass about halfway through when he arrived, the small congregation gathered together in the front two or three rows.

Chiesa Nuova, the 'New Church', had been built in 1615 as the Oratorio di S Filippo Neri, the imposing mother church to oratories worldwide. But in this city of ancient churches it had always remained Chiesa Nuova. Jimmy didn't like it, it was too ornate. Everywhere was paintings, flourishes and gold leaf. It distracted the eye from the altar.

He sat down in the back row of the pews far away from the congregation and altar. The priest saying Mass wore red vestments. It must be the feast of a martyr, red was for blood, violent blood, and death.

He sat searching for words.

'Dear Lord...'

Dear Lord why is Anna here? No, not that. God knew, but he wasn't about to share the information. Dear Lord, keep me good as a detective. No. Dear Lord, keep me bloody good as a detective. No, it wasn't that. You got it by working at it, it didn't come any other way. Dear Lord, make me wrong about this pope thing. But God didn't change things. He wasn't a slot machine – put in a prayer and get out what you want. If God had been like that then all he'd ever get was, Dear Lord, please give me something good for the two thirty at Kempton Park. So, what were the right words? Jimmy switched off his mind, and when he did, the words came.

'Dear Lord, keep in your mercy, compassion and forgiveness Bernie and Michael, and take them into the love of your everlasting kingdom of peace and happiness.'

You didn't ask for yourself, you knew what you were. You left yourself to God and hoped for mercy and maybe, if you were lucky, other people prayed for you. The ancient formula, spoken without thought, came automatically to his lips.

'May their souls and the souls of all the faithful departed, through the mercy of God, rest in peace. Amen.'

He looked at his watch, he was hungry. He'd had no lunch and it was now three o'clock. When the Mass ended he would go somewhere and get something to eat. He turned his attention to the priest and switched off his mind. The priest was speaking rapidly in some language that wasn't Italian. He was oriental. Jimmy looked at the people in the front rows. They were oriental, probably pilgrims with their own priest. He looked back to the priest. He found no difficulty in following what was being said. He knew the words of the Mass almost by heart, but from constant repetition not from any study or interest in what it all meant. That had come in Ireland, after Bernie and Michael's deaths. Then he had started to listen. Why had he waited for them to die before he had begun to listen?

Jimmy sat and watched the altar.

It was something someone had said. The thing he wanted to bring out into the open was something someone had told him. No, not someone, more than one person. He had been told something very important and told more than once, and by more than one person. He concentrated and as he did so whatever it was slipped away.

He gave up. It would come when it was ready, if it came at all.

He got up and quietly walked to the nearest candles. They were in a black, wax-spattered affair by a massive round pillar. Above them, on a plinth, the statue of a saint looked down. Jimmy put some coins in the slot of the money box, picked up two candles, lit them and put them among the others. There were always candles burning. People always wanted something from God, a big favour, a small favour. And when only God could help, you reached out to him like you did to all the powerful ones. You got a friend of his to put in a word for you. Jimmy looked at the statue.

'Whoever you are, if you were ever in trouble, please, please pray for me and Ricci. Pray that we can do what we need to do, and that we can do it in time. Amen.'

He crossed himself and looked back into the church. The priest had come down from the altar and was distributing communion at the altar rail. It was nothing to do with him, he was a spectator, uninvolved. It was their Mass, not his.

Jimmy went out of the church into the sunshine. It had only been a little prayer to a very minor saint whose name he didn't even know. But it was something. It was the best he could manage in the circumstances. Now he could go and get something to eat and try to work out, why Anna and why now? Maybe he could dredge whatever was at the back of his mind out into the open before he heard from Ricci. He had the feeling that when Ricci did get in touch things would begin to hot up.

Chiesa Nuova was on the Corso Vittorio Emanuele so he had a choice of places to eat but he just wanted a simple meal somewhere quiet. He went round the back of the church into a maze of little streets where he could find the kind of place he wanted.

It was something he'd heard, just one thing, like Anna was just one thing. One thing that might tell him what he needed to know, but what? What had he been told?

The *Ride of the Valkyries* jangled in his jacket pocket and the man at the next table, smoking a cigarette with a glass of red wine in front of him, looked across.

'Shit.' Jimmy put his fork on his plate, took out the mobile and answered it. 'It's still playing bloody Wagner, when are you going to...' He stopped and listened. 'Why won't they?' He listened again. 'Oh, fuck.'

If the solitary drinker at the next table spoke English he didn't seem to mind the language, but it wasn't much of a place, so it probably didn't matter one way or another. 'Look, we'd better meet, this needs sorting. Where are you now? I'll be there in about ten minutes.'

He had only eaten half of his spaghetti but it would have to be enough. He went to the bar and paid. Then he left and set off for the Campo de Fiori.

Cars weren't allowed in this busy market square but Ricci's big black Lancia was outside the bar with the blue light still on the roof to identify it as a police car. There was no sign of the driver. Inside Ricci was sitting holding his usual Campari Soda, a beer was on the table. The waiter nodded as he walked past him. He didn't smile, but he definitely acknowledged his arrival. Jimmy sat down.

'He nodded at me.'

'Why not? He's seen you before.'

'He used to ignore me.'

'Maybe now he thinks you add a dash of something to the

place. To be so out of fashion in a place like this might be the way to be in fashion. Who knows, crumpled-scruffy might be the new black.'

Jimmy took a drink.

'Why won't they?'

'Because I'm unofficial. I'm on leave pending a medical report and when I'm at work I'm nothing to do with terrorists. As for you, you don't even exist. I found out who was on the team, phoned one of them off the record. I told him I was working for the Minister in an unofficial capacity and asked for a contact inside the investigation so we could share information. Fifteen minutes later I get a call that slams the door on me.'

'Why didn't you go straight to the Minister?'

'We were in a hurry and going through the Minister would have taken too much time. I was wrong.'

'Well, what's done is done. We need access to progress reports. We need information as it comes in. We need to ask questions and get them answered.'

'I put a message into the Minister's aide. He'll get back to me.'

'He'll get back to you? You just left it at that? We're sitting here with no police hook-up. Little sister is on the move and all we've got is that the Cherub will get back to you?'

'Well, what else could I do? And he was quick with the Anna stuff in the first place.'

Jimmy left it.

'We've got to phone McBride.'

'Why?'

'Well, who the fuck else is there?'

Ricci looked around. Jimmy had let his voice rise and in this place just about everybody spoke English.

Jimmy noticed and continued more quietly.

'She must have a direct line to whoever set this up with the Minister. When we asked for a Vatican contact we got her. Whoever she is she's more than just a simple academic and part-time rector. She's a player of some sort. So if we ask her for a police contact inside the investigation she might be able to get somewhere. We need access to up-to-the-minute reports with a first briefing not later than ten tonight or we could be dead in the water.'

'How do you work that out?'

'Think about it. Anna wouldn't move until she was needed, and she wouldn't be needed until the team were about to arrive. She already has a safe house for them…'

'We don't know that, maybe that's what she gone to do, not pick up the team.'

'So what's she been doing since she arrived, sightseeing?'

'Okay. She's got a place for them somewhere in or near Rome and she's on the move, so they must be on their way.'

'If she's moving, they're moving. That means a timetable. Day one, the day she left, would be to get where she's going to make the pick-up and make sure everything is okay. Day two, she would have taken delivery of the team and got them to a hotel. Day three, arrange transport and brief them on the safe house and anything else they needed. Day four, move to the safe house. That takes us to today. They're here now so little sister will have flown. We need to know how she travelled, where she travelled and who she met. We need names and descriptions. We need details if she hired a car. If she's gone they might use it. They'll be careful but they won't know they're blown so they'll not change identities. Whatever names they used to come in will be the ones they'll still be using. Somewhere they'll have left information about themselves.'

Ricci took it up.

'And they can't just come to Rome and, bingo, they kill the pope. There's a plan to go with the timetable. They need him where they can get at him and it has to be foolproof. That might give us time and with the right resources it could be enough. Our problem is we know they're here but we can't look for them. The police have the resources but they don't even know they exist, so it comes back to getting alongside the team looking for Anna and doing it quickly enough to get action. Right?'

But Jimmy didn't answer, he was thinking of something else.

'What is it?' Ricci asked.

'Something you just said. Nobody can just come to Rome and kill the pope. Not even an Intelligence-backed team. If they're here now it's because they're ready. They have it worked out or they wouldn't have come.'

Ricci could almost hear the cogs turning in Jimmy's head.

'Maybe you were right and she hasn't gone for the team. Maybe she's been waiting for something else.'

'Which would be?'

'What about equipment? If they're a hit-team going up against the level of security that surrounds the pope, they're going to need some very fancy equipment. They'll need the sort of equipment that will get them past some very heavy security. If we could work out the how, that could give us the when and where. What would punch a hole in the security? Not a grenade or a gun, because it has to be certain. It has to be a very special piece of kit, not the kind they'll be able to bring with them if they come by plane. It will have to come in separately and get picked up at this end.'

Jimmy was thinking out loud and Ricci didn't like the way his thoughts were going.

'Give it up, Jimmy, let's go to the police with what we've got. We'll never be able to sit here and work it out.'

'We could try.'

'One minute we can't do this fast enough, then it's, let's sit and think about it. Stop trying to be Sherlock Holmes and let's go with what we've got.'

Jimmy nodded. Ricci was probably right. There would be time to think after he had phoned McBride. But it still wasn't right.

'Alright, I'll phone McBride.'

'Good.'

Jimmy finished his drink.

'Okay, let's go to my apartment and phone her.'

'Like shit we'll go to your apartment, use your mobile.'

'I can't.'

'Why?'

'I don't have her number. It's beside the phone in the apartment.'

'Oh, Christ, I don't believe this.'

'I told you. I never use a mobile, only the landline.'

'God give me strength. Come on, I'll drive you.'

Jimmy got up slowly.

'You sure? How many Camparis have you had? Are you okay to drive?'

'I'll risk it, Jimmy. I think it's worth it to save the pope's life, don't you? Now come on and stop pissing about.'

'If you say so. But take it easy.'

'Go to Hell.'

They left the bar. The waiter watched them go. What could two people who were so different find to talk about he wondered. They were certainly an odd couple.

Chapter 17

RICCI WATCHED JIMMY put the phone down.

'What did she say?'

'I told her what we'd got so far, how Anna turned up and our theory...'

'Your theory, Jimmy, you're the brains, remember?'

'I told her Anna was on the move and what we think is happening...'

'What you think is happening.'

'...and she just said, stay where you are, give me your number and I'll phone you back as soon as I can.'

Jimmy sat down. His eyes were far away.

Ricci waited for a second.

'So we wait here?'

'She didn't seem interested, she just listened. Why didn't she have any questions?'

'You told her what you think and then told her what you wanted, an urgent message passed to the Minister. What do you expect her to do, spend time cross-examining you? She's getting on with it, exactly what you asked her to do.'

Ricci wasn't wrong, but he wasn't completely right either.

'I suppose so.'

Ricci was restless. Waiting, doing nothing, wasn't something he was good at.

'Shall I make us coffee? Do you want a coffee?'

Jimmy gave him a vacant stare. He wasn't really back yet.

'No.'

'Neither do I.'

It wasn't easy with Ricci just standing there. He wasn't going to settle until he was occupied.

'I'm not happy about this.'

Ricci gave an ironic laugh.

'Not happy? That's a bit of an understatement, isn't it? We start with the outside possibility of a murder, move on to four possible murdered cardinals, and then go right to the top of Seria A with an attempt on the pope's life probably by a foreign Intelligence service. What's there to be happy about? Even if you're right, we don't have enough time or resources. We have nothing that's concrete evidence. All we have is your theory, which is pure *Looney Tunes*, if it wasn't for a lot of circumstantial.'

'We've gone wrong.'

'What?'

'We've got too close.'

'Enlighten me.'

'Cheng and the other cardinals. Do you remember what we were looking for, a connection?'

'Sure, and you thought you'd found one. Fixing the next conclave.'

'If I'm right it isn't about killing cardinals or even killing this pope. All along it's been about fixing the election of the next one.'

'And to get a conclave you have to have a dead pope. But that still leaves the question – how, after they've killed this one, can they influence who gets to be the next one?

According to you, they've worked out how it can be done. You haven't and I don't think you ever will, because you're wrong.'

'It keeps coming back to fixing the conclave somehow.'

'Only because you say so.'

Jimmy didn't like it but Ricci was right.

'Okay. Forget the conclave and tell me how they're going to kill the pope. They have to have something special, something that makes it failure-proof.'

Ricci tried. It wasn't easy but he tried.

'We agree that they need special kit. What special kit would be good enough to make killing the pope a sure thing, other than nuking the bloody place?' He brightened. At least he could try to get a rise out of this stupid ex-London bastard. 'Is that it, Jimmy, you think they're going to launch a nuclear missile at the Vatican? Oh no, that won't work, will it, because you don't need to bring a team in if you're using nuclear missiles, do you? And that can't be right because it won't fit your theory. And we all know that the most important thing is that everything has to fit your theory or it can't be right, can it?'

Jimmy looked at him.

'Finished being funny now?'

'No, I'm not. I feel like I'm being sucked into your head, that everything I do and think about is crammed inside your nut. This whole idea of killing the pope is a million-to-one shot at best. But I go along with it because it's where you want to go and I was told to follow. Alright, if it turns out that Anna really has come to bring in a team the odds go down to maybe a thousand to one that the pope is the target. But why do they have to be after the pope, if they're after anybody? Why can't they be terrorists on the run that Anna is moving around? Why not a bomb on the Metro, like Madrid? If it's terrorist related it could be almost anything. Why do you have it that it must be killing the pope?'

Ricci was letting his anger and frustration show as well as the tiredness of working non-stop on an investigation where all the usual support was missing. Jimmy's voice, however, was flat; he was just talking the thing through.

'Because that is the only way it connects with Cheng's death. And Cheng's death is what we're supposed to be looking into, or had you forgotten?'

'Yes, I'd forgotten. Because as far as I can see the two things are about as connected as my mother and the Queen of England. But then, if you wanted it they would be connected, wouldn't they, because they're both women.'

Ricci got up angrily. The whole thing was beginning to prey on his mind. Jimmy went on in his matter-of-fact way.

'When that Turkish gunman shot John Paul II he did it in St Peter's Square.'

Ricci sat down, his anger gone. He had needed the outburst but now it was over.

'That could never happen again. Nobody could get close enough.'

Jimmy leaned forward.

'Okay. There's no way a gunman could get close or a sniper get into any of the buildings to get a clean shot. The ground is too well covered for a grenade or a bomb. So you don't come at the pope from the ground.'

Ricci suddenly saw where he was going.

'Oh, Christ, you don't mean from above?'

'Why not? Why not a smart missile from a hand-held launcher in a helicopter? If this has the kind of backing we think it has then that sort of kit could be made available. The team would just have to be two, a pilot and the button man. They can hire a helicopter but they'll need the missile and launcher sent in. It's not exactly something they can shop for once they get here or bring with them on the plane.'

'Jesus.'

'It was your idea really, you thought of the answer.'

'Me?'

'Yes, the missile idea. Come at him with a missile, and enough of a missile to make it certain. A tank-busting missile into a popemobile would make it certain.'

'Christ.'

'What do you think?'

'What I think is, if you're right, thank God we can get it stopped.'

Jimmy looked surprised.

'Oh yes, and how do we stop it? We haven't told anyone except McBride and we don't know what she can do even if she believes us. At this moment in time the Minister doesn't even know that we think the pope may be a target. Nobody's told him.'

Ricci felt uncomfortable.

'No, I know we haven't. Look, I thought I'd get nowhere with the Minister. All we've actually got is that maybe the deaths of some old cardinals were suspicious. Maybe they were connected if a conclave were to be called. When you come right down to it, before Anna turned up what did we have, what concrete evidence was there?'

'The Glasgow business.'

'A fire set by hooligans, a call that might have been nothing to do with us, just a local matter.'

'Your arty police mate.'

'Which will look like a perfectly genuine transfer. I couldn't go to the Minister with that. He'd have laughed in my face and got me kicked off the case for wasting his time.

'We have Anna. She has to have surfaced for something.'

'The problem is that almost all of this is only held together because you say it is. The connections don't exist as hard evidence. It's all in your head.'

'Not Cheng. I didn't make up the autopsy, or that he was a cardinal or that there were three other dead cardinals, and I wasn't the one who said a conclave connected them. Glasgow may be exactly like you say, but I really did speak to someone who knows about that fire and getting that information really did get me put in hospital. I didn't bring Anna into the frame and I didn't get her on the move. What I've got in my head is why it should all hang together. If you can come up with something better let me hear it.'

But Ricci didn't have anything better and he knew Jimmy was well aware of that.

After a pause, Ricci got back into it.

'What were you saying just now?'

'About?'

'About Anna maybe not going for the team.'

'The kit. If they're going after the pope with some pretty sophisticated kit they would need the stuff to be here when they arrive. We've no idea where they're coming from but it's unlikely they'll travel by car and bring it with them. It makes a lot more sense to have it here. Maybe Anna's gone to take delivery of the kit, which means the team might not be here yet and maybe we have a little more time.'

'So we stick with setting up the meeting with the Minister. Which means we sit here and wait for a call from your professor.'

Jimmy nodded. They had to wait for McBride.

'Well I hope she's operating with more than prayers, candles and hope.'

'I have great faith in prayer, candles and hope, especially when they're mixed in with Professor McBride.'

Chapter 18

THEY HAD BEEN waiting for an hour. Ricci had taken to wandering in and out of the kitchen. He had opened the fridge and looked inside three times. It was the same each time. He had stood and looked at the phone but it had refused to ring. Jimmy was sitting at the table staring at nothing. Ricci had begun to hate the room. Now he was ready to hate Jimmy because apparently he could sit still forever doing nothing.

'Are you thinking or have you just switched off? Maybe you're dead. Should I close your eyes?'

'The United Nations.'

'What?'

'What would you say is the most powerful non-national body in the world?'

'Is this a game to pass the time or are you thinking up some way of bringing the UN into your master plan? Why not? Come one, come all, the more the merrier.'

'You asked me, so I'm telling you. I was thinking about the UN. Why is it in New York?'

Ricci sat down, defeated.

'How the hell should I know?'

'Shouldn't it be in The Hague? The League of Nations

before the Second World War was.'

'Maybe it was built in the US because Europe was a heap of rubble.'

'They could have put it in some country that had been neutral in the war. Why were the headquarters of a supposedly neutral international body like the UN built in New York?'

'Why not?'

'Do you think the Americans would have allowed it to be built in Moscow or Peking?'

Ricci knew the answer to that one.

Then he noticed Jimmy's face. Was there the beginnings of fear in his eyes? All this about the UN wasn't just to pass the time. Jimmy was going somewhere with this, somewhere that scared him, and that scared Ricci.

'Come on, Jimmy, why is New York important?'

'Did the Americans want it in New York because that way they could make sure it never worked against them: where, if it became necessary, absolutely necessary, it could be closed down? Look at what John Paul II did to the Soviet Union. He made possible something the US, with all its money and firepower, had been trying to do for nearly half a century.'

'So?'

'What if a pope decided to jump the other way? What if a pope set out to act against the US, to push them off the top? There are over one billion Catholics worldwide and the number is growing all the time. What if they were mobilised in a way that threatened the US?'

'How, threatened the US?'

'I don't know.'

'That's ridiculous, why would any pope...'

'I don't know why, no one does. But given the right circumstances it could happen. No one predicted the fall of the Soviet Union but it still happened.'

'The UN, the Soviet Union and dead popes. Tell me where you're going with this. That phone could ring at any time and I need to know where we stand before it does.'

'I don't think that it's an anti-tank missile that's coming in.'

There was a question. Ricci didn't want to ask it but he had to.

'Are you're saying that this might be about moving the Vatican from Rome to America? Are you telling me it's a US Intelligence thing to take over the papacy?'

'I'm just saying it could be. All along there's been something nagging at me, something I couldn't figure out. Let's say you can fix a conclave, that you get to pick the next pope. What does that get you?'

'It gets you the pope you want.'

'But only for as long as your man is pope. It also makes you plenty of enemies. People would find out what you've done, because even if you can fix a conclave you can't fix the whole Vatican. They'd look at it and they'd work it out no matter how clever you'd been.'

'Fine, so now you've just demolished the only idea we have because anyone big enough to pull this off doesn't just want the next pope. They want the whole bloody show, they want the…' Ricci voice trailed off. The line of Jimmy's thinking about the UN was beginning to sink in. Jimmy waited a second then went on.

'I don't think this is about putting one papacy in their pocket. I think it's about doing to the Vatican what the US did to the United Nations, effectively cutting off its balls. Somebody in the US learned a very important lesson from what happened to the Soviet Union. Now I think they're doing something about it.'

There was a silence.

'So you think it's the Americans? The Americans are going

to steal the Vatican?' Jimmy nodded. 'Okay, if that's the way you want it. But don't you think the rest of the world might have something to say about it?'

'Oh yes, the world will go bananas, but not at the Americans.'

'No? Who then?'

'Whoever sets off the dirty nuclear device here in Rome. The pope dies and who knows how many others, but the main thing is that the pope dies, and the whole of the Vatican goes with him. If the bomb doesn't kill them the radiation will. No more Vatican.'

'My God, you can't mean it? You can't ask me to believe that the US would do something like that?'

'It does the job, can't you see it, it does both jobs. It kills the pope and it makes the Vatican and I don't know how much else of Rome uninhabitable for years. Wherever the next conclave will be held it won't be here. It will have to be somewhere else, and my guess is the good old US of A.'

'No. You're way off on this, you have to be. No one's mad enough to pull a thing like that, and certainly not the Americans. They'd have to take on the rest of the world.'

'Why? If the bomb is brought in by terrorists, if it's clearly a terrorist attack by an Islamic group? That would be great for the Americans. It would make Catholics worldwide start baying for blood. It would draw a line between Islamic countries and the West that would make the Cold War look like a walk in the park. The gloves could come off and their War on Terror would be back in gear and firing on all cylinders. They could do anything they liked, no one would even blink an eye. Ever since Iraq the US has been struggling to get anybody else to commit the way they want. If this happened there'd be all the troops and weapons needed to fight World War Three, with America waving the flag.'

Ricci was trying hard not to be convinced.

'Not even the Americans would go that far, not the CIA in its wildest dreams would think up...'

'Ever since 9/11 it's been on the cards. A small nuclear device slipped into a Western city and detonated. If the CIA thought it would happen eventually, why not make sure it happened in a way that worked for them instead of against them?'

The room took on a strange silence as the two men looked into the future Jimmy had just described.

'You're wrong,' said Ricci. 'Killing the pope was too far out for me, and this goes way beyond that. I don't buy any of it, especially not moving the Vatican. Killing the pope to make the world take sides, maybe, but to move the Vatican? I don't buy it at all.'

Jimmy's mind began to run. He put his thoughts into words as they came.

'This is terrorist-related now, we know that through Anna. She's not Intelligence and never had any connection with any Intelligence service. But according to US reports the Geisller Group were hooked up to al Qaeda and al Qaeda has so many offshoots they could have met and worked with any number of people who were members of Islamic extremist organisations...'

The phone rang. Ricci watched as Jimmy picked it up and listened.

'Thanks.' He rang off. 'We've got a briefing in one hour.'

'Police headquarters?'

'No. The Duns College rector's office.'

They stood for a moment.

'Jimmy, you must be wrong about this.'

'You thought of it first. It was you who gave it to me.'

'Me?'

'You said, nuke the Vatican. You meant it for a joke, but I

realised it made sense. As a way of doing the job it was certain and it was do-able, especially if you used suicide bombers.'

'Christ.'

'So, we assume I'm right, pray that I'm wrong and do whatever we have to do.'

'Which means, how do we stop it?'

'Come on, we don't need the car. We'll walk and you can think about it on the way.'

As they left the apartment a thought came to Ricci. Maybe Jimmy wasn't joking when he talked about prayers and candles. Maybe that was when you needed to listen to him most.

'So we think the safest way to bring it in is by sea. Road or air have to be too risky. If Anna has gone to pick up the bomb then she'll have gone to a port. If she came to Rome it will be one near Rome. She'll use the same name so long as she thinks it's safe.'

'And the police will keep a tight lid on it. They need her to think she's safe.'

'So we ask the police to check hotels in ports, starting with ports nearest to Rome.'

They came to the top of the stone staircase and walked along the corridor towards the rector's office. When they reached the door they stopped and Ricci knocked. A man's voice answered. They went in. From behind the desk the bland Monsignor smiled at them.

'Sit down, please.'

'I was told we were getting a briefing from the team who's looking for Anna Schwarz.'

'And so you are, Inspector, so you are. The Minister asked for an up-to-the-minute report and I have been asked to deliver its contents to you.' The Monsignor picked up a sheet of paper from the desk. 'I was told you would only want relevant information. Needless to say, I was not the one who decided what was and what was not relevant.' He looked at the paper and began to read. 'A woman calling herself Anna Bruck hired a red Fiat Punto from Hertz Rent-a-Car at their Rome central office four days ago using the address of her apartment in Rome and a current European driving licence. This afternoon at seventeen fifteen the car was returned to Hertz at their Florence airport office. It is now being examined but first reports say there were no fingerprints nor any other traces in the car to make an initial forensic confirmation that the woman who hired and returned the car were one and the same person, or that either was actually Anna Schwarz. Descriptions from Hertz in Rome and Florence were vague: a young woman of about the right age, about the right height, who wore dark glasses and a yellow headscarf. Her hair was described by the member of staff in Rome as blonde, by the one in Florence as fair. In Rome they thought she was wearing lipstick and other make-up and Florence couldn't remember. Both were shown a photo of Anna Schwarz and both were unable to confirm or deny it was the woman they dealt with. No further trace of the woman has been found. Enquiries are continuing.'

The Monsignor put the sheet of paper on the desk and sat back. Ricci looked at Jimmy.

'Now what?'

'If she picked up what we think was coming she took it to Florence airport and handed it over some time this afternoon before taking the car back to the Hertz office. That means that whoever took delivery probably came into Florence by air, hired a car or van, met her and took delivery.'

'So our package is on its way to Rome?'

'Yes, or it's already here.'

Ricci felt a cold sweat forming on his brow. He had thought Jimmy was wrong, had forced the connections further than they would go. Now it looked as if he was right. Anna had sat tight until her team was due then gone to Florence and handed over what she had collected for them. It could be anything; an anti-tank missile and launcher, a grenade launcher, a weapon of some kind. But it could also be a small nuclear device that would start World War Three and set the West against Islam, and America shouting 'charge'. For Christ's sake, Jimmy mustn't be right. Pray that he's wrong. Maybe it was only prayer that was left.

'Can you get a message to the officer in charge of this investigation?' Jimmy asked.

The Monsignor pulled out a mobile and began to key in a number.

'What is your message?'

He finished dialling and held the phone to his ear.

'Get the car checked for any signs of radioactivity. If there is, then check for anyone who flew in to Florence today and rented a car or van. Tell him it's terrorist-related and it's as bad as it sounds. That he should take whatever action he thinks fit.'

Somebody answered the call.

'Hello. Yes, it is, I have a message which is to be passed to the officer leading the search for Anna Schwarz. He is to check the car she used for radioactivity and if he finds any he is to cross-check the names on passenger arrivals with car or van rentals at the airport.' He listened for a second, then looked across at Jimmy. 'How long before?'

'Up to six hours, that should be enough, but if they turn up nothing then keep going to twenty-four hours.'

The Monsignor passed on the answer.

'If there is radioactivity present in the car the threat is real and present and he should take whatever action he thinks fit.' He held the mobile away from his mouth and looked across again. 'Anything else?'

'If he finds any likely matches among the rentals the vehicle and its contents will be headed for Rome or are already in Rome.' He looked at his watch and turned to Ricci.

'How long to drive from Florence to Rome?'

'From the airport it would be three to four hours, depending on how fast you drove and where in Rome you wanted to get to.'

Jimmy worked out the timing. They got the bomb before five p.m. and it was now eight thirty.

'If the radioactivity test is positive they should start turning Rome inside out.'

The Monsignor passed on the message then looked back.

'I'd like to know the outcome of the test as soon as they have it.'

'Do you have a number they can reach you on?'

Ricci gave the Monsignor a number.

'It's the mobile I gave you.'

Jimmy nodded.

'Then that's it.'

The Monsignor gave the number then slipped his mobile inside his jacket.

'Is there anything further, gentlemen?' They couldn't think of anything. 'In that case I will wish you good evening.' He stood up, picked up the paper from the desk, folded it and put it into an inside pocket and went to the door. He looked at his watch. 'I'm meeting friends, drinks and *Il Trovatore*. I'll just make the interval.' He smiled and left, pulling the door shut behind him.

'Who the hell was that?'

'He's a man who thinks to live modestly is to live well.'

'Stop playing fucking games. Who the bloody hell is he?'

'He's the one McBride sent to give me the information on the other cardinals. He was the one who confirmed the link between them and Cheng. She must have arranged for him to get the report and brief us.'

'And?'

'And what?'

Ricci rubbed a hand across his forehead. Jimmy thought he didn't look too well. The strain was really beginning to show.

'You okay?'

'No I'm not okay. I've got a bloody headache.'

'You should take something.'

'I am taking something.'

'You get lots of headaches?'

'Ever since I met you.'

Jimmy smiled.

'Yeah, people tell me I have that effect.'

'Look, stop fucking me around will you? We tell that guy to pass on a message that something radioactive could be on its way to Rome, that it's as bad as it can be, and he doesn't bat an eye. Then when he's finished he tells us he's off to drinks and the opera. No shock, no questions, no nothing. Doesn't that strike you as very strange behaviour?'

'It should, shouldn't it? But somehow it doesn't.'

Ricci got up angrily and began to walk around the small office.

'Stop being cryptic and give me a straight answer. My family live in Rome for God's sake. My parents and a sister. Should I be scared shitless for them and all the others if those guys you're so sure are coming set off their bomb before they can be picked up?'

Ricci slumped back down into his chair. He was tired and

his head felt like someone was driving a red hot spike into it.

'Headache bad?'

'Never mind my headaches. Why do you think he wasn't interested that a terrorist nuclear device might be about to arrive here in Rome.'

Jimmy gave a shrug. Ricci asked too many dumb questions to answer them all.

'Either he knows something that we don't or he was trying to make a point.'

'What point?'

'That he doesn't like me.'

The headache and the frustration combined to silence Ricci. He leaned forward with his head in his hands.

'You should see a doctor.'

Ricci ignored him, so Jimmy sat back and waited.

Jimmy guessed the Monsignor was the kind of man who liked to let people know when he didn't like them. But in his case he couldn't do much about it because he was under orders to help. So the drinks and opera with friends could have been an 'up yours', which would become clear later. And he did it because he knew something Jimmy didn't. But what did he know and, more importantly, did he really not care about the bombing thing?

Ricci sat up again. He looked dreadful but he was ready to get going again.

'Do you think there's a bomb?' Jimmy asked him.

Ricci slowly shook his head.

'No, at least not a nuclear one. When we get the test result we'll be certain one way or the other. If there's nothing, you're wrong. If there is, then God help us all. But I think you're wrong.'

'How long before we hear? You think less than an hour?'

'The police have the car, all they need to do is get something to test with. That shouldn't be too difficult.'

'Shall we wait here?'

'No, I need some air. They've got the mobile number, so it doesn't matter where we wait. This dump depresses me.'

Jimmy looked round. It was a dump, and yet from the outside it was what the tourists wanted the Vatican to look like. It was just as well that they never got into the place. The inside would be a real disappointment. It was like the Catholic Church really. What you saw from the outside was impressive but it wasn't what you got if you came inside.

'Well, are you coming?'

'Sorry, I was thinking about something.'

'You think too much, you know that? You spend too much time in your own head.'

Suddenly somebody had switched a light on and Jimmy could see more clearly. He looked at Ricci who had stood up and was waiting.

'You think so? You really think so?'

'No. I don't think so, I bloody well know so.' He went to the door. 'Come on, let's get a drink. I'll get a taxi home and pick the car up tomorrow.'

'If there is a tomorrow.'

'There'll be a tomorrow, there's always a tomorrow. You're good, Jimmy, very good, but you're wrong on this. Dead wrong.'

No I'm not, thought Jimmy. I was wrong, but now I think I'm right. Yes, I'm pretty sure I'm right.

Chapter 19

'MY TROUBLE IS I don't listen to people. People keep telling me things and I just don't listen. I guess I try to live in my head too much.'

'I told you there was nothing I could do.'

'I know. You told me. You told me more than once but I just wouldn't listen.'

Jimmy took a drink from his beer and Danny reluctantly took a sip from his coffee. The barman read his paper and the few regulars talked, smoked or stared into space. The bar was just the same, dull and shabby, and the sunshine still didn't get any further than the narrow gap between the apartment roofs. Jimmy liked it.

'Where's Ron?'

'At a lecture.'

'But you've bunked off?'

'I do sometimes. It doesn't matter now, does it?'

'I suppose not.'

'We're starting on Dogmatic Theology.'

'Good.'

'What do you mean, good? You wouldn't say good if you'd just started on Dogmatic Theology.'

'So what's your favourite?'

Danny thought about it.

'Maybe Church History. Know what happened and why it happened and you begin to get some idea about why things are the way they are. Church History helps.'

'I know what you mean.'

Danny got up.

'Back in a minute.'

He walked off towards the toilet.

Jimmy liked Danny. In many ways they were the same. They both wanted to know why things were the way they were. With Danny it was the Church, with Jimmy, just at the minute, it was the investigation. He thought about how Ricci had reacted the previous night in the bar when the call had come through. The test had been positive, there had been something radioactive carried in the red Punto. Rentals at Florence airport had turned up a van rented by two Asian men travelling on British passports who had flown in from Pakistan. Ricci had gone all nervous on him and had ordered a large whisky.

'Christ, Jimmy, I was wrong and you were right. Christ, Jimmy.' He had put his mobile on the table. He wanted to call somebody, his family probably. He wanted to say, 'Don't ask questions, just pack a small bag and get out of Rome as fast as you can.' But if every copper who was looking for the men and the van did that, Rome would be in total panic inside one hour and the chances of nailing the terrorists would have gone. Jimmy remembered watching him. He hadn't made any call. He'd drunk his whisky, picked up his phone and put it away, and asked what should they do.

What did he think there was for two men sitting in a bar in central Rome to do? The police had all they needed. And he had been right. There'd been nothing for them to do.

Ricci was the one they'd phoned to say they'd got them. They'd been picked up as they approached Rome. Now they were somewhere being interrogated. It was all simple and straightforward. Jimmy smiled, remembering how Ricci had been after the danger was over. He had banged on about how they had been cut out of it, as though it had all been done deliberately to spite him.

'I should have been there. It was us who worked out what was going on. We did the detective work. We worked it out all the way from Cheng to Florence airport.'

Jimmy liked how it was 'us' now, how they had done it all together.

'They just took our message and watched the Florence to Rome road for God's sake. Traffic probably made the collar.' God, was he pissed off, and he wouldn't leave it alone. He had kept on about it.

'This way we get nothing and the team chasing Anna gets it all. They get to be heroes, and the best of it is, they didn't even do what they set out to do. They missed Anna. She's free and clear but they're bloody heroes and no one even knows who we are. We get nothing.'

He could have asked Ricci whether saving Rome from a terrorist nuclear attack was getting nothing. But Ricci hadn't been in the mood to appreciate the irony. Maybe he had wanted a James Bond ending, with him as James Bond. What they got was what you always get – the bad guys got picked up and the good guys went home. And that's what he had done, finished his drink, gone home and left Ricci in the bar. For Ricci, last night meant it was over.

But today Jimmy knew it wasn't over.

Danny came back.

'You want another beer?'

'No, I'm okay with this one. Don't much feel like drinking

or talking. I'm not good company today.'

'Thinking about the investigation? I thought you said it was sorted.'

'I know.'

'Then leave it alone. What time's your meeting?'

'Two o'clock.'

'You'll tell her how it went?'

'I think she probably knows.'

Danny looked at his coffee trying to make his mind up whether to say what he was thinking. He decided he would.

'Jimmy, you told me it was all over. But you didn't tell me what happened. You didn't tell me how it finished, and that's okay because I don't want to know. But I'm still worried about you. One minute you're telling me some weird story and saying how you want me to watch your back because it's all big deal stuff and very hush-hush. Then all of a sudden it's finished. Everyone's gone home and the show's over. Whatever this is about it's not that bullshit about Archbishop Cheng and papal conclaves. I think this is about you, and that's me as a copper speaking as well as a friend. I think you're still in trouble. The machine is still chewing you.'

Jimmy looked at him. Was he a friend? When had that happened, if it had happened? Or was it just words? What the hell, friend or copper, either or both, Danny was right. He should have listened to him from the beginning. In a way it *was* all about him, and he should have seen it long ago. It was pointed out to him often enough.

'No, Danny. It really is finished and it's not something you need to worry about. Not as a copper, not as anything.'

Danny gave a shrug.

'Okay, if you say so. But you're going to pack it in, aren't you? Whatever it was, it's made you change your mind about becoming a priest.'

'I don't know. Let's just say I'm asking the question, although whether I still have a choice may be in someone else's hands.'

Jimmy looked at his watch. It was nearly time to go but all he wanted was to stay and just sit. He had been up all night going through the whole thing from beginning to end and now he was worn out. Now he just wanted to rest. He picked up his glass and finished his beer. He began to get up.

'I better get going.'

'Okay, see you around.'

Jimmy put his hand in his pocket pulled out some coins and put some on the table.

'You won't be having another will you?'

Danny smiled his big smile and Jimmy smiled back.

'Do I ever?'

'See you, Danny.'

'See you, Jimmy.'

Jimmy picked up the bottle and glass and took them to the bar and walked away. The barman glared at his back, then went back to his paper. Danny watched him go. Just before he reached the door the *Ride of the Valkyries* jingled. Jimmy stopped, took out his mobile and held it to his ear as he walked out of the bar into the street. As he walked past the window Danny could see he was listening to someone. God go with you, Jimmy, Danny thought. Then he added, not that it will change anything even if He does.

'Come in, Mr Costello. You asked to see me. Was it to bring me up to date?'

'Wouldn't you say that you were pretty well up to date?'

Professor McBride was still neat, still just back from the laundry, and Jimmy was right. She wouldn't say. She sat and waited. He had asked for the meeting. It was up to him.

'What happens now?'

'In what way?'

'Now that the Vatican has become a nuclear power...'
He paused just long enough to know that he had scored,
'which you realise puts it in breach of the UN Nuclear non-
Proliferation Treaty, and I don't know how many others.'

She didn't say anything. Her expression never changed.
Whatever had been there in her eyes had flickered and gone.
But it had been there and she knew he had seen it. She didn't
try to be clever. If he knew, he knew.

'When did you know?'

'I worked it out last night.'

'May I ask how?'

'Detective work, just straight detective work. You'd laid it
all out nicely for me to see. All I had to do was go over it.'

'But something gave it away. What was it? Do you mind
me asking?'

'No, it's why I wanted to meet, I wanted you to ask. I
wanted us to talk. It was the red Punto that finally did it, but
I think I was on my way for a while. Certainly after Anna
went walkabout I knew there was something I should have
been seeing. But the Punto was the clincher. That meant I was
right. There was something I'd missed, something that was
there all along. After I was sure of that it was just a matter of
going back over the whole thing and looking at it in the right
way, which we both know was not the way it was shown to
me in the first place.'

She turned it over in her mind. Then she relaxed.

'You just can't get the staff you know, and you can't do it
entirely by yourself can you? There's always some little thing
that you delegate and that's where it all starts to unravel.
Some little thing like hiring a car.'

'The guys who came in rented a van so whatever they

picked up wasn't carried in the rental car. There wasn't enough room.'

'You would have thought I could have handed that to someone without any mistake getting made. She rented a Punto, did she?'

Jimmy nodded.

'A red one, maybe it was her favourite colour, whoever she was.'

Professor McBride made a dismissive gesture with her hand.

'A secretary. She was fair and the right sort of age. I had a false driving licence made up in the name of Anna Schwarz. On the day I needed the car to be hired I told the secretary that a Sister Anna Schwarz had a small problem. She needed a hire car quickly but had been called to a meeting and she couldn't be in two places at once could she? Would she phone Hertz and rent a car in Anna's name and then go and pick it up using her driving licence, which she had left with me. I gave her cash to cover the hire.'

'If the whole thing was straightforward and payment was in cash no one would look too closely and no one would be any the wiser.'

'Yes.'

'What about the name?'

'What about it?'

'It's not exactly Italian is it?'

'Names don't mean much. Is Costello an English name? The secretary spoke like a Roman, dressed like one and the licence had a Rome address. The name wouldn't matter. She was supremely ordinary, nothing would go wrong.'

'Except she wore a yellow headscarf with the dark glasses and that got remembered.'

'Yellow! She wore a yellow headscarf?'

Jimmy nodded.

'When she picked up the car and dropped it off, it was in the police report. You can't blame her, she wasn't a professional, just someone you used. A woman who's an expert at staying invisible doesn't wear a yellow headscarf and dark glasses to rent and return a car.'

'No, she certainly does not. But I couldn't very well have edited her choice of clothes even if I'd thought I had to. Yellow! How unfortunate, no wonder it set you to thinking.'

'It was just one more thing but it meant she wasn't the real Anna Schwarz whatever the forensic said. Wasn't it all a bit risky, so late on in the whole thing? The renting of the car in Anna's name was important. What if the secretary had said no?'

'I'd done it before, so I knew it could work. We really did have a sister, a missionary sister who was visiting Rome, who needed a car and suddenly got called away. She lent me her driving licence and I rented the car in her name. No one looked too closely, and my black face wasn't so different from her black face, so no one made a fuss. I knew the secretary, she's a nice girl, co-operative, always keen to help. I knew if I asked in the right way and said how much the imaginary Sister Anna needed the car she would agree, and she did.'

'I see, a simple but effective lie.'

'A lie? How was it a lie? In a sense, a very real sense, Anna was in Rome and I needed her to rent a car.'

'But she wasn't a sister.'

Professor McBride let that one pass.

'She did what I asked her to do, she rented a car for Anna Schwarz. Unfortunately she rented a Fiat Punto and wore a yellow headscarf to do it. Oh well, as I said, I couldn't do everything myself, could I? And it served its purpose.'

'You used what came to hand. Cheng, me, Ricci, the China-

watcher, the Monsignor, the secretary. What was available.'
She nodded, a bit smugly Jimmy thought. He could use that.
He would use it to get the leverage he needed. 'What are you
really? And don't tell me you're a simple academic.'

'Sorry to disappoint. I am an academic, Mr Costello. But
also I occasionally get asked to do things that need to be
done, and this needed to be done.'

'When did you get the traces of radioactivity planted?'

'She came back from renting the car and I'd told her to
put it in my parking space and bring the keys to me. I had
already arranged for someone from the Instituto de Technica
to pick up the car, plant the radioactivity, and bring it back
when I needed it to go to Florence airport. I don't know what
he used. He said it would show up clearly but wouldn't be at
all dangerous when the car was used again.'

'Didn't he ask why you wanted traces of radioactivity in
the boot of a rental car?'

'Of course. I told him to mind his own business.'

'That's it? You just told him to mind his own business?'

'More or less. I told him that if he wanted to know, he
should enquire from the Minister direct. Naturally he chose to
leave it alone.' She allowed herself a smile as she went on. 'I see
now, of course, that I should have told her that Anna needed
a station wagon or something like that. But you can't think of
everything, can you, and we were so close to the end.'

'Who told you it was coming?'

'The Chinese.'

'The Chinese!'

'Chinese Intelligence. I'm afraid I don't know what their
official name is. Two years ago a government scientist was
approached to sell a small amount of weapons-grade plutonium. He was probably approached because he had already
sold bits and pieces of know-how. Chinese Intelligence were

on to him and had him under surveillance, so when he was approached they quietly picked him up and told him they wanted the sale to go through.'

'Go through?'

'Yes. If an organisation was looking to build a bomb it had to be terrorist-related. With the way things are today if they didn't get what they wanted in China they might very well get it elsewhere. A decision was made to sell the plutonium and then track what happened to it, where it went, who was involved and what was the probable target.'

'A bit risky, wasn't it?'

'The alternative was to refuse, which would make the organisation who wanted the material look elsewhere, and perhaps succeed. A dirty nuclear device set off in a major Western city has been a prime aim of terrorist groups for some time. One day it was going happen, the materials and expertise were becoming increasingly available. This way the Chinese stood a fair chance of preventing such an attack. And if they failed, well, the target wouldn't be a Chinese city would it?'

'It's still a big risk. Why take it?'

'The Chinese economy was booming and just as they were about make it into the top grade of economic nations they didn't want all the tables to be kicked over.' Jimmy's face showed how unconvinced he was. 'Let me put it this way, Mr Costello. That we are having this conversation and not dead should be confirmation enough that they made the right choice.' When she put it like that, thought Jimmy, you could see she had a point. 'Once they'd decided on their course of action they needed to alert someone in Europe to deal with this end of things.'

'This end?'

'They were sure the target city was going to be European.'

'Why certain?'

'They were certain, that's all.'

'All you know or all you'll tell?'

'It works out the same for you either way.'

Jimmy decided not to press the point. He had his own ideas about it anyway.

'Okay, so who did they contact?'

'People here in Rome close to the Church establishment.'

'The Church? Why the Church?'

'They were enabling someone to build a nuclear device aimed at a European target. They were prepared to take the risk. How many European governments do you think would have agreed with them?' She didn't wait for an answer. 'They needed someone who would have a significant presence on the ground wherever the bomb turned up. Someone who could support their agents, who would be already there in sufficient numbers to get information and move freely. They needed to be absolutely sure that once the bomb arrived they could keep close to it and get hold of it before it was delivered to whoever was going to set it off. The Catholic Church is the only organisation that fits the bill. We have personnel, a great many personnel, in every European country that would be on the bombers' list. We have the communications infrastructure. We could provide transport and all the non-specialist resources they would need. They would have the specialists, the people who knew how to handle the bomb when they got it and the Intelligence resources to make sure they could track it. They came to us.'

'How? How did they come to you?' Professor McBride was about to answer when it dawned on Jimmy. 'Wait, I know. They sent Cheng. He was their messenger.'

'He was being rehabilitated, he was available. They were prepared to trust him and they knew we would trust him.

He was ideal. Also, who would notice another archbishop coming to Rome, even a Chinese one.'

'What did they ask for?'

'That as soon as they knew the destination we should help in making sure the bomb could be intercepted, quickly and without involving the local police until it was absolutely necessary. We agreed. The necessary communications were set up, then we waited. They tracked the plutonium to Pakistan where the bomb was to be assembled by a Pakistani nuclear scientist who was willing to sell his services. That was eighteen months ago. The Chinese waited until the bomb was ready. It didn't take long. It didn't need to be a sophisticated device or even very powerful. It just had to be nuclear. From Pakistan it was sent by lorry to Lebanon in a packing case marked as machine parts. In Beirut it was delivered to a man who had been recruited to arrange for the shipment of the case by sea to an Italian port.'

'A terrorist?'

'Perhaps. He was a shady character, part gangster, part fighter, part middle-man. A man who was paid by many groups to do things from arms smuggling to car bombing. He had the experience to handle a job like shipping the goods and not get caught. He got the crate onto a ship and then flew to Italy where he thought he would take delivery of the packing case and get it to the hand-over.'

'Thought he would?'

'Once the Chinese knew it was coming to Italy we were told to expect him. We were told the airport and the flight and we were there when he arrived and kept him in sight until the Chinese were ready. They knew which port and the arrival date, so they waited until the boat was due to dock. They let him pick up the crate and then moved in and took it off him. They interrogated him, got the details of where the bomb was to go and how the hand-over would be made and what the final target was.'

'He just volunteered that information, I suppose?'

'We never asked. It was something we were prepared to leave to the Chinese. Whatever methods they used they were able to give us all the information we needed. With their information we knew how to finish what the Chinese had started. We told the Chinese how we thought it could be dealt with. They agreed, so we put our plan into action. We arranged for everything to be in place.'

'And "everything" included me and Ricci?'

'Yes.'

'And Anna's stuff? That was all part of it?'

'Yes. We had you and Inspector Ricci looking into Cardinal Cheng's death. That meant we could feed you information as and when we wanted. Each piece of information moved you on to the next step. When we were ready we arranged for it to appear as if a known terrorist was in Rome, which gave us the police we needed. The hire car took everyone to Florence airport when the hand-over was due to take place. It was just a matter of bringing everything together at the right time.'

She was obviously reflecting on what had happened. She was pleased with herself.

'It was the opioid that was found by the autopsy that gave me the idea. That was a fortunate opening.'

'It was your plan?'

'The matter was entrusted to me. I had help of course but basically, yes, it was my plan.'

'Did the Chinese know who the suicide bombers would be?'

'No. The Lebanese had been given an airport and flight number and was told to wait at Arrivals with a card with a name on it.'

'What name?'

'Does it matter? It would certainly have been false. It was merely to allow the bombers to make the correct contact. Our job was to provide a replacement for the Lebanese who would use his papers to make the hand-over at Florence airport. We had the police already mobilised, so it was just a question of getting them to move in and make the arrest. Anna supposedly surfacing gave us the police, the Punto got them where we wanted them and the radioactivity finished it off. You and Inspector Ricci were our trigger to move the police in. Once you knew Anna had dropped her car there and had the police check it for radiation the whole thing ran itself. It was a pity that the car chosen by the secretary was too small to have carried the bomb. But its only purpose was to provide the evidence of a nuclear device, which it did, so no real harm was done. I doubt the police will spot the mistake in a hurry. They'll be too busy congratulating themselves on the arrest. When they find out that the radioactivity is the wrong sort it won't matter, everything will be over.'

'So it was all a set-up?'

Professor McBride nodded and had the good grace to smile. It was an excellent plan and she was rightly proud of it.

'You were vital, Mr Costello. We needed someone who would be good enough to follow the trail, to make the connections we wanted made. Inspector Ricci was necessary because we wanted you to think the investigation was genuine, if unofficial. He was also useful in getting police information to you and getting your information to the police. But essentially he was window dressing so you would buy into the fiction.'

She gave Jimmy a moment to think about it. She obviously wanted him to be impressed. And he was. She had been good, very good.

'Everything you were told was true. The interpretations you put on the information you were given were your own. Admittedly they were what we wanted you to arrive at, but you did so using your own detective skills, you made your own deductions.'

'No lies?'

'No, Mr Costello, no lies.'

'What about the fire at the ice-cream factory in Glasgow?'

She paused for a moment, the ice-cream factory could very well be a moot point.

'That was organised by a third party…'

'I know, Special Branch.'

'Yes. I wasn't aware of your Glasgow connection. I had no way of knowing that you'd actually go to Glasgow and find out what had happened.'

'And what did happen?'

'That was Fr Phan.'

'The China-watcher?'

'I had to be sure and keep the people involved in all of this to a minimum but as Fr Phan was already involved I told him what was needed. I asked him to use any UK Intelligence Service favours he was owed to arrange something in Glasgow which would enable a message to be sent to Inspector Ricci. Nothing too violent and definitely nothing life-threatening, but enough to add weight to the idea that Cardinal Cheng had been murdered.'

'And the other cardinals, the ones your Monsignor told me about.'

'All dead as described, but none murdered, natural causes in all cases.'

'But he told me they were all in positions of influence if a conclave was called to elect a pope. No lie there?'

'No lie at all. Every cardinal is in that position during a conclave, nothing the Monsignor told you was an untruth. You were always and at all times free to put your own interpretation on the information you were given.'

'But what actually happened was that it was always the interpretation you kept sticking under our noses.'

'True, but you were told nothing that was not true.'

'But I was told in a way that was untrue. Isn't that a sin?'

'A point you would have to have clarified by a moral theologian, Mr Costello. Moral Theology isn't my field, I'm afraid.'

Jimmy was finally beginning to understand. There were no lies, that was the key. She was telling him facts, but she was still at her old game. She was pointing his nose where she wanted it to go, and that was still in the wrong direction.

'The Anna thing was clever, I liked that. She was never here was she?'

'No.'

'But you did it neatly. It was real enough to get your police team up and running. Where is she?'

'Does she have to be somewhere?'

'Oh, yes. You may be good but not even you could just reach out and lay your hands on her fingerprints and DNA.'

'At this moment she is about to take her initial vows as an enclosed sister. She is, and has been for some time, in a convent in Bavaria.'

'So what was the story there?'

'There is no story. No story for you, that is.'

Jimmy had her. She had made her mistake. She had told him a fact she couldn't spin. Now he knew he could get it all: the truth, the whole truth and nothing but the truth, so help him God.

'There's a woman called Anna Schwarz in a convent in

Bavaria. I would guess there are plenty of people who would think it worth the time and effort to check.'

'And there are plenty of convents, Mr Costello. I don't think anyone would find anything.'

'But if someone tells the Intelligence community they'll start looking. I don't say they'll find her. I'm sure your nuns will be as good as the monks were with the Nazis they moved around after the war. But she'll have to give up any idea of a settled religious life. Is that what you want for her?'

She wasn't so pleased with herself any more.

'No.'

'Then tell me about her, where she fits in.'

'She's not part of this, she wasn't ever in Rome.'

'You put her in this, not me. You had the DNA and fingerprints planted. If you made her a part of it, I want to know what that part was.'

'Why is it so important for you to know? It's all over now.'

'I need to know where I stand in all of this. There's been some very nasty people involved and I'm satisfied that they wouldn't think twice about what happened to one individual if they thought he had information they didn't want shared with anyone else. I was involved. I want to know all that I was involved in. Tell me about Anna.'

It didn't take more than a couple of seconds for her to decide.

'Eva and Anna were chalk and cheese. Eva was wild from being a teenager, Anna was always quiet. Eva's parents hoped her going to university would help her settle down. As we know, it did the reverse. Anna was pious, she wanted to be a nun. She was waiting until she was old enough and was sure she had a vocation. She used to go and stay at a convent and talk to the other nuns and the mother superior. She was pretty close to being admitted when Eva and her friends did what they did and went on the run. Eva turned up one day and got Anna on her own. She demanded her help and gave Anna no choice. Help or I'll kill Mummy and Daddy, and then I'll kill you. What could Anna do? She helped. She got the men places to stay and got herself and Eva into a retreat house. It was perfect. The men didn't know where they were, and who would look for a terrorist murderer in a Catholic retreat house? Then that idiot Geisller tried the bank business. Eva realised at once that if he tried again without her, they'd be taken. They met up and she planned the supermarket robbery. Once that was over they had enough money to travel so they set off to find the real strongmen, the ones who were organised and ruthless. Anna went home and her parents arranged for her to go into a convent. They realised they'd effectively lost one daughter. They didn't want to lose the other to a long prison sentence. In a convent she'd be safe and they could visit her if they were very careful.'

'And the mother superior agreed to take her?'

'Of course, Anna had done nothing wrong.'

'Nothing wrong! She acted as transport officer for a gang of murdering thugs.'

'I mean she had committed no sin. She was guilty of assisting the group and no doubt under criminal law she could be tried for complicity after the fact in a murder and for actual complicity in armed robbery. But she had been given a choice between two evils, help her sister or see her parents murdered and be murdered herself. She chose the lesser of two evils. To do that is not a sin. She may have been guilty according to the law, but to the Catholic Church she had not sinned.'

Jimmy the policeman would have laughed at such reasoning. Jimmy the priest-in-training could see how it worked for a truly Catholic mind.

'The Geisller Group dropped out of sight and Anna settled down to a life in the convent but she never felt safe. At any time Eva might have turned up and demanded her help again. Then Eva was shot outside a railway station and the threat was gone. For Anna and her parents the nightmare was over.'

'Do you know who did it, the shooting?'

'No, but given who she was running with it could have been anyone.'

'But with Eva dead Anna could pick up the threads?'

'That's right, and when the mother superior felt that emotionally and spiritually she was ready she agreed to let her begin her training.'

'And she was to hand when you needed a known terrorist for your piece of theatre.'

'Yes.'

'And that's all of it?' She didn't answer. Jimmy waited, but she still didn't answer. 'Only the thing is, I got a phone call as I was coming here from Inspector Ricci. He had been following up on things. The two men, it turns out, were British Asians, one from Manchester and one from Luton. Both were students at Birmingham University and both sang like canaries as soon as they were questioned. Yes, they were suicide bombers and yes, they had tried to detonate the bomb when they were stopped by the police. But the bomb didn't go off.'

If this information surprised her, she didn't show it.

'Didn't it? Maybe the fuse or whatever it was failed.'

She could keep up a charade just as well as Jimmy.

'Do you want to know why I think it didn't go off?'

'If you want to tell me.'

'Because there was no bomb in the van. What they got

at the airport was a case, a packing case marked machine parts. They thought it was a dirty bomb. The man who gave it to them had the right identification, they just took delivery. Then they set off for Rome and ran straight into the police, who were waiting for them, just like you'd planned.'

'So you think there was no bomb?'

'Oh yes, there was and is a bomb. And now you've got it.'

'I assure you that...'

'Wriggle all you like, piss me about with half-truths and fancy words. You personally haven't got it but the Vatican has it, or knows where it is.'

Professor McBride let the thing go. If he'd worked it out he'd worked it out. Just listen to what he thought he knew and what he wanted.

'This only makes sense if you switched the bomb when it was picked up in Italy. After the bomb was safely in your hands you could let things go on because nothing bad could happen. The suicide bombers would get caught and everything would be neatly wrapped up.'

'Neatly wrapped up?'

'You had the proof, the proof of who was really behind it. You had the bomb, you had the Chinese who had sold the plutonium, the Pakistani scientist who had put it together and the Lebanese who was supposed to collect it and pass it on. You could actually prove who really did it. If the bomb had gone off in Rome there would have been a beautiful trail from Pakistan down to Lebanon, both in the terrorists' back yard. Then it had gone on to Italy where a couple of radicalised young British Muslims carried out the actual attack. It would have come out as a straight al Qaeda sponsored attack.'

'But you think something else?'

'I think it was set up by the CIA to set the Christian world against the Muslim world, to make everyone take sides so that the War on Terror could be fought to a conclusion. If I wanted to radicalise every Muslim you know what I would do? I'd bomb Mecca, preferably during the hadj. That would radicalise every Muslim across the globe – moderates, secular, Westernised, the lot. Turn it round, make Rome the target, and you get the same result.'

She looked at him with genuine surprise as he went on.

'You didn't get anything from the Chinese. Somehow you got wind of it, someone leaked the plan to you so you had to see that it never happened but you couldn't afford to point the finger at the American government. The only way was for you to let it happen and then step in at the last minute and take the bomb. Then you'd be in a position to say, "We know all about it and we can prove it, so don't ever try anything like it again, anywhere." The Chinese choosing the Vatican to help out was just crap, like the target could have been any European country was crap. The Vatican was the target from day one.'

The surprise had left Professor McBride's face. Now there was a slight hint of worry. She had been right to find out what he thought he knew. He was good, but he had gone too far, he had overshot. He hadn't let her point his nose for him, he'd gone where he wanted to go, not where he was supposed to go. Now he posed a real danger. What he knew could be his death warrant.

'I'm afraid you're quite wrong, Mr Costello. The American government, I assure you, through their Intelligence services or in any other way, would never contemplate using a nuclear device against the Holy Father...'

'No lies, remember. Don't take to sinning at this stage of the game. The truth, the whole truth and nothing but the truth. You said you had me brought here after I'd done my placement in London. But the timescale doesn't fit does it? You had to know before the Chinese were approached, if it was my letter of application that brought me to your attention. You had to know there was going to be an approach to the Chinese.' He paused, he was just about sure. 'It was the Chinese who got tipped off, you told them that an approach would be made. You told *them*, they didn't tell *you*.'

Her reply was quiet.

'Yes.'

'And Cheng was acting for you both. He was your secure line of communication?'

She nodded.

Now was the time. Now he could tell her what he knew, what he had worked out.

'It was the Americans, wasn't it? Unite the West against Islam and move what was left of the Vatican into their own backyard. Once there, it could be a rallying point for the religious crusade that was going to break out. One billion Catholics worldwide baying for blood. So would a lot of other people, half the bloody world probably. The Americans had to be sure they would be the ones leading the pack.' Jimmy was trying very hard not to let his anger take over. He wanted to be right more than he wanted to be angry. 'For Christ's sake, stealing the Vatican is like…' he struggled for words, '…it's like stealing God. Only the Americans would be so fucking arrogant as to think that they had the right to…'

She didn't interrupt because of Jimmy's language. She interrupted because he needed to know the truth, the real truth, and he needed to know it now.

Chapter 20

'WE WERE TOLD very early in the planning. But it wasn't as you think...'

'What is it about you Americans, why is it never America's fault? Why can your people never be the bad guys?'

'I assure you, Mr Costello, it is not some patriotic, blinkered view which makes me say it was not America...'

Jimmy sneered at her. His anger was taking over. He wanted it to.

'America, always banging on about being leader of the Free World. America doesn't want to be leader of the Free World, it wants to be the owner of the Free World. They think they can do anything they like with the Free World so long as it suits their interest.'

'Mr Costello.' There was a sharpness in her voice that stopped Jimmy. 'Mr Costello, it was not the Americans.'

Jimmy shut down his anger. This woman was hard to call. She said she'd told him the truth and in a way she had, in a twisted Catholic sort of way. Was she telling the truth now or was she still trying to give him the run-around? No, he was sure. It had to the Americans, it wouldn't work for anyone else. No one else benefited if the Vatican was hit by a nuclear device. He was right, it had to be the Americans. She was trying to send him somewhere else. Well, let her try, she had tried before.

'Prove it to me.'

She paused. She had to prove it to him, that's what he didn't realise. She really did have to prove it to him.

'You know I never wanted you for this, I told you that didn't I?'

Jimmy nodded and smiled. It was the smile he had started working on about a hundred years ago.

'Yes, you told me I wasn't a nice person.'

'Oh you're not, Mr Costello, but that wasn't why I didn't want you on this.'

'You told me that as well. I was mentally unstable, I might have another psychotic attack and balls everything up.'

'Please remember that I have never lied to you. Before I told you that, I said clearly that I had no medical knowledge. My subsequent assessment of your behaviour when you attacked those two men all that time ago was something that might have happened. One possible explanation, although I must say I think it a very unlikely one.'

'You never thought I might have a second episode?'

'I didn't think you'd had a first one. I think you are one of the most well-balanced people I have ever met, if self-confidence can be taken as a barometer of mental health. That little bit of make-believe was to slow you down, to give you something else to think about.'

'You really didn't want me for this?'

'Not because of any shortcoming on your part, rather the reverse. I didn't want you because I thought you were too good, and this conversation has confirmed I was right. I wanted someone good enough to follow the clues I would feed, who would work out it was a bomb coming in and when they were told of the car at Florence airport would ask for it to be checked for radioactivity. That way the police could come flying in to the rescue when they were needed. You did all that beautifully. But I wanted someone who would stop when it was over, just as Inspector Ricci did. You didn't stop, Mr Costello, you went on. You worked out that just stopping this one bomb wasn't enough. We wanted enough evidence to make sure that the people who planned it could never try anything like it again. Now we have the evidence and, as you've worked out, we have the device. Nobody except us and the people behind this will ever know what it was really all about.' She paused to let it sink in. 'Except you. You know what it was really all about, Mr Costello.'

Jimmy's faith in his judgement shuddered a little. When he spoke it was very slowly.

'If not the Americans, who? And don't try to give me terrorists.'

'Just as a matter of interest, why not?'

'Because from start to finish no real terrorists were used. Real terrorists would have used their own people. They might have bought the scientist but they certainly would have used their own to move the bomb from Beirut to Italy. The two British students were new recruits, untrained. They were stooges. And why the Vatican? If terrorists had a nuclear bomb and could move it they'd send it to an American port and let it off as soon as the ship docked. They wouldn't even have needed to unload it. They would have made their point. We can get to you. Nowhere is safe now. It would have been America, not the Vatican.'

'Very well, I think I have to agree with you that it cannot be terrorists, at least not what people call terrorists in the current sense.'

'So if not America then who?'

'I can't tell you, Mr Costello.'

'Can't or won't?'

'Can't *and* won't. I am not allowed to tell you. I have undertaken to keep that information secret. There is no way I will give you a direct or indirect answer to the question. I'm afraid it is something you must work out for yourself.'

The awful part, she thought, is that now I have to make him believe me. He only has my word for it that it is not the Americans, but he has to believe me enough to work it out. And please God he's good enough to work it out.

She waited.

'I have to ask you a straight question and I have to have a straight answer. Maybe then I'll know enough to decide what I might do, if I do anything.'

She nodded. She knew what was coming. If she answered his question properly, he might finally accept he had made a mistake. Although whether that was better than how things stood at the moment was very much a moot point.

'Were the Americans involved?'

Professor McBride was ready for it.

'There are Christians in America who believe that the Second Coming of Christ can only take place after Armageddon. They would welcome anything that brings Armageddon closer. They might very well view the prospect of the Middle East conflict going nuclear as one way of bringing about Armageddon, thereby bringing the Second Coming. There are also Americans who would welcome any action which polarised opinion between the Muslim and non-Muslim world and allowed the War on Terror to be waged without restraint. This is all common knowledge, Mr Costello, you do not have to have spent a lifetime watching the international political scene to know that these are realities and they are at work. I wouldn't rule out an unholy alliance between the military hawks and Christian fundamentalists, but they would not be supported in any way by the government.'

'Or the Intelligence agencies?'

She knew it had to be the truth this time, just the truth.

'One cannot rule out that within the Intelligence community such an option has been discussed.'

'So?'

'So, yes, there were almost certainly people in America, important, influential people who would not have been party to any planning of such an operation but would do nothing to stop it. Such people would have been ready and waiting to persuade the American government that, if it had happened, it should be used to the benefit of America. That what was done could not be undone and the best use should be made of the situation on the ground. It would have been a powerful argument but, as it is, we will never know what might have been the ultimate outcome.'

Suddenly something she had said switched that light on again in Jimmy's brain and he could see his mistake. He could see who benefited.

'This wasn't about starting Armageddon, was it?'

She could see he was getting there now.

'It was about stopping it.'

She sat in silence. He was there.

'The Israelis. If the world thought terrorists had nuked the Vatican the Israelis could call it a first strike and reply by hitting Iran. If they took out an Iranian target with a strategic nuclear attack that would send the message from Egypt to Syria and beyond – we will use a nuclear response to any attempt to create nuclear weapons in the region. No Western government would object. The Israelis would be the good guys. But what they'd really be doing would be showing they'd take out any facility in the region they thought was being used to develop a nuclear weapons capacity. They'd be making sure the status quo remained, with Israel as the only nuclear power in the region. The bloody Israelis. Why didn't I see it?'

'Because you wanted it to be the Americans, Mr Costello. So many people want the Americans to be the bad guys and you've just found you are one of them.'

'The bloody Israelis.'

'No, you're close, but it wasn't the Israelis, not the government anyway. It was the picture you tried to draw of the Americans, a combination of a radical splinter group in their military and an extreme religious political group. Between them they dreamed up the plan and set it up. Fortunately for us one of the military involved told his wife. She couldn't accept that the loss of so many innocent lives justified what they were planning to do. As it happened she had studied Ancient History when she was at university and spent quite a lot of time in Rome. I'm not sure that the loss of so many historical treasures weighed with her just as much as the innocent lives. Anyway, whatever her reasons, she didn't dare go to her own people because that may have placed her husband in danger, so she went to a priest friend and asked him what to do. He contacted... well, never mind who he contacted. The matter arrived at the Collegio Principe and we took it from there.'

'The Collegio Principe, your college?'

'Yes, my college, not the Vatican. The Vatican was never involved.'

'But...'

'You assumed that, because they kindly made this room available, I worked for the Vatican. It suited me to allow you and Inspector Ricci to make the same wrong assumption.

I assure you the Vatican was in no way involved. It was a matter of politics, power and religion, so it came under our remit of action.'

Jimmy sat trying to see it.

'But, surely, Fr Phan, the Monsignor, surely...'

'The Collegio enjoys excellent relations with many institutions in Rome as it does with many governments and government agencies. They are always willing to assist if the project in hand seems to justify support.' She waited and gave him time.

'So what are you, some sort of...' But he didn't know what sort of.

'I told you, Mr Costello, we study politics, power and religion. What good would all those centuries of study be if they resulted in nothing but words? Study leads to knowledge and the proper use of knowledge is action, right action. What good would the CIA or any other Intelligence service be if all it did was put its knowledge into words and never take any action? We knew the people planning the attack were going to approach the Chinese because she told the priest they had identified a nuclear scientist who was known to have sold bits and pieces. We acted on our knowledge and took the necessary right action. We warned the Chinese. The rest you know.'

'The rest I found out.'

'If you prefer it that way. If the attack had gone ahead the political group would have pressured the Israeli government to follow it up in the way you have described.'

'Like the US scenario? What's done is done, let's make the best of it.'

'Yes.'

'And would they have gone ahead?'

'Oh I think so. It was a very good idea and very well done.

It would certainly have been taken as an Islamic terrorist attack and it gave them a way of justifying strikes against any nuclear weapons facility their neighbours in the region tried to build.'

'And they could go on killing each other with conventional weapons?'

'Regrettably that would seem to be the likely outcome.'

'What about the Chinese, won't they want the plutonium back?'

'They can have it any time they ask for it, but they have plenty. I think they'll prefer it to stay where it is and do the job we want.'

'Why did they want Chinese plutonium? Couldn't they have got some from inside Israel?'

'I don't know, but they couldn't have used it. If the bomb had gone off it would have left a nuclear footprint. The radiation could be examined and the source of the plutonium identified. If they used their own plutonium the Americans would have recognised the footprint as Israeli because they gave Israel the bomb in the first place. The source had to point to a terrorist bomb, which meant it had to come from somewhere like China, India or Pakistan. It had to be an illegal sale.'

Jimmy sat back. It was all over.

'What will you do now, Mr Costello? You have some dangerous and very powerful information. There are those who would pay well for what you know.'

'I don't need any more money.'

'A sentiment as refreshing as it is rare. So what will you do?'

'Well I can't go on studying for the priesthood can I? I was brought here to do a job for you, not really to train as a priest.'

'Yes, I'm sorry about that, but I had no choice. We needed someone and you fell into our lap, although now I regret not making a stronger argument against using you.'

'Me too. What about Ricci?'

'He thinks it was all over when the bombers got picked up.'

'But when he finds out that the crate doesn't contain any bomb... what is in it by the way?'

'Machine parts, tractor machine parts I believe.'

'Well, he'll find out and he'll start thinking. He's not such a bad detective. He might very well get as far as I did.'

'I doubt Inspector Ricci will get very far with it. The two bombers were just targeted as students who could be radicalised. They were unsuspecting young men carefully selected and trained well away from any real Islamic group. They'll admit to everything. They'll glory in what they tried to do. The police may well give them a real bomb, with a faulty trigger of course, and let them have their day in court and their years in prison. It would seem to be the best ending all round. They get to be heroes of Islam, the police get to be heroes of democracy, we get our evidence. Only the fanatics lose out.'

'For the moment.'

'Sadly, yes, only for the moment. The search for a nuclear capacity in the region by those states determined to remove Israel from the map will continue. Our success, I agree, can be looked on as a mixed blessing.' Jimmy stood up. 'Are you going, Mr Costello?'

'If you've told me everything I should know. Have you?'

'You were not supposed to know anything other than what you were told.'

'No lies, remember, have you told me everything I should know, yes or no?'

She paused before answering. He was asking a direct question and it required a direct answer. God, she hated telling the truth, the whole truth and nothing but the truth. It made things so very difficult. Sometimes you just had to give in to temptation and take the easy way out.

'Yes, I have told you everything you should know. But you still haven't told me what you intend to do.'

'No, I haven't have I?'

Jimmy turned and left the office.

Professor McBride sat for a moment then picked up the phone, dialled a number and waited for it to be answered.

'Come to the Duns College rector's office.' It was an order. 'I don't care who you're with and what you are talking about. I want you here in no more than half an hour, understand?' She listened for a second. 'I don't care if the Minister will think it rude. Tell him anything you like, tell him your wife just had twins, tell him you've just been elected pope. Just get here.'

Across Rome, in a splendid office, the bland Monsignor stood up, made embarrassed excuses and left. How he hated that woman. Why, oh why had the Church allowed females into positions of power and influence? As he hurried through the marble halls he longed for the days of his youth when women cooked and cleaned and had babies and it was a simpler, easier world for men.

Professor McBride sat back. She would not leave the office until she had seen the Monsignor. It was silly perhaps, bordering on the superstitious, but even going down stone steps could be fatal. A slip, a fall, who knows? As a little girl she had been told that God watched out to take you unawares in your sin. It had been a way of frightening her into going to confession, just a silly tale, she knew that, but things from your childhood stuck.

She would sit and wait and not leave the office until the Monsignor had come and heard her confession and given her absolution. As she sat she prepared for her confession. It had only been a small lie. The trouble with lies was that you never knew what they might lead to. A lie linked you to consequences over which you had no real control. Better to be on the safe side. She sat back and began to say the rosary to herself in her head, waiting for her confessor to come and make things right again.

Chapter 21

JIMMY GOT UP from his chair, went to the door and opened it. Ricci was standing there.

'Come in.'

'I got the report this morning,' Ricci was saying before he was even over the threshold.

His voice was flat, almost dazed.

'About the crate? It was tractor parts. There was no bomb. It was switched somewhere along the line. I found out about it for definite two days ago.'

'What are you talking about?'

'The crate the police picked up in the van, it wasn't a bomb. Have you just seen the report?' Ricci didn't seem to know what Jimmy was talking about. 'Isn't that the report you meant?'

Ricci shook his head.

'My medical report, the one I said they were doing so I could go on leave and do the investigation.'

'The cover story. What about it?'

'Can I sit down?'

'Sure.'

Ricci went to an armchair and almost fell into it. He held

his head in his hands for a moment. Jimmy was beginning to feel worried, he didn't look at all well. Ricci raised his head. There were tears were running down his cheeks.

'I'm going to die, Jimmy. It says I'm going to die.' Jimmy didn't doubt what he was saying for one second. Ricci was going to die. Shit, he didn't need this, he had his own troubles. Ricci wiped his face with a hand. 'I didn't know who to talk to so I came to you. I don't know why, we're not friends, we hardly know each other. I have no right to…'

'That's okay, you needed to tell someone. Tell me.'

Jimmy went to the table and pulled a chair round to face Ricci and sat down. Ricci pulled out a handkerchief. It looked like silk and it was a pale lemon colour. He wiped his eyes and cheeks.

'I've been getting these headaches and over the last few days I've started to be nauseous. I went to see my doctor today. He said he was glad I came because he'd got the medical report he'd asked for. My medical report.'

'The one you said was a cover?'

'That's right.' Ricci put his head in his hands again. 'Oh God, it hurts.' Jimmy waited until he was ready to go on. 'I said I thought the report was just something he had been asked by the police to pretend to have done, and he said, no, there really was a report and the police hadn't asked him to do anything except…'

Ricci seemed even more confused. Jimmy eased him on.

'Except what?'

'Except to wait to give me the report until I made my next appointment to see him. Why was he told that? How did anyone know I'd make an appointment to see him?'

Jimmy didn't like this. A cover story should just be a cover story.

'Tell me what happened.'

Ricci began, he wanted to talk.

'I go for a check-up every six months, I don't have to but I do. I like to stay on top of things, take care of myself. Not the last check-up, but the one before that, I was okay except my blood pressure was a bit high. I'm fit, I work out, there was no reason why it should have been high. The doc said it wasn't something I should worry about but he would check it again next time. Six months later it was still the same, so he said he wanted a blood sample to send away for tests. I told my boss about it. He didn't need to know but I told him. I wanted him to know I kept in shape, that I looked after myself. Anyway, I forgot all about it until I was told I'd been given leave and the Minister's aide wanted to see me. I was going on special assignment and I would be put on indefinite paid leave with a story that I was awaiting the results of medical tests which might indicate a serious illness. I thought it was just a cover story. But it wasn't. They did some tests and now the report's come back.'

Ricci could see Jimmy was thinking so he waited.

Jimmy's mind was running ahead of itself. He needed timings.

'How long was there between you giving the blood sample and getting told about the assignment?'

'I don't remember.'

'Remember, it's important.'

Ricci's head went back into his hands, then he suddenly stood up. He was very pale. He looked like he was going to throw up.

'Where's your…'

Jimmy pointed and Ricci went, holding a hand over his mouth. He came back wiping his mouth.

'I just retch, nothing comes up. The doctor said it was to be expected.'

Ricci sat down again.

'How long between the blood test and getting the assignment?'

Ricci forced himself to concentrate.

'About two weeks, maybe a bit more, it's hard to remember. I didn't take much notice.' The tears came back. 'I don't know what to do. What do you do when they tell you you're a dead man?'

He looked lost, bewildered.

Jimmy looked at him.

If you're a dead man then you may not be the only one. Jimmy's mind was in overdrive. It had to be connected, this had to be part of things. Ricci was chosen because someone knew he wouldn't be around for very long after it was all over. But Jimmy hadn't got a terminal illness so what was the plan for him? Ricci started to get up.

'I'm sorry, I don't know why I came here. I just needed to talk to someone. I don't want to tell my family, not yet, not while I'm like this. The doctor says there'll be a lot of pain but they can control it with morphine. I've only got a couple of months.'

Jimmy leaned forward, put a hand on his shoulder and gently pushed him back into the chair.

'It's alright, you need to talk to someone, I understand.'

Ricci was breaking apart. Jimmy didn't like that, he needed to know what was going on. He didn't want him in pieces.

'There's so much I was going to do, there's so many things. I have a girl, you know, a nice girl, not just someone to sleep with. We've talked about getting married, having a family.' Ricci was not looking anywhere. He was really talking to himself. That was fine, thought Jimmy, let him talk. It's good to talk.

So Ricci talked about the future there would never be and

Jimmy listened, his mind racing.

They had Ricci sorted from day one. He was chosen because he was already taken care of. Nature had done it for them. Jimmy wasn't really listening as he looked at Ricci, who was now telling him about how he would have to go into a hospice, something about dying in a haze of morphine. It was tough but you had to go when you had to go and you didn't get a choice about how you went.

Jimmy went through it as Ricci spoke. He could see it now. This was the last little bit, or almost the last, and he hadn't seen it coming. There was no way he could have seen it coming. They chose Ricci not because he was a clean copper. They chose him because he would soon be a dead copper and wouldn't be around to tell anyone anything when it was over. In a couple of months he'd be so shot full of morphine he would do well to remember his own name. In the meantime he wouldn't give a damn about what was in the crate. He wasn't a threat to anyone. He was dead, and waiting to lie down.

'The doctor says I can have a brain scan, but it won't help it will just confirm...' He was better now, he was talking himself through it. Soon Jimmy could get rid of him and get on with what he had to do. Now he knew about Ricci he knew what had to be done. Ricci took out his damp handkerchief again and blew his nose hard. Then he wiped his eyes. Jimmy noticed because he did it the wrong way round and that meant he was on autopilot, but that was okay because it also meant he was getting ready to leave. Ricci was sorted, it was tough on him, but he was sorted. But what about me? I'm healthy, there's nothing wrong with me, at least nothing that will conveniently get rid of me. He looked at Ricci, thinking: Your troubles will soon be over, mine are just beginning. Ricci was sitting staring at the floor. What the hell was he waiting for?

Suddenly Jimmy thought of Bernie. Bernie would have been beside Ricci. She would have an arm round him and she would have listened, really listened. And Michael, Michael would have found some words, the right words. What had he done? He had thought about Jimmy Costello. This guy's going to die, die in a haze of morphine or die conscious and in agony, and that was some shitty choice. And all I did was close the book on him and think, how does this affect Jimmy fucking Costello? Oh God, will I ever change, please God, help me bloody well change. Jimmy went and sat on the arm of the chair and slowly put his arm around Ricci's shoulders. Ricci didn't move, he didn't respond in any way. He just looked at the carpet. Jimmy wanted to think of the right words, he wanted to listen, he wanted to help. But Jimmy's mind wasn't having any of it. Jimmy's mind was running. It didn't care what this new Jimmy wanted, it was running and Jimmy knew he'd soon have to join it. He wasn't Bernie and he wasn't Michael, he was Jimmy Costello, and would be for the rest of his life. For the rest of his entire fucking life.

Jimmy was waiting when Danny came into the bar. He walked to the table and sat down. There was a whisky in front of Jimmy and a bottle of beer and a glass on the table. When Danny sat down Jimmy pushed the beer and glass towards him. Danny looked at them before he spoke.

'I hope this is as urgent as you made it sound, man. I had to miss a Christology lecture, an important one. I was looking forward to it. "What was the Nature of Christ's Humanity Before the Incarnation?"'

'Deep stuff, I'm glad I'm out of it.'

'So you're out of it? You made up your mind?'

'Somebody made it up for me.'

'Your rector?'

'In a way. Cheers.'

Jimmy took a sip of his whisky. Danny looked at the beer.

'I drink coffee, Jimmy.'

'You hate coffee.'

'Maybe so, but it's what I drink.'

'This is special, this is goodbye. Drink your beer, or would you prefer whisky? Or maybe white rum?'

Danny smiled a big smile.

'You know damn well I'd prefer white rum but I guess I'll settle for this.' He took up the bottle and glass and carefully poured the beer. 'Cheers.' Danny took a long drink then closed his eyes for a second. Jimmy waited. 'The first in over five years, man. That's how much I'm doing for you.'

'I appreciate it, Danny.'

'You damn well better.' And Danny took another small sip. Jimmy put his hand inside his jacket and pulled out a brown paper envelope. It was thick. He put it on the table and pushed it across to Danny. Danny picked it up and opened it. It was full of euros. He put it back on the table.

'Who?'

'Who what?'

'Who do you want me to kill? Your rector?' Danny laughed. 'I'll do it, of course, but you don't need to pay me. It'll be a favour to a friend.'

They both laughed.

'It's to pay off my apartment to the end of the tenancy.' Jimmy put his hand into his pocket and pulled out some keys which he put on the table. 'I want you to clean it out. Get rid of anything, absolutely anything that could help anyone who might come looking for me. Clean the place out, Danny, and I mean really clean. Get a professional firm in if you think you need to.'

There was no laughter now. Danny looked at the black

holdall on the floor beside Jimmy's chair. He was on the move and travelling light. He was running.

'I understand. I'll see to it.'

'Slow them down, Danny, make them work for it.'

'Who is it? Who's going to come looking for you?'

'Someone I won't see coming and someone I can't stop.'

They sat in silence. Jimmy took a sip of his whisky and Danny took a drink of his beer.

'Listen, Jimmy, there's nothing really keeping me here. I could leave tomorrow if I wanted. Why not come to Jamaica with me? I have friends there who could look out for you.' He smiled, 'I could even watch your back like you asked me to.'

Jimmy thought about it. Maybe they'd leave him alone, maybe no one would come for him. He was small-fry, not important, maybe they would leave him alone. And maybe he'd get made bloody pope. If they came they would ask around. They would ask among the mature students and they would find that he hung around with Ron and Danny. Then they'd find that Danny had left suddenly and gone back to Jamaica about the same time he'd gone. That would take them to Jamaica because that would take them to Jimmy.

'It's a thought, Danny. Do you think your old police buddies could really make it safe for me? I think the people who come, if they come, will be tough nuts and good at what they do.'

'I think it may be the best chance you've got, if you really are in the kind of bind I think you are.'

'Okay, Danny, I'll do it your way. I'm going today, as soon as I leave here. How long will it take for you to clean up my gaff and get away?'

Danny thought about it.

'Maybe three to five days if you want your apartment done thoroughly.'

'Right. How will I contact you in Jamaica?'

'When you get in, ring this number and I'll come out to the airport.' Danny had pulled a small notepad and a pen out and he jotted down a mobile number. He tore out the page and handed it to Jimmy who took it, looked at it and then stuffed it into the side pocket of his jacket. 'Any time of the day or night, just call and I'll come and get you.'

'Thanks.'

'Why didn't you get out when I told you to, man? I told you they would chew you up and spit you out but that they wouldn't spit you out alive. Why didn't you get out when you could?'

'I know you told me, I just wouldn't listen. I never listen. I live too much in my head, I guess.' Jimmy picked up his drink and finished it. Then he stood up. Danny was a good friend. Going to Jamaica would take them to Jamaica and might slow them down. If they came. But Jimmy knew they would come. He was a nothing, but what he knew about them wasn't nothing. They would come alright. 'So long, Danny. I'll see you in Jamaica in about a week, two at the most.'

Danny didn't get up, he just stretched out his big hand. They shook hands.

'Go carefully, Jimmy, and God go with you.'

'Light a candle for me.'

'I'll light two.' He smiled and Jimmy smiled back and then turned and walked out. The barman looked at him as he left. Why hadn't he brought his glass back? Why couldn't he be bothered to bring his glass back to the bar? He looked at the table. Damn, there was no tip. The mean bastard had slipped out because he hadn't left a tip. He glared at the door for a second then went back to his paper. Danny pushed the beer away, it was better than coffee, but only just. He got up. He would go to church and light those candles, although he knew two weren't enough. There were probably not enough candles in all the churches in Rome to make sure Jimmy was going to be okay. But what could you do? Jimmy was Jimmy and he always would be.

Epilogue

'IF THAT TIDE of European money they say washed over Ireland got as far as Mayo it didn't do as much as wet the soles of my boots.'

'The trouble with the Celtic Tiger was that its mouth was over in Dublin and Cork and it swallowed what money there was. Connaught is at the other end of the beast and we all know very well what the other end deals in.'

'Shite.'

'Is that a comment, Noel, or are you agreeing with him?'

'Neither.'

'Maybe it's both.'

'It was bloody foreign charity that's what it was and what's worse, it was charity that went to the wrong people. Charity is for the poor, and it certainly wasn't the poor who got it.'

'Well it's been and gone, so there's an end to it.'

There was a pause until one thinker asked a question.

'But tell me, if we're the arse-end of Ireland, where's the tail? There's nowhere after us until New York.'

'The Celtic Tiger never had a tail, it ran short of money somewhere in Roscommon and wasn't able to afford one after it got here.'

'So wouldn't that have made it a Manx Tiger?'

'What?'

'It's Manx cats that have no tails.'

'And I have no more beer in my glass. So if none of you mean buggers are buying there's nothing for it but to use my own money.' The speaker got up and took his empty glass to the bar. 'Another pint please, Noel.' The small group of thinkers and drinkers left at the table in Maloney's lost interest in European finance and, as the talk had been of money, the conversation naturally turned to farming. The man at the bar nodded to a middle-aged man in a crumpled tweed jacket sitting at a table by himself with a half-finished glass of Guinness in front of him. The man nodded back, but without any real enthusiasm.

When the pint came he asked quietly, 'Do we know yet who he is or why he's here?'

The barman waited until he had handed over a note for his pint of Smithwick's before he answered.

'He's an Englishman, London by the sound of his voice, and he doesn't seem to be here for anything in particular.'

'Doesn't fish?'

The barman shook his head.

'Golf?'

Another shake.

'Maybe he paints.'

'Well I hope it's watercolours because we've seen nothing but rain for the past month.'

'Maybe he's a writer. I can't see why anybody would come here from England if it's not for the fishing or the golf, so maybe he's a writer. I wonder what he writes. What did you say his name was?'

'I didn't, but it's Costello.'

The barman put the man's change on the counter. The

Smithwick's drinker continued to speculate.

'I've never heard of anything written by anybody called Costello, but he might write under another name.'

'Maybe he's come here to be left alone and not have people poking around finding out who he is and what he's doing here.' The drinker took his change and his pint, ignoring the barbed answer.

'Well, he's made a poor choice if he has. There hasn't been a secret kept in Eriskenny since Cromwell was Catholic.' And he rejoined his friends. At his table, the man glanced at the group of thinkers and drinkers. They were locals, friends and neighbours having a drink together. They probably met like this most nights of the week. God knows there wasn't much else to do in Eriskenny except stay home and watch the TV. He gave his mind up to Eriskenny. It was an ugly little town on the main road to nowhere. It had a run-down, hopeless air about it. It survived on an agriculture which itself struggled with the wet, rock-strewn land. The wide main street was a collection of shabby little shops selling just about everything a householder might ever need, from paint and paraffin to lace curtains and china tea sets, with the odd funeral wreath here and there. Among the shops were scattered no less than seven bars. The man took a sip of his Guinness. He didn't really like it, that was why he drank it. The way he looked at it, because he didn't really like it the pints lasted longer and he could get through the night on just three pints. Maybe he would change to Smithwick's. It might be alright, and if he took a good long walk in the mornings and again in the afternoons maybe after three pints of bitter he would be ready to sleep.

He took another glance at the men at the table. They certainly weren't furious drinkers. Their pints seem to last longer than his and he was deliberately slow. How could a place like Eriskenny support seven bars? He did a quick calculation. Allowing fifty per cent of the population were women and three quarters of what was left were kids that meant there was one bar for about every twenty adult males. That couldn't be right. Yet that seemed to be how it was. The bars were all much of a muchness, crude drinking shops that looked none too clean. And here he was, like he had been now for a week after he had settled on Maloney's as the place to spend his evenings. And there was Maloney's group of regulars. Six of them tonight. Some nights there was a couple less and some nights another two or three would come and form a second group. When that happened it was Maloney's on one of its big nights. Suddenly the man who had just bought a pint got up and came to his table.

'I hope you don't mind me coming over but, as you've been here a few nights, we thought we should say welcome like and maybe buy you a drink.'

He stood and waited. The crumpled man looked at him then at the group. They were all looking at him, the youngest, a lad of about eighteen, gave him a big smile and called across, 'Welcome to Eriskenny.'

The others nodded, endorsing the sentiment but they didn't smile as if to distance themselves from the impetuosity of youth. The crumpled man seemed reluctant to speak and looked back to the man standing at his table who realised it was his initiative so he had to make the next move.

'What'll you have, sir?'

'No.' The man standing blinked at the sharp emphatic response, but the crumpled man's voice changed as he went on. 'Let me buy you all a drink, that would be better. You've said welcome and I appreciate you saying it, so let me say thank you and buy you all a drink.'

The young man shouted across, 'Good luck to you, sir,'

then to the barman, 'mine's a whiskey, Noel, a double.' The oldest man of the group, eighty if he was a day, looked at the young man.

'Yours is a pint like it always is, Seamus Dooley.' Then he turned to the stranger. 'All pints, thank you, four of Guinness and two of Smithwick's.'

The crumpled man looked to the bar.

'And you, you'll join me?'

The barman nodded. This was turning into a big night.

'Thank you, sir, I'll have an orange juice.' The man started to get up. The barman stopped him with a gesture. 'No need, sir, I'll bring them over.' The man standing at the table made the invitation which would cement the night and turn it into an occasion.

'Would you care to come and join us?' And he waited.

'Thank you, if you don't mind I'll pass on that tonight. I'll be going soon and I have a few things I have to think about before I go. Another night, perhaps.'

'Any time, sir, any time at all, and thank you for the drinks.' And he returned to his friends where the talk subsided to whispers and sly glances. A writer. The consensus was definitely a writer of some sorts. Someone in the cultural line anyway. An educated man, educated, like a priest.

Jimmy sat with his thoughts. Not that they were particularly good company, but he sat with them anyway. He didn't hear the lowered tones or notice the glances, he was doing his thinking. Six weeks had passed since he caught a train out of Rome to Milan. He had flown to Paris and then travelled to Roscoff where he caught the ferry to Cork. Now he was back in the west of Ireland. Was he safe? He was not. Was he happy? He was not. Did he have any idea what he was going to do? He did not. He had a small piece of information lodged in his brain and it was going to kill him as certainly as if it was a malignant tumour. He was on the run, but he wasn't an Anna Schwarz. He didn't have the Catholic Church to hide him away where no one would ever find him. The question he thought about was the same one he had started with on the day he left Danny in the bar. What next, where to go next? The door of Maloney's opened and an old man in a black cap and black raincoat walked in. Jimmy recognised him at once. The old man walked to Jimmy's table and sat down.

'Hello, Jimmy. How are you?'

'Well, thank you, Father.'

'Good, I'm glad you're well. I've come across to give you something.' Jimmy looked at the old priest. He had talked to him so often over cups of tea in the comfortable presbytery when he had first come to this part of Ireland, to another dead and alive little town on another main road to nowhere. It was the old priest who had finally persuaded him to apply to Duns College. 'I've something for you. It came today and I thought you should have it right away.' He began to fumble around inside his raincoat.

'How did you know I was here?'

The priest stopped fumbling.

'This is a very small world and I'm a parish priest. People talk to me and I listen. How would I not know you were here?'

The barman brought the drinks to the next table where they were taken and raised to Jimmy with various toasts to their benefactor.

'To you, sir.'

'Cheers.'

'God bless you.'

The barman came to Jimmy's table.

'Can I get you something, Father?'

'No, no, I'm in and out, Noel. Just talking to my man here and then on my way.' The barman left them to their talk and the priest began to fumble again. 'It's in here somewhere.' Finally he pulled out an envelope and passed it to Jimmy. 'It was in a letter sent to me from Rome and I was asked to pass it on if I knew of your whereabouts.'

'And you knew of my whereabouts?'

'Twenty miles, Jimmy, just twenty miles, why wouldn't I know? If a cow farts or a sheep coughs I know about it.' Jimmy took the envelope and put it in his jacket pocket. The priest stood up. 'Well, I've done what I came to do. Goodnight, Jimmy. You know where I am if you need me.' He turned and headed for the door.

'Goodnight, Father.'

The old priest nodded to the barman and left. After he had gone Jimmy sat for a while and finished his Guinness. Then said his goodnights, and left. Back at the B&B he sat on the bed, pulled the envelope from his pocket and looked at it for a while. Then he tore it open and took out the sheet of paper.

Duns College
Viale Santo Maria Magdalena 21
Vatican City
00 135 Rome

Dear Mr Costello,

I have no way of knowing whether this will reach you but I have sent copies of this letter to three places where you might be found.

I feel you are owed an apology. I apologise. I regret that, like Anna Schwarz, I was given a choice between two evils but I think I made the right choice. Nonetheless you were used and have been put in harm's way as a result.

I assure you that all records of your presence in Rome have been erased from any file or storage system to which I have access. Officially, you were never a Duns student and never in Rome. However, I cannot erase memories, so your existence as a student in Rome remains with those who knew you while you were here.

Before I met you I only knew you as you had been, as you were remembered by the people who had known you as a policeman in London. You know better than I what picture that would have drawn of you. But having met you and known you a little as you are now, I think you are trying to change, to live a life your late wife might be proud of.

I know it is not easy and I also know that what I did has made it that much harder for you, perhaps impossible.

I cannot undo what has been done, and if I could I wouldn't. What was done had to be done. But now I can offer my help.

If you would like some time to think again about the priesthood I would be happy to arrange a placement for you with a parish priest. It would be somewhere discreet but I cannot promise total anonymity. Alas the Collegio Principe has many resources, but not a Witness Protection Programme.

I know that a parish placement is not much, but it may help you to get closer to where you thought you were going when you first applied to Duns College.

If you take up the placement and decide to reapply to Duns College I think I can assure you that acceptance for training will be a formality. Further than that I cannot go.

Concerning the other matter, I regret I cannot help you. It is not that what I have in my possession is not enough to help you, unfortunately it is too much.

However, if you came to Rome I assure you there would be the fullest co-operation of all agencies with which we have influence to ensure your safety while training.

With my prayers and every good wish,

Professor Pauline McBride

Jimmy put the letter on the bed. He didn't want to think about it tonight. If it was going to be part of anything then that was still in the future. He would leave it for tonight. He thought about Danny and Ron and Ricci. What were they doing? Ricci was dying, probably in a haze of painkillers. Ron was studying. Danny was back in Jamaica, maybe still waiting for him to turn up. Had they found Danny yet, had they come and watched him? Had they talked to him or hurt him for information he didn't have? Or maybe he'd picked up with his old partner, the white rum. Maybe now he drank and slept well and had given up on his friend from Rome.

Jimmy got up, picked up the letter, folded it and put it in his pocket and slowly began to get undressed with one simple thought.

Forget Rome. Rome was yesterday and yesterday is finished and gone. Think about today and get ready for tomorrow. You do what has to be done in whatever way you can. You use whatever comes to hand. Whoever comes to hand. You... And then the words stopped and thinking finished. You did what you did and you tried to live with it. He switched the light out, got into bed and tried to pray.

'Dear God, take Bernie and Michael into your mercy and...'

But he still didn't know if he was talking to nothing and there was no Michael and Bernie any more. Was there a God? Maybe when you died that was it. No eternity, no Heaven, no Hell. Nothing. How could you know? Well, whatever Bernie and Michael got, he would settle for the same and fuck the rest. God, eternity, the Church, the whole lot. Fuck you and... And nothing. You couldn't turn life off at the switch. So he lay still and waited for sleep in the full knowledge that soon he would wake up to another day, and it would all go on again, day by day, until it ended. He began again to pray.

'Oh my God, I am sorry and beg pardon for all my sins...' It wasn't what you wanted, but it was all that was on offer, so you took it, and you did what you had to do.

Shortlisted for the CWA New Blood Dagger
Award 2009

Bad Catholics

James Green

ISBN 1 906817 07 3 PBK £6.99

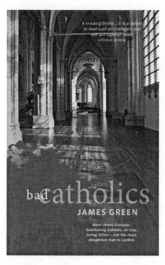

It's a short step from the paths of righteousness...

Jimmy started off a good Catholic altar boy. Yet growing up in Irish London meant walking between poverty and temptation, and what he learnt on the street wasn't anything taught by his Church. As a cop, he did what he could to keep his patch clean, and if some called him corrupt and violent, his record was spotless and his arrest rates were high.

It's a long time since he left the Force and disappeared, and now Jimmy is trying to go straight. But his past is about to catch up with him. When one of the volunteers at the homeless shelter where he works is brutally murdered, a bent copper tips off the most powerful crime lord in London that Jimmy is back in town. However, Jimmy has his own motives for staying put... and can he find the killer before the gangs find him?

The first in the Jimmy Costello series.

Luath Press Limited

committed to publishing well written books worth reading

LUATH PRESS takes its name from Robert Burns, whose little collie Luath (*Gael.*, swift or nimble) tripped up Jean Armour at a wedding and gave him the chance to speak to the woman who was to be his wife and the abiding love of his life. Burns called one of the 'Twa Dogs' Luath after Cuchullin's hunting dog in Ossian's *Fingal*.
Luath Press was established in 1981 in the heart of
Burns country, and is now based a few steps up
the road from Burns' first lodgings on
Edinburgh's Royal Mile. Luath offers you
distinctive writing with a hint of
unexpected pleasures.
Most bookshops in the UK, the US, Canada,
Australia, New Zealand and parts of Europe,
either carry our books in stock or can order them
for you. To order direct from us, please send a £sterling
cheque, postal order, international money order or your
credit card details (number, address of cardholder and
expiry date) to us at the address below. Please add post
and packing as follows: UK – £1.00 per delivery address;
overseas surface mail – £2.50 per delivery address; overseas airmail
– £3.50 for the first book to each delivery address, plus £1.00 for each
additional book by airmail to the same address. If your order is a gift,
we will happily enclose your card or message at no extra charge.

Luath Press Limited

543/2 Castlehill
The Royal Mile
Edinburgh EH1 2ND
Scotland
Telephone: +44 (0)131 225 4326 (24 hours)
Fax: +44 (0)131 225 4324
email: sales@luath. co.uk
Website: www. luath.co.uk